"Brilliant! Leslie Langtry has once again penned a 'gotta read every page' drama. I loved it, and the end as brilliant...Agatha Christie would be proud!"
—*Kings River Life Magazine*

"Darkly funny and wildly over the top, this mystery answers the burning question, 'Do assassin skills and Girl Scout merit badges mix...' one truly original and wacky novel!"
—*RT BOOK REVIEWS*

"Those who like dark humor will enjoy a look into the deadliest female assassin and PTA mom's life."
—*Parkersburg News*

"Mixing a deadly sense of humor and plenty of sexy sizzle, Leslie Langtry creates a brilliantly original, laughter-rich mix of contemporary romance and suspense in *'Scuse Me While I Kill This Guy.*"
—*Chicago Tribune*

"The beleaguered soccer mom assassin concept is a winner, and Langtry gets the fun started from page one with a myriad of clever details."
—*Publisher's Weekly*

BOOKS BY LESLIE LANGTRY

Merry Wrath Mysteries:
Merit Badge Murder
Mint Cookie Murder
Scout Camp Murder (novella)
Marshmallow S'More Murder
Movie Night Murder
Mud Run Murder
Fishing Badge Murder (novella)
Motto for Murder
Map Skills Murder
Mean Girl Murder
Marriage Vow Murder
Mystery Night Murder
Meerkats and Murder
Make Believe Murder
Maltese Vulture Murder
Musket Ball Murder
Macho Man Murder
Mad Money Murder
Mind-Bending Murder
Mascots Are Murder
Mosquito Bite Murder
Manga and Murder
Mayor for Murder
Mardi Gras Murder
Munchies and Murder
Memories Are Murder
Method Actor Murder
Marked for Murder
Mythic Melee Murder
Monster Mash Murder
Merry Christmas Murder
Match Box Murder (novella)
Museum of Murder

Greatest Hits Mysteries:
'Scuse Me While I Kill This Guy
Guns Will Keep Us Together
Stand By Your Hitman
I Shot You Babe
Paradise By The Rifle Sights
Snuff the Magic Dragon
My Heroes Have Always Been Hitmen
Greatest Hits mysteries Holiday Bundle

Aloha Lagoon Mysteries:
Ukulele Murder
Ukulele Deadly

Other Works:
Sex, Lies, & Family Vacations

MUSEUM OF MURDER

A Merry Wrath Mystery

USA TODAY BESTSELLING AUTHOR
Leslie Langtry

MUSEUM OF MURDER
Copyright © 2024 by Leslie Langtry
Cover design by Janet Holmes

Published by Gemma Halliday Publishing
All Rights Reserved. Except for use in any review, the reproduction or utilization of this work in whole or in part in any form by any electronic, mechanical, or other means, now known or hereafter invented, including xerography, photocopying and recording, or in any information storage and retrieval system is forbidden without the written permission of the publisher, Gemma Halliday.

This is a work of fiction. Names, characters, places, and incidents are either the product of the author's imagination or are used fictitiously, and any resemblance to actual persons, living or dead, business establishments, or events or locales is entirely coincidental.

SPOILER ALERT!

This book describes, sometimes in detail, the murders in previous books in the series. Therefore, if you haven't read them yet, you may want to reconsider reading *MUSEUM OF MURDER* until you've caught up. You have been warned.

MERIT BADGE MURDER (#1)

MAP SKILLS MURDER (#7)

MYSTERY NIGHT MURDER (#10)

MACHO MAN MURDER (#15)

MASCOTS ARE MURDER (#18)

MANGA AND MURDER (#20)

MUNCHIES AND MURDER (#23)

METHOD ACTOR MURDER (#25)

MONSTER MASH MURDER (#27)

CHAPTER ONE

It wasn't the first time I'd seen it, but I still couldn't believe it! It was like looking in a mirror…without the, um…mirror. I was staring at a life-sized mannequin of myself. Then I reached up and poked myself in the shoulder. The other me was standing on a "road" in front of my car as it screamed in horror at the scene. I recognized Carlos the Armadillo as he lay on his back in front of my car.

The mannequin they had for Carlos looked a little different this time and seemed a little more lifelike. I bent down and pressed my index finger against his cheek.

I shot up to a standing position. What the hell? That wasn't firm plastic I'd touched! It was human skin! And the man lying in front of me wasn't a mannequin. He was real and very, very dead.

ONE WEEK EARLIER…

"What do you mean they're making a museum about *me*?" I asked after a moment of stunned silence. It was such shocking news that I nearly dropped my lava-covered rag.

The girls exchanged knowing glances usually reserved for my impending death from old age at thirty-two. We were just cleaning up after a rather unfortunate Girl Scout meeting. Kelly, my co-leader, had gotten the flu this morning, and she was in charge of the snacks. This was a serious offence in a troop that held snacks as sacrosanct. But still, Kelly wasn't bringing anything, which meant I scrounged around in my body-sized freezer until I found five dozen frost-covered pizza rolls. Fortunately, I had a gallon of ranch dressing, which went a long way in hiding the taste of freezer burn.

The girls were working on their Thinking Day project, where each troop presents a booth representing a foreign country at a one-day event at the local expo center. The troop had picked Iceland and had built a replica Eyjafjallajökull volcano, and they'd decided it had to be a *working* volcano. Unfortunately, we ended up spending the better part of an hour cleaning "lava" off the ceiling.

And then there was the idea that we should serve hakarl, or rotten shark. Lauren, our junior zookeeper, announced that she was watching the Shedd Aquarium in Chicago to negotiate for the corpse of any shark that might kick the bucket. I was a bit concerned that Betty would send an assassin for the job, but Lauren insisted that most shark deaths were suicides, which for some odd reason made everyone feel a little better.

The girls had insisted we make hakarl authentically by burying the big fish's corpse in the ground for six months, unearthing it when the toxins (because of course, there are toxins) decayed. We'd cut it up and serve it as diced cubes with a little toothpick bearing the Icelandic flag. The girls showed me a mock-up made of tofu. I had to admit, it was festive.

When the girls realized we only had a month until Thinking Day, they said they were going to order harkarl in bulk online. I ran to my purse and pulled out my credit cards, stuffing them into my back pocket. They weren't going to use my credit card this time!

And now we were talking about a museum about me.

Betty rolled her eyes. "Oh sure, it's *always* about *you*."

I was confused. Moments earlier the girls had told me there was going to be a museum about me. "But you said…"

Mayor Ava held her hand up to silence me. "It's not about you, exactly. But it also is because you are always murder-adjacent."

"Explain," I insisted.

A museum about me would be bad. I'd been a spy for the CIA for seven years, and most of my cases were still classified. If Langley heard about this, I'd probably be on a hit list tomorrow. I've been on the hit list before. I didn't like it.

Lauren spoke up. "It's called the Museum of Murder. It's because we have so many murders here."

"More than any other town pretty much anywhere." Betty pulled a stiletto out of her pocket and began repeatedly opening and closing it quickly, which was annoying. "In the last eight years, which is how long you've been here, there have been sixty murders. When you compare it to Iowa statistics, you get thirteen percent. Which is a lot. Which is also awesome."

I'd been here eight years? I counted on my fingers. Huh. She was right.

"You're involved in all of those murders," two of the Kaitlyns said in unison.

"Literally," the other two said.

I had four Kaitlyns in my Girl Scout troop. They looked exactly alike, had M as their last initial and, as near as I could figure, operated on an elaborate hive mind system.

My name is Merry Wrath Ferguson, and I was once a CIA operative, until the vice president "accidentally" outed me to get back at my senator dad. After accepting a huge settlement and the sad fact that I would never again work in my chosen profession, I moved back to my small hometown of Who's There, Iowa, where my best friend, Kelly, decided we should start a Girl Scout troop.

The rest is, apparently, a history that would soon be on display. Sixty murders? That was kind of hard to believe. Then again, bodies tended to fall around me like mice on Chechnya's *Mice Rain From Sky Making Harvest Lucky Day*. Of course, the mice don't literally fall from clouds. A guy named Oskar drops them from a biplane. And no, the mice don't survive the fall, which is probably for the best since Chechens are a superstitious people and would take it as a bad omen if the mice hit the ground running.

"Who's building this museum?" I asked after a moment.

Ava shrugged. "No idea. The donor wishes to remain anonymous."

"We'd found out the money was transferred through forty-seven shell corporations, so we can't trace them yet," Betty admitted. "Which is pretty cool because forty-seven is my lucky number. Because of samurai warriors and stuff."

"The dude Betty likes, Conrad, is into samurais," Inez said.

Betty's eyes flashed. "I don't like boys."

Inez wasn't intimidated. "Whatever."

According to the girls, Betty had become obsessed with a boy named Conrad, who I'd just met over the holidays. Recently it made her glitchy, which made me nervous. I reached over and calmly took the stiletto from her, just to be safe.

"Why"—I shoved the knife into my sweater pocket—"is the city supporting some mystery backer who's so dodgy he has to filter the funds through forty-seven shell companies?"

Lauren shrugged. "He gave money to Ava's campaign."

Ava threw her arms up. "I know I'm supposed to say that's bad. But why? They're *giving* me money!"

Hmmm...we might need to see if there's a way we could stage an intervention without the other city officials finding out. Especially the city council. Those people were always trying to figure out how to remove Ava from office...mostly because they were all afraid of Betty.

"What's this museum called?" I wondered. The Merry Wrath Museum had a nice ring to it, even if I didn't want a museum.

"The Who's There Museum of Murder!" Two of the Kaitlyns grinned.

"That's totally awesome, right?" the other two finished.

Ava held out her hand. "Come on, then. We have to go to city hall."

I looked up at a bright-red stain on the ceiling, which would never, ever come out. "What? Now? Why?"

"Because there's going to be a press conference in fifteen minutes, and the donor who's launching the museum wants to see you there or they won't give us the money." The mayor motioned me towards the door, and after grabbing my coat and hat, we made our way to my silver minivan. Betty, Inez, and Lauren went with me. The others went with Ava in a very expensive Rolls Royce that had the mayor's seal on it.

"You ordered the hakarl, right?" I heard Inez whisper to Betty in the seats behind me.

"Of course," the girl said. "I even put the card back in her pocket after. She'll never know."

CHAPTER TWO

To my complete surprise, city hall's grand rotunda was packed. It looked like half the town was here. I spotted my husband, Rex, the town's detective, who stood next to Officer Kevin Dooley, village idiot and resident paste connoisseur. On his shoulders sat four uniformed hamsters, all improbably named Officer Hamlet. The rodents gave me a short nod as I joined them.

"Hey!" I sidled up to my husband and squeezed his hand. "Where's the rest of your team?"

Rex smiled and squeezed back. "Troy and Joanna are covering the office. Officer Dooley and I are representing."

Looking around, I saw there were a number of faces I'd never seen before. New people to town, I wondered?

"This must be a big announcement," Rex whispered. "There are a lot of people from out of town."

I knew what it was about, but since I was still in denial, I denied telling my husband about it. What was he going to think about a museum of murder? Since these crimes were all committed on his watch, I didn't think it was going to be his new, favorite place.

Ava didn't so much as climb the stairs to the risers but ascended them with great drama and stepped on the stool behind the mayoral podium. Betty came to the front of the stage and whistled loudly. The crowd was silenced and waited for whatever was going to happen.

"Do you know anything about this?" Rex whispered.

I couldn't ignore it any longer. "Oh yeah. It's apparently all about me," I admitted.

Betty shot me a glare, and I took that as my cue to be silent.

"Thank you all for coming," Ava said. "Before we begin, I have an important announcement. Who's There is all about inclusivity. So we are introducing a new interpreter who will interpret for a sadly underserved population."

"Sign language?" Rex's eyebrows went up.

A man stepped next to Ava and gave her a smile.

"Today, we are announcing…" She turned to the man.

He proceeded to neigh and whinny like a horse. It made sense in a way that no one else would understand. The girls were nuts about horses and believed in unicorns. Looking around the room, I spotted a Shetland pony. Apparently, this was all for its benefit.

"The newest, great thing for Who's There!" Ava smiled and turned to the horse guy, who neighed and whinnied some more.

The mayor went on. "Funded by a really rich, anonymous donor is the Who's There Museum of Murder!"

The horse man looked a bit surprised but continued interpreting, which I thought was very professional of him.

The packed room burst into loud applause. A man next to me, who I didn't know, seemed confused.

I leaned toward him. "New in town? It's okay. You'll get used to that."

He wore a concerned frown. "Um, yes. Just moved here from Chicago. I wanted to get away from all that noise to a nice, quiet little town."

"As you all know," Ava continued, "there have been a *lot* of murders in town over the last eight years. Sixty, in fact. And I'm proud to say that we make up thirteen percent of all murders in Iowa!"

The townspeople applauded loudly. If there was anything that got a small town excited, it was being the best at something. When I was a kid, May Merriweather won the first prize at the talent show of the Iowa State Fair for her interpretive dance of a rather violent Iowa Hawkeye vs. Iowa State football matchup. The town had a billboard made that stood outside of town for twenty years until a twister took it.

"Did she just say this is basically the most murdery town in the state?" The new-to-town guy's face looked like he'd just witnessed mice raining from the sky. It really was a shock the first time you saw it. It also helped to have a sturdy umbrella. Oskar never had very good aim due to being legally blind. Still, he could fly a plane and wasn't afraid of mice…which were the only requirements.

I cast a sideways glance at my husband, who wore a neutral expression. That seemed like a good thing! I probably shouldn't have worried. Rex was a smart guy who could roll with almost anything. I mean, the man allowed four hamsters to be considered police officers just to make the village idiot happy. I looked over to see the four Hamlets scanning the crowd for possible disruptions. One of them appeared to be holding a miniature walkie talkie, as if he was ready for action at the drop of a hat.

"The Museum of Murder," Ava went on, "will feature murders from the distant and present past," the mayor said.

"Present past?" Rex mused.

"Shhh…" I pressed my finger to my lips. "She's on a roll."

"Ah." My husband grinned. "So that's why this is about you."

The new guy couldn't help but overhear. "*You're* responsible for all the murders in town?"

I tried to reassure him. "Well, not really. I just always happen to be in the vicinity of most of the dead bodies, so technically I don't think that counts."

The man visibly gulped. "I just bought a house here! And I thought that Welcome Wagon, Helping Hands and Tentacles, was just part of the town's quirky charm!"

Helping Hands and Tentacles was Betty's mom's pet project. Carol Anne had allegedly been kidnapped by aliens often enough to know that they needed a little guidance and a friendly face when moving to Earth. I was just guessing, but the lack of aliens lining up to live here was probably why she was now visiting humans who'd just moved to town.

Ava grinned. "And now, to talk about this exciting project, please help me welcome Mrs. Merry Wrath to the stage!"

People turned to me, clapping, as the interpreter let out a very loud whinny, followed by a belch. Was that supposed to be my name? And why was she calling on me? I only found out about the project mere minutes ago! I didn't know anything about it. What was I supposed to do? Talk about the forty-seven shell companies?

"Mrs. Wrath," Ava glowered. "The mayor demands your presence on the stage."

Betty appeared at my elbow. "Don't make me make you."

I actually went. I literally walked up onto the stage, not having any idea at all what I had to say on the matter.

"Merry Wrath is a serial killer!" a voice shouted.

Ah. My sister-in-law Ronni must be here. She and her twin, Randi, were on the verge of delivering two sons, soon to be named Blasto and Blasto, to Ron and Ivan, a pair of Chechen muscles-for-brains, who were also their husbands.

"Mrs. Wrath, everyone!" Ava motioned to me, and the horse interpreter did that loud whinny and belch again.

I hoped the thunderous applause would last forever, because I had no idea what I was going to say. This was worse than the time I had to give a speech to a powerful committee at the UN, disguised as Sandra Bullock, about how the movie *Speed* could be seen as a metaphor for peace in the Middle East. That, at least, went smoothly.

This however…I think I'd rather eat hakarl, made from a suicidal shark and prepared by thirteen-year-old girls who didn't know what they were doing.

CHAPTER THREE

Betty had warned me on the way up that the mystery donor needed to see me at the event as a requirement for their backing of the museum. For a moment, I almost refused, thinking this might be what I needed to get out having the museum here in the first place. But Betty didn't take no for an answer, and so there I was, walking up on stage, hopefully getting noticed by whatever sadist came up with this idea.

"Hello," I said after Ava shoved the mic into my hand. "I'm Merry Wrath Ferguson, and I guess they're opening a museum of murder here…"

I wasn't quite sure what to say next, so I just gave two thumbs-up. This could be a solid strategy depending on where you were. For example, in most places, the gesture is considered positive. But in Bangladesh, it's a very rude insult, and in certain parts of Chechnya, it means *your mother hates your goats*, which is pretty much the worst insult you can make and is surprisingly worse than *your mother hates you*.

"That was Mrs. Wrath—who was actually here and not a hologram." The girl reached out and pinched me, causing me to jump. "See?" Ava took the microphone and shoved me aside. "Are there any questions from the media?"

A petite pink-haired reporter I knew as Medea Jones (who hated me more than goats) leapt forward. "Medea Jones, *Who's There Observ*er. Are all these murders based on the immense damage and destruction Ms. Ferguson has caused this community?"

All eyes swiveled to me. Ava looked at me. "Is it?"

I stepped forward. "I have nothing to do with this museum, so I don't really know what it's about. And what do you mean, the destruction I've caused this community?"

Medea didn't answer, instead scribbling something way too long to represent what I'd actually said.

A man in his fifties stepped forward. "Nick Zimmer, *Nickel Shopper,* formerly known as the *Penny Shopper*. Will the museum have coupons to advertise in the *Nickel Shopper,* formerly known as the *Penny Shopper*?"

I looked to Ava, who nodded. "Of course."

The *Penny Shopper* was a weekly sort of newspaper that had all kinds of classified ads and coupons in them. As far as I knew, no one ever read it.

I raised my hand then, realizing I didn't need to do that, called out, "Why did you change the name to the *Nickel Shopper*?"

The man rolled his eyes. "Inflation." Then Nick Zimmer faded into the crowd.

"Everyone knows that," Ava scoffed. "He wanted to call it the *Quarter Shopper,* but Betty didn't like that, so he didn't. She said it has something to do with Malthusian Economic Theory."

I was pretty sure that wasn't right, but just in case it was, I said nothing. There was no point in looking bad in front of the girls who were, apparently, way smarter than me.

A beautiful woman with a thick mane of glossy hair stepped forward. "Lucinda Schwartz, Channel Four ABC Affiliate." She gave me a little wave, and I smiled back. We'd known each other since high school, and she'd since forgiven me for setting her hair on fire when we were lab partners.

Ava straightened the medieval mayoral chain of office she often wore around her neck. This was TV media, and I guess she wanted to appear mayoral.

Lucinda held up her mic. She must be good because I didn't see a cameraman anywhere. "Is the rumor true that Sheldon McBride is the mystery backer for this museum?"

A gasp ran through the audience, and I know because I'd gasped too! Sheldon McBride! Was he really behind this? Sheldon grew up in Who's There and then left upon graduation to seek his fortune somewhere other than Iowa. He went to Yale, got a PhD from MIT in thermodynamics, and promptly invented the flying car, which revolutionized travel.

Okay, so he didn't invent the flying car. That was just wishful thinking on my part. But he did invent the next best thing—a car that ran on a hybrid ethanol. You couldn't make Iowans happier than that. Iowa was the largest producer of this biofuel and wanted everything run with it. (A guy in Cedar Rapids even invented an ethanol-run toaster—which, in fact, turned out to be a terrible idea.) The ethanol car made Sheldon a hero and put Iowa on the international stage in auto engineering.

The car was a sleek model that somehow used less ethanol to go farther than any electric hybrid or on regular gasoline. Sheldon unfortunately named it the Corn Hole, for reasons he never explained. I often wondered if he'd named it after the dive bar outside of town.

Iowa had embraced a number of environmentally friendly things, like wind farms. But it didn't embrace pure electric cars. In fact, you'd be kind of hard-pressed to find charging stations for Teslas out here, especially in rural areas.

The Corn Hole was considered a huge breakthrough and made Sheldon insanely wealthy. He was also very reclusive to the point where no one really knew what he looked like. The man lived in an unknown location, somewhere in Nevada. He never granted interviews and was known for backing some strange museums in the past, like the suddenly more relevant Central Florida Leprosy Museum, the IBM Selectric Typewriter Whiffletree Mechanism Museum, and Willie Smith's Largest Lump of Lard Museum in Nebraska.

Lately there'd been some rumors that he'd invented a very small camera drone and a flock of robot turkeys that were powered by ethanol. No one knew if these were real. We'd just have to wait until they came out, I guess.

Did Sheldon put up the money for the murder museum? Was he watching me right now? That would be really cool and also a bit disturbing.

Ava held her hand over the mic as Betty appeared at her side. The two leaned their heads together and appeared to be deep in discussion. I tried to lip read but only made out something that appeared to involve arson, one dozen lobsters, and Taylor Swift. After a moment, Ava took her hand off the mic.

"No comment."

This caused a loud buzz as people excitedly embraced this possible news. Lucinda turned back to a cameraman I still couldn't see, brought the mic to her lips, and said, "Who's There's young mayor neither confirms, nor denies that billionaire recluse Sheldon McBride is behind this new Museum of Murder. This reporter remains on the case. Back to you, Scott and Andrea."

She then marched through the crowd and out the door. I still hadn't seen a cameraman, but a small drone suddenly dropped from the ceiling before flying towards the door that Lucinda had just closed and smashed into it. There was a brief spark before the door burst into flame.

Maybe the ethanol drone wasn't a rumor after all.

As the screaming commenced, Rex calmly walked over to the door with a fire extinguisher and put the fire out. Officer Kevin Dooley and the Hamlets immediately taped over the doorway with CAUTION tape, until Rex told him to take it down as it was a working exit. I gave my husband two thumbs-up, and a pair of young Bangladeshi men I hadn't noticed earlier scowled and aimed the same gesture back at me.

Ava leaned toward me and held out her phone to show me I'd already gotten a one-star review on some app. "You have to stop being rude to the interns from Bangladesh. I'm already getting complaints."

A second small drone descended from the ceiling. It stopped in front of my face and hovered for a few seconds before flying out the door that had now been chopped open with a fire axe.

I stood there, staring after it. For a moment there, I could swear it had winked at me.

CHAPTER FOUR

The press conference appeared to be over, so I jumped off the front of the stage and went to apologize to the Bangladeshi interns. They were very nice about the whole thing. I found out that the city was putting them up in the Radison for a week, and then they were going to move them somewhere more permanent. I wished Pantu and Bal good luck, but as I walked away, I could swear that one of them mentioned my old house and eminent domain. I could be wrong. I'd have to talk to Ava about that.

"I think you should know..." Ava appeared at my side, and the interns vanished. "The museum goes up next week."

My jaw dropped open, and I forgot all about the interns. "How is that possible? It was only just announced!"

"This was the *public* announcement." Ava rolled her eyes. "We've actually known about this for about six months."

What? "Why didn't you tell me before now?"

"Because the owner, who is also the donor, told us not to. Anyway, the exhibits have been made and are ready. They just need a week to install it."

I guess there was no point in holding out hope that it would never get built. "Where is it going to be?"

Ava pointed to her left. "Next door in the old community center. We're building a new, awesomer one outside of town. It's going to have rooms to meet in but also a creative hub."

Lauren joined us. "Isn't that cool? It'll have a 3D printer, a sound and video recording and editing studio, a sewing room, and an auditorium!"

That did sound cool. "I suppose that will be ready next week too?"

"No," Ava corrected me. "It'll take a couple of weeks for that."

"Everything is pre-fab these days," Betty said. "No one just builds a building from scratch. That would be dumb."

It did seem more efficient. "About this museum, do we have a list of the exhibits?"

The girls nodded. They did not, however, provide me with the list.

"We have pictures and everything!" Lauren grinned but did not produce those photos.

"Can I see them?" I pressed.

The three girls stepped away and began whispering conspiratorially. After a moment, Ava said, "No." Then they walked away.

"Hey, hon." Rex joined me. "Ready to go?"

On the way home, I asked him if he'd known anything about the museum.

He denied it. "Just what you've told me and what was said at the announcement tonight."

"How do you feel about that?" I turned to him. "Having a museum dedicated to all the murders in town?"

He pulled into the drive and turned off the car. "I'm not thrilled. It's a little too gruesome for my taste. On the other hand, it would be a big deal if Sheldon McBride was supporting it. And it should bring the tourists. The local businesses will be happy about that."

Two pickup trucks pulled in behind us. We met Rex's twin sisters and their husbands, Ron and Ivan, at the door. Rex ushered everyone inside to avoid the cold. Once everyone was settled with hot cocoa, he asked why they were here.

"Wives are upset," Ron said.

Ivan nodded. "They do not like museum coming here."

We looked at Randi and Ronni.

"I wouldn't exactly say upset…" Randi started with a warm smile.

"I would!" Ronni shouted. She always shouted. "We could've done that! We could've made a murder museum! You should've asked us first!"

Randi and Ronni were the owners of *Ferguson Taxidermy – Where Your Pet Lives On Forever!* And while I'd never heard of them mummifying the townspeople's' cats and dogs, they did do a very lucrative business creating anthropomorphic scenes where animals did people stuff, like a scene from *Beach Blanket Bingo* done with wildebeests as Annette Funicello and Frankie Avalon, or *Psycho* with a cast of moray eels.

Most of their orders came from Japan.

I guess they were saying that they could have done a museum of murder, featuring the same thing but with animals. To be completely honest, I think I'd like that better.

"Merry had nothing to do with it. At any rate, it's all been done," Rex soothed. "Maybe you could do a special exhibit for them sometime?"

"That is good idea, little brother!" Ron beamed before crushing Rex in a bear hug and lifting him off the ground.

"I want to hug little brother too!" Ivan joined in, and my husband was crushed between them.

Randi brightened. Ronni scowled. Ron and Ivan put Rex down.

"I think that's brilliant!" Randi jumped up and hugged her little brother before looking to placate her twin. "Besides, we're going to have our hands full soon!" She patted her baby bump.

"She means of babies," Ivan explained, as if we needed it. "Babies can fill up two hands."

Ron nodded. "Or three!"

"You can't really do anything about the museum," I said. "Believe me, I'd rather it didn't happen at all."

My phone rang, so I stepped out of the room to answer it.

"The girls don't have school tomorrow," Kelly sighed. "And cookie sales start in a couple of weeks, so I thought we could have our annual cookie meeting at your place."

Girl Scout cookie sales! My troop lived for that time of year. That would distract them, and maybe I could see those photos of the exhibits!

"But we just had a meeting on Iceland," I worried. "Will they show up for another one so soon?"

"Yes. Besides, I wasn't there and we need to get this done."

The next morning, the girls arrived as Kelly and I set up in the living room. Once everyone was sitting in a circle on the floor, my co-leader started to hold up the new order forms, when the mayor interrupted.

"What do you think of this?" Ava held up a T-shirt that said *Museum of Murder* in red, dripping letters.

"Isn't that a bit disturbing?" Kelly looked dubious.

"The donor gave us permission to design all the merch," Betty explained. "We're going to do T-shirts, insulated mugs, cups, salt and pepper shakers, gun holsters…everything. It'll be a big moneymaker."

I raised my hand. "Who did they give the permission to? You guys or the city?"

She shrugged. "What's the difference?"

"There's a big difference. If you guys get this wrong, the donor could pull out of the whole project," Kelly warned.

"Unlikely," Inez said. "Betty had a lawyer look over the whole deal. We're getting more out of it than the donor is."

"What lawyer?" The last thing I needed was for these girls to lawyer up…on anything.

"A Russian dude," Betty said, "who owes Grandpa a favor."

I decided at that moment that I didn't want to know. Not that I was afraid of the Des Moines Russian mob. In fact, I had a couple of friends involved. I just didn't need the drama after finding out there was going to be a murder museum and I was one of the main exhibits.

"And then there's this one." Ava held up another shirt.

A black T-shirt had *Who's There? Enter if You Dare* in the same, bleeding letters.

"I'm sensing a theme here…" I muttered to my co-leader.

"I think this is my personal favorite." Ava held up a shirt with my face on it, wearing a sinister expression that even frightened me.

Who's There's Murder Woman! This was also in bloody letters.

"Seriously?" I broke in. "I'm not a murder woman…whatever that is!"

"I think it'll be a best seller!" Inez insisted.

I folded my arms over my chest. "Well, you can't use it. I won't give you permission."

The girl folded her arms, mirroring me. "You already did!"

"No," I said evenly. "I most certainly did not."

They held up a Girl Scout permission form that had been doctored to read: *i, mrs. Wrath, give my permission for the fellowship of the robust otter, llc, to use my likeness in any way imaginable, forever.*

Huh. It did look like my signature.

"When did I do that?" I didn't remember doing that.

"Remember that sleepover we had a couple of weeks ago?" Betty asked.

I did remember that sleepover. We ate twenty cheese and pepperoni pizzas, told ghost stories, and attempted to learn snowshoeing, with such disastrous results that I vowed never to do it again.

"I remember everything about that sleepover," I declared. "Except for signing that."

"Well duh! That's cuz you were asleep at the time," Inez countered.

"Anything I signed in my sleep isn't legally binding." At least, I didn't think it was.

"Igor says it is," Betty said. "And since he's a lawyer, we will go with what he said."

"But if you really don't want us to make money for orphaned kittens…" two of the Kaitlyns said.

"We won't use that design," the other two finished. "We promise."

Inez, Betty, and Lauren stared at the Kaitlyns for this breach of a long-standing, unwritten policy that it was them against us. The girls didn't back down. Lauren walked over to them. I guess she'd picked a side.

"Fine!" Ava tossed the shirt aside. "I guess you won't like this one either, then."

She held up a T-shirt of me behind bars with a savage-looking dagger between my teeth, asking, *Why Isn't She Locked Up?*.

"Your sister-in-law did that one," Inez added.

Of course she did. "Any other designs featuring me as murder woman?"

The girls all shook their heads.

"Good." I started to speak but was cut off.

"What if we did something representational of you that isn't completely you?" Betty wondered. "I really think the Murder Woman idea will take off."

"I don't think the Girl Scout Council would allow Murder Woman to continue to run a troop." Ha! Take that!

That seemed to stop them in their tracks. They wouldn't want to give up their leader. These kids loved me!

"We'd still have Mrs. Albers," Lauren reasoned. "And maybe you could be like…a consultant."

I turned to my co-leader, who had, for some reason, declined to comment on any of this.

"I'd hate to have to be responsible for all those permission slips on my own. Besides," she went on. "Cookie season is starting, and I don't want to do that all by myself."

"And…" I added. "I'm her best friend. So…"

Kelly cocked her head to one side. "I don't think I should take that into account. It might make me look biased."

I clapped my hands together. "Right! We are here to talk about cookie sales!"

"I'm not sure we've resolved this," Kelly interrupted.

"Yes. We have. Should we go on? Because I have the cookie forms right here." I produced a large envelope. "And if we don't plan this now, all the other troops will get the jump on us."

That started a near riot, mostly because there was a troop of cute Brownies at the girls' elementary school who would have no problem hoovering up all the orders. Their cutthroat instincts kicked in, and we began to discuss how we could crush the competition of small, adorable children.

CHAPTER FIVE

Considering the dedication my troop had to the things they are passionate about (often to the verge of psychotic obsession), I shouldn't have been surprised when the museum was actually up in a week. I'd admit that I was proud of their dedication to goals, whether it was setting up a new museum of murder, blackmailing area Boy Scouts into buying their cookies, or selling personally crafted conspiracy theories on the dark web.

A lot of work had been done while I'd fretted and gotten all the cookie sales stuff together and did my annual winter gun cleaning. It wasn't long before the old community center was completely renovated, and rumor had it that the exhibits were fully installed.

It was nice of the mayor to invite me to the *Super Secret Sneak Peek for Shetland Ponies* the night before it opened. I put on a little black dress, and Rex suited up.

Two of the Kaitlyns were at the front door, each wearing a headset and carrying a clipboard. In spite of the fact that we were the only ones there, they still made us line up behind the glittery pink velvet rope stanchions.

"Betty's orders," one said.

The other continued, "You have to follow the rules."

The girls made Rex and me stand there, in the cold, for five minutes before one of the Kaitlyns whispered something into a headset while the other one nodded. It felt like a bit of a power trip on their behalf.

"You're cleared to enter," they said in unison. "Fiona the Shetland pony is already inside."

"The pony got to go in before me?"

One of the Kaitlyns nodded. "She's very high maintenance. Fiona didn't want to get her hooves dirty standing out here."

I still hadn't seen anyone else, and I was worried about one thing. "What are you guys doing for security? What if someone tries to crash the event?"

The Kaitlyns simultaneously gave a loud, very specific whistle, and Ron and Ivan burst through the doors. They were wearing black *Museum of Murder Security with Mayor-Ordained Permission to Use Unnecessary Violence* T-shirts. The scowls on their faces were replaced with disappointment when they saw it was only us.

Ron turned to the girls. "You want us to bounce?" He waved a hand at me.

Ivan seemed thoughtful. "We would not want to fight family. But little girls are paying to us a lot of money, so we will."

"If we have to," Ron added.

The Kaitlyns shook their heads, and one said, "No, we just wanted to show Mrs. and Mr. Wrath our security system."

My name was Ferguson, but trying to get my troop to call me that was as futile as making a Russian figure skater likeable. I had long suspected that once kids name their adults, those names never changed.

Ron and Ivan puffed out their chests.

"Did you hear?" Ron smacked Ivan on the arm. "We are security system!"

Ivan nodded eagerly. "Is promotion!"

Ron liked this idea. "Maybe we get health insurance!"

The Kaitlyns looked at each other and shook their heads before saying, "Maybe."

We were still the only people here.

"Are we late or really early?" I asked.

"It's just you and your plus one." Kaitlyn nodded toward Rex. "And the mayor and the troop."

"And the donor drone," the other one said. "But that's all."

"You can go in," the other Katilyn said ominously. "Betty is waiting."

We entered the lobby, which was all black and white tile, from the floor to the ceiling. It was extremely disorienting, and that was saying a lot since I was once a guest at a wedding between a foul-mouthed Republican parrot and a Democrat penguin who came down the aisle in full drag, beak-syncing to "I've Been to Paradise, But I've Never Been to Me."

Betty dropped down from the ceiling on a cable, wearing the now characteristic black T-shirt with bloody letters that said *Murder Inc*. I was guessing she didn't know that phrase had a different meaning, something I'd need to talk to her about later. Betty unhooked her carabiner, dropped to the floor, and pointed to the main doors.

"Nobody's been inside yet. For some reason, Ava thought you should be the first. She's in the basement checking out the offices with the other girls."

"Nobody's been inside the exhibit hall?" Rex wondered.

"Not since the trucks unloaded and set up this morning. The donor drone is inside." The kid opened the door. "Oh, and Fiona's in there somewhere. You should get going. The donor drone is waiting for you." She leaned forward conspiratorially. "Whatever you do, don't make fun of its accent."

"That's not at all weird," I muttered.

"It's totally weird," Rex muttered back.

We looked at each other and stepped inside. We appeared to be in a large entryway. On the wall was a map of the exhibit, which I went to read.

Damn. It was all there. You started at the most recent murder and worked your way back to my very first body in Who's There. My heart sank. Every single exhibit appeared to include me.

"I guess that answers that," Rex sighed.

We heard the whirring sound before we spotted the drone.

"G'day!" an Australian voice said cheerily. "Welcome to the Museum of Murder!"

The voice came from a drone that looked just like the ones we'd seen at the announcement. The only difference was it was sporting a black bowtie and a short, rather androgynous wig of auburn hair.

"You talk?" I looked around in case I was being punked.

"So, you're an Australian?" Rex asked the drone as if it was the most normal thing in the world to do.

"No," the drone replied. "I'm using an AI filter so you won't figure out who I am. Aces, right, mate?"

I nodded. "We did stuff like this in the CIA to hide our identities."

"Defo!" The drone seemed to bob up and down as if it was nodding. "So…what d'ya think?"

Someone worked very hard to make this happen. The girls were very proud of it. How could I say I hated it?

In the end, I settled. "We haven't seen it yet."

"Oh. Right, mate. We'll have to fix that! Follow me." The drone plunged into the exhibit hall.

I suppose a lot of people would love to have a museum about them. Kim Jong-un had six hundred and thirty-two Museums for the Worship of Dear Leader buildings in Pyongyang alone, complete with warning signs posted everywhere telling people they would be shot for eating the exhibits. Putin had one in Red Square featuring all the taxidermied bears he'd ever ridden shirtless.

I didn't want a museum.

"The rooms start with the latest murder and end with the first," the drone said, which we already knew.

He wasn't wrong. The first room we came to looked just like the first floor of the haunted house my troop had a few months ago, complete with the body of the dead city building inspector we'd found on the floor, surrounded by zombie mannequins. And there were the statues of my co-leader Kelly and me. My best friend was standing in the doorway, looking appropriately horrified, while "I" looked a little bored with the whole scene.

Rex crouched down next to the body. Everything was there, as if we'd traveled back in time to that actual moment.

"It's pretty realistic," he said.

"Oh! Blimey! Where are my manners?" the drone said in a British accent. "Detective Ferguson, I presume?"

"This is my husband, Rex." I felt like an idiot introducing my spouse to a drone. "My plus one, as the girls said."

The drone seemed to frown. "Forgive my incredulity, but I didn't mean for you to bring a date. It was quite imperative to get your reaction alone."

"Okay, we can leave." I started to turn back. "Because I'm not staying without him."

"No! My apologies. This is, of course, fine." There was a pause. "Actually, this is good. Because he can attest to the veracity of the exhibits."

"Thanks," Rex said wryly. He waved at the scene. "Everything is perfectly in place. Which makes me wonder how you were able to see the police report?"

The drone seemed to smirk. "Freedom of Information Act, dear chap."

That was interesting. Maybe we could find out who requested the information. Rex smiled as if he thought the same thing.

I stepped towards the hovering equipment. "I have to ask. Is the AI making you talk in the vernacular, or are you just doing it to throw us off?"

"It is the exclusive prerogative of the AI. I do not really talk like this, but it is a nice touch, don't you think?"

I didn't answer. I looked around the room and spotted a large turkey vulture pouting in one corner. The girls must've told the donor about it, because Rex had kept it out of the report for fear of getting them in trouble.

"Come through, please!" The drone flew ahead to the doorway, and we found ourselves on a theater stage that was all too familiar.

An excellent likeness of Dante, the theater director and actor, lay on the floor of the stage as his wife Ophelia clutched her turban, wailing dramatically. My mannequin stood off to the side, hands on her hips as if irritated with the whole thing. I didn't remember acting like that.

I sighed. "You've got this murder scene right." A thought occurred to me. "But there was a murder that happened between this one and the last one."

"Ay, there was, lass," the drone said in a lilting Irish accent. "You see, we only had so much room. In order to make it authentic, we could only make nine exhibits. As for the others, we are going to cycle exhibits out. Since you've been involved in so many murders, this should keep the museum fresh for years!"

Great.

"You know Ophelia still lives here and runs the program," I said as I walked over to the statue of Iago the stage pig. I looked back at the drone. "She'll probably think this is insensitive, throwing her husband's murder in her face like this."

"Actually, Mrs. Oxnard gave us her blessing," the drone replied.

I reached down to touch the pig statue, and it squealed loudly before nuzzling my leg.

"Iago?" I looked at the drone. "You're keeping a real pig in here?" I scratched between his ears.

There was a whinny, and it sounded like an army was on our way. From the far door, Fiona came running in. She spotted Iago and ran over to him. The two began snorting to each other in a way that appeared they liked each other.

"Officer Dooley," the drone said, "loaned him to us. It was ever so nice of him."

I was about to ask who was going to clean up after the pig but decided I just didn't care.

The drone flew on, and we followed it. In a weird way, it was kind of fun seeing which murder would be next.

We walked into the next room and found ourselves in the dining room of my old neighbor's house, with my old neighbor's body lying on the floor, glaring at the ceiling. Every single 1970s knickknack the woman had had seemed to be here. I was going to ask where the drone had found *Nixon – an Honest Man* salt and pepper shakers when I spotted Kelly's mannequin, again looking appropriately dismayed, and mine, throwing her hands in the air, eyes rolled up to the ceiling. Why did I always look annoyed? At least the method of murder was spot on, which made me wonder if this guy had access to the autopsy photos too.

"Looks like you've been very thorough, Mr...?" Rex started.

"Tis Seamus. Although I may not be a man at all. I may be..." There was a pause before the drone began speaking in a Spanish accent of a female. "A senorita named Maria Conchetta Arabella Concepcion!"

There was a whirring sound, and two huge gold hoop earrings popped out of the machine as the bowtie appeared to be sucked inside the mechanism. The drone seemed very pleased with itself, if that was possible.

I couldn't help but think about who had requested the files. Usually it was the media, like a newspaper or something...

"Medea!" I shouted, fists in the air. "You got Medea Jones to request the files!"

The drone hovered in one place and said nothing. I wondered how I could torture a drone to get the intel I needed. Would a car battery with rusty cables work? Waterboarding would just short it out. Then again, there was a whiff of ethanol in the air. I wonder how it would react to a flamethrower. Then I realized I didn't *have* a flamethrower. I'd have to find matches. Maybe the gift shop had them.

It had to be Sheldon McBride. Who else, besides Lucinda, would have an ethanol drone? I decided to keep this to myself until I was certain. And without waiting, we went into the next exhibit.

There she was. Deliria, the queen of horror, lay on the floor, surrounded by mannequins of teens in cosplay costumes, holding comic books and gaping. Stewie stood over the body with a knife, which wasn't accurate. I felt like that was a little win for me. That is, until I spotted my mannequin standing off to the side in that stupid beetle costume. And I'd hoped the humiliation of wearing that had died on that day with Deliria.

"Oi!" A Scottish voice this time. "Whad'ya ken so far, ya silly bastards?"

Just to be difficult, I didn't answer and plunged into the next room—my high school gymnasium. A pair of feet stuck out from behind the curtain on the stage, and the passed-out bodies of my classmates lay all around us. "I" stood on stage with Kelly, Kevin Dooley, and the girls. In this one, I was scowling with my hands on my hips.

"Where are the other bodies?" I turned to the drone. "There were multiple murders in this one."

The drone looked around. "Och! Excuse me a wee meenit."

The next thing we heard was a furious Scotsman screaming at someone about being fired. When that was over, the drone turned back to us. "Just a wee problem. Some eejit will lose his spoondoolies." Then the drone buzzed over to the punch bowl, where a small familiar mannequin was dumping something from a bottle labelled LSD into the punch. "Lookit! We have stuff that's pure dead brilliant!"

"You can't include Betty spiking the punch with LSD." I put my hands on my hips, mimicking my dummy. "The police left that out of the report so as not to implicate the girls."

The British accent reappeared. "Ah. I wondered why it had been left out. But I am afraid Miss Betty was quite insistent."

Of course she was. I looked to the doorway to see a little brown head disappear.

Rex shook his head. "I'm afraid you have to take this one out."

"*No!*" Betty shouted as she ran over to us. "I need this to back up my resume!"

"The CIA doesn't take thirteen-year-olds," I said.

She shook her head. "Not yet they don't."

"See?" the drone said. "It's decided."

Rex sighed. "All right. But that might be what it takes to push your parents over the edge and finally send you to that military boarding school in Texas."

There was a moment of silence.

"Fine!" Betty snapped before stomping away.

"Texas military school?" the drone asked.

My husband nodded.

"Out it goes!" The drone was silent for a moment. Probably emailing orders for fake Betty's removal.

"Out of curiosity," I asked, "what are you going to do with the Betty mannequin?"

The drone turned toward me. "I am not certain."

"Well..." I looked around. "I'll take it off your hands...if you were going to get rid of it anyway."

Betty ran back into the room, scooped up her doppelganger, and glared at me. "I'm taking it. I can use it...for a thing."

She marched out of the room, head held high.

Rex nudged me. "What exactly did you want that for?"

I shrugged. "I have no idea, but I'd have come up with something."

My husband waved his arms around him. "This is impressive. They have really done their research."

I had to admit. Whoever it was had done a great job. The gym looked very real and even was decorated with streamers and a banner that read *Go Fighting Whorish*, referring to the unfortunate mascot—a blend of Who's and the main nationality in town.

Unfortunately, this was worse than I thought. I couldn't wait for the tour to be over. Only five more exhibit halls to go. I closed my eyes, crossed my fingers, and prayed on the life of Putin's current bear, Little Putin Jelly Bean Toes, that things wouldn't get worse.

CHAPTER SIX

I turned to the drone. "Surely there are other things about Who's There's history that would be better in this museum?"

Hopefully it wouldn't ask me what those things were, because I had no clue.

The drone said nothing. It just hovered there, staring at me.

"Merry's right," Rex agreed. "This just seems like a questionable idea. Not all the details are correct. What if it inspires lawsuits against my department?"

"The donor," the drone explained, "will back the department with the best legal representation it can find."

Aha! It had to be Sheldon McBride! Only a rich guy would promise something like that. But how could I make him admit it?

"Now that that is settled, shall we move on?" the drone said in a now gender-neutral, accent-less voice. "Please keep up." It zoomed ahead into the next room.

Rex and I exchanged glances before entering the next room, where we were transported to a dusty parking lot behind the Corn Hole bar. An unfortunately familiar dumpster had a pair of legs sticking out. It was Azlan—that is, Wally (his American name), or a representation of the Chechen strong man I'd been embedded with. He'd come to town to threaten me and ended up dead in a dumpster. Ron and Ivan, who'd accompanied him as mindless muscle, had been blamed, and I'd worked hard to get them out of jail by proving Wally had killed himself.

A mannequin of Hilly Vinton was walking away, appearing to brush her hands together, as if she had been the killer. Technically, the CIA assassin, who wasn't an assassin because the CIA doesn't have assassins because that would be illegal (but totally was), had helped Wally kill himself.

"You can't have that in here." I stepped closer to the manikin of my friend. "Hilly works for the CIA. They'll close this place down in minutes!" *Hey! That might work for me!*

It was the best of all the mannequin we'd seen so far. This thing really looked like the statuesque brunette.

"We didn't put that there!" The donor zoomed over, closing in on Hilly's head.

"And yet, here she is," I pointed out.

All of a sudden, the statue moved. It turned and grinned at me. I didn't realize they were going to use animatronics! That's pretty cool. I might have to change my vote on this...

"Hey, Merry! I got you!" Hilly beamed.

The drone screamed in horror.

Hilly glanced at the machine then back to me. "Want me to *milk the marsupial*?"

Hilly liked using euphemisms for wet work. A while back, the CIA had adopted the euphemisms, assuming no one would realize they were speaking in code. Unfortunately, everyone knew immediately what they were saying, which caused a dramatic drop in *marsupial milking*, so they dropped the whole procedure. Hilly kept it going, and no one stopped her because she's scary.

The drone backed away slowly.

"No," I sighed. "Whoever's behind this will just send another drone. You really had me going for a moment!"

The assassin grinned again. "I'm a bit rusty. I haven't stood that still since that time I had to pretend to be a marble statue at the Coliseum for that job in Rome."

The drone hovered uncertainly. "I don't believe you!"

Hilly didn't seem offended. "It's true. I was the bust of a woman. It was tricky, pretending to have no digestive system, hips, or legs, but I nailed it."

I learned a long time ago to just go with whatever Hilly said. She always assumed that we knew exactly what she was talking about.

"You aren't supposed to be here!" The drone seemed to regain its thoughts. "Security!"

Hilly shrugged. Ron and Ivan burst into the room, fists up, ready to rumble. They stopped when they saw the assassin.

"Who is here?" Ron looked around. "Who to bounce?"

The drone nodded toward Hilly. "That woman! She's trespassing!"

"But that is *Hilly*," Ivan explained.

"She wasn't invited!" the drone screeched.

"We do not fight Hilly." Ron folded his large arms over his chest. I suspected this was because he knew she could kick their collective asses.

"It's okay." I held up my hands. "Hilly is a close, personal friend. I can vouch for her. She's been involved with half of these murders anyway." I thought for a moment. "Not, like, she's the killer. More like how I'm involved…"

We heard Betty's voice echo from somewhere. "She can stay!"

The drone sighed. "I suppose there isn't anything we can do about it now, is there?" he asked a bit hopefully.

"Nope." Hilly began doing lunges and stretching. "This is pretty awesome! Maybe someone will do a museum like this about me!"

It seemed unlikely, because for that to happen, the CIA would have to admit that she's been killing for them for years.

"By the way," I started to say. "Isn't it weird how this is the Corn Hole bar and that ethanol car is called a Corn Hole?" I turned to the drone to study its um, features. Just in case it gave something away.

"Not at all," the drone said. "It's a common name. Anyone could've thought that up."

"But only Sheldon McBride did," I said.

The drone and I stared at each other for a long time.

Finally I said, "Do you have something you want to admit to…Sheldon?"

The drone said nothing. Like, really said nothing. I worried that I'd shorted him out. In fact, we waited for several minutes with no response. It just hung there, mid-air, in total silence.

Hilly walked over and smacked the drone hard on the back. There was a strange beeping, and for a moment I thought it was going to explode. After what sounded like a burp, it spoke again.

"Thanks," the drone said. "I needed that."

"Before you blipped out," I pressed, "you were about to confess that you are Sheldon McBride."

"No I wasn't," the drone insisted.

"Yes you were," I fought back.

"I most certainly wasn't going to admit to anything!" the drone shouted.

"Stop making the anonymous donor angry!" Betty's voice came from an unknown location.

I looked around at the others. "Really? No one's going to back me up here?"

My husband and former colleague said nothing. My brothers-in-law fled. The cowards.

"Fine. I guess we should keep going."

This wasn't over!

"This way," the drone said as it made a beeline towards the next door.

"Thanks a lot," I muttered to Hilly as she fell into step with me.

She brightened. "You're welcome! What did I do? You should tell me so I can do it again!"

If the dead Wally exhibit was a bit of a yawn, the next one was very exciting. The whole room was laid out like a Clue game board. I suppressed a shudder. I remembered this case all too well. Six people were murdered before I figured out who the killer was. I still felt a little bad about that.

Still, the layout was really cool, with nine rooms drawn on the floor and a square for the staircase in the middle. There were four mannequins in all, with a man in the dining room, slumped over a table, a woman in the study with a trophy sticking out of her neck, a man passed out on a sofa in the conservatory, and a woman lying prone at the foot of the staircase.

Rex and Hilly frowned. They hadn't been part of this one because it was outside of Rex's jurisdiction, and Soo Jin and the girls had accompanied me instead. There was a scratching sound in the walls. A little door flipped open in the conservatory, and a white, lop-eared robot rabbit stuck its head out to study us.

"Gertrude!" I shouted. "You've really thought of everything!"

"Yes, well." The drone hemmed and hawed. "We had trouble replicating the second floor and the two murders there, I'm afraid. But we do have a monitor in the study where you can see mockups of those murders. The rabbit is not the actual Gertrude but one that looks like her, named Pete."

I walked over to the body representing Dennis Blunt on the couch in the conservatory. The dummy did look like the arrogant young man. He really looked asleep...and poisoned by an aerosol spray. At least they didn't have the second floor where Thad Gable had drowned face down in a bowl of lube jelly. I never did fully explain that to the girls. I hoped I never would have to.

Rex was exploring the room, studying each fake corpse. "I kind of wish I'd been on this one with you."

The drone seemed pleased. "If you think this is great, wait until you see the next one!" It dove with glee toward the next doorway, and once again, we followed.

This museum seemed to go on forever. I was less frustrated than when I'd entered. Now I was curious about what was next. In fact, it was a little fun. Not that I was about to admit that to Rex or anything.

I studied my husband as he looked around. He must be having a little fun too...even if he wouldn't admit it.

As if he knew what I was thinking, Rex looked at me and winked. Yeah. He was enjoying this.

Hilly, on the other hand, was doing back flips through the doorway until she disappeared.

I don't know what I was expecting, but it wasn't the next room. In one corner, there was a mockup of a shed with just Ike Murphy's feet sticking out. That was good because he'd been bludgeoned with an ax. But the best part was the rest of the room, which was done up to look like the first floor in the Peterson house—the first nice home in Who's There, owned by the town's founders.

This room featured the century-old mysterious ax murder of Mehitable Peters. A mannequin representing her was on the floor with an axe buried in her plastic head. A rigging system ran along the wall with a surprised llama at the other end.

Rex had seemed to relax a bit. Because it happened a century ago, he wasn't involved in Mehitable's murder. Maybe he was getting perspective on the whole thing. Hilly, however, was trying to ride the llama like a cowboy.

"Um, excuse me…" The drone zoomed over to her. "Could you get off the fake llama, please?"

Hilly hopped off and closed in on the machine. "Hey, how come I'm not in most of these?"

"You were in Wally's vignette and the theater one," I explained. "You weren't here all the time, or you would be."

Hilly whipped out a notebook and spoke as she wrote: *Be here all the time.*

The drone hovered in front of me. "Well, what do you think so far?"

It seemed like there wasn't any point in fighting it anymore. "It's better than I expected. If you're going to lay my life bare to the public, that is. At least it isn't as bad as when I was outed in Chechnya and trying to flee the country for my life."

"Hey!" the drone said. "That's not a bad idea! Please see that I get a detailed account of that!"

I narrowed my eyes. "This is the Museum of Murder, not the Museum of Merry Wrath Ferguson."

The drone stared at me. "I don't see why we couldn't do both."

Okay, now I was mad. I may not be able to get at the donor, but I could take his drone apart, piece by piece. I started towards the thing, but Rex got in between us.

"It's okay," he said quietly to me. "I'll handle this." He turned to the drone. "I think one museum is all we can handle right now. If you want to pursue this, I can tell you from experience that the CIA doesn't like outsiders spilling national security secrets on classified activities."

The drone looked disappointed somehow. Or maybe I just hoped he was. "All right. Let's check out the last exhibit before we hit the gift shop. I know the girls are excited for you to see what they've done there."

Was I imagining it, or was he moping on the way to the doorway?

"Thanks." I took my husband's hand and squeezed.

"Don't thank me yet. While you were looking at the exhibit, he said something about a new museum where the proceeds went to the police department. I could still sell you out."

He winked.

"At least we have only one exhibit hall left," I said. "We're almost done."

Hilly ran after the drone, shouting, "You need to make a museum about me!"

It was the exhibit I was most dreading. The room had a replica of my first car, with a mannequin representing Carlos the Armadillo, after I'd accidentally hit and killed him. It was still murder because Carlos had been pushed into the path of my moving car.

My first brush with murder in Who's There. To the right of the outdoor scene was a mockup of my house, as if someone had cut it in half and exposed only the kitchen, where Yakuza boss Midori Ito lay dead on the floor.

I wasn't sure they could do this. Technically, both murders had taken place in Who's There, but both victims were people I'd worked under as a spy. The CIA would have something to say about this. They'd even sent my former handler, Riley Andrews, back to deal with it at the time.

Of course, he'd long since left the CIA and was now a private investigator in town. And technically, I hadn't killed Carlos. I hadn't killed Midori either. I *had* killed two Russian goons in a shootout not long after that. But that wasn't really murder, and I was grateful that wasn't in this museum.

I relaxed and closed my eyes for a moment, happy that this trip through the past was over. Now we just had the gift shop, and I was certain there wouldn't be anything dangerous in selling souvenirs.

CHAPTER SEVEN

"And this," the drone said as it led the way, "is the gift shop."

We walked into what appeared to be the biggest room in the whole place. It was laid out like a department store...like a murdery Macy's. The gory T-shirts were front and center and sold for fifty bucks a pop. It was kind of impressive, in a disturbing, yet awesome way.

"Ooh!" Hilly squealed as she ran over to a miniature souvenir dumpster. "I need this!" She held it aloft and studied the legs coming out of it. "Reminds me of good times!"

Did I mention that Hilly's modus operandi was dumpsters? It was her favorite place to dispose of bodies. Usually, the CIA didn't like someone behaving in the same way over and over. But Hilly was almost as terrifying to them as the Dominatrices who ran Human Resources, and she had an extremely malleable moral code, so they let her do whatever she wanted.

Hilly looked around. "I'm going to need forty-seven of these!"

"That's a random number," I said.

"Why would you say that?" Hilly wondered. "It's the perfect number for anything, from how many pet beetles I have to how many electrical outlets in my apartment."

"You've counted the number of outlets in your apartment?" Rex asked.

She stared at us blankly. "Of course I did! Who doesn't? What's really weird is that people always ask me that question."

Betty appeared at our side, carrying a small wand in her hand. She looked like she was getting ready to audition to be Voldemort. The kid took one of the dumpsters and waved the wand over it. The wand projected an image in the air with the total cost for forty-seven souvenirs, plus tax.

"That'll be $1,180," she said.

Hilly handed over a credit card. Betty scanned this with the wand, and the transaction was approved.

"Where did you get that?" I held out my hand for the device.

Betty held back, refusing to give it to me. "It's the latest technology. The donor gave it to us. It isn't in use anywhere else in the world. This is a prototype."

It had to be McBride. I held out my hand more insistently. Grudgingly, Betty handed it over. The minute it touched my hand, a hologram popped up that read *Merry Wrath, Original, $10,000*.

"I'm for sale?" I gaped.

Betty snatched that away. "Oh sure, it's all about *you*."

This whole place was about me! "Why only 10K?" I was worth more than that.

The girl shrugged. "Don't blame me. It's what the market will bear. Ask the drone."

We turned to look at the drone, which seemed to be very interested in some board games based on the island murders. I walked over to check them out.

"Hey, this is laid out exactly like a Clue board. You can't sell this. It's probably a copyright violation."

"My legal team went over everything in here to make sure we could sell them," the drone argued. "You really like to tell me what we can and can't do, don't you?"

"Merry?" Rex called me over to a large glass counter flanked by two huge glass display cases.

They were filled with a very odd collection of what at first seemed like random things, all with very large price tags attached.

After studying the case, I stood up and looked to the girls. "What's this?"

Ava and Inez came over.

"Oh, those are real artifacts from the nine murders," the mayor explained. "Pretty cool, huh?"

"Are you promoting this as the very garrote that killed Barry Goetz in the high school gym?" Rex's eyebrows went up.

Museum of Murder | 45

"Lying to customers can constitute fraud, especially if they found out the garrote is in my evidence lockup."

The two girls looked at each other.

"Is it?" Inez asked.

"Of course it is," Betty, who'd joined us out of nowhere interjected, wiggling her eyebrows. "You don't need to look. Or even do a complete inventory on everything you have in the fourth room down the hall from your office on the left."

Rex sighed. "It kind of feels like I do need to do exactly that."

"I wouldn't recommend it," Betty said. "There might be booby traps."

"What booby traps?" Rex narrowed his eyes.

The kid shrugged. "How would I know what kind of booby traps you'd have in there? I don't work there!"

I peered into the glass. "That does look a lot like the knife that killed Deliria." I spotted something small and furry that was priced at $800. "How did you get Tinkles' fur? She's been dead for over a century!" If that was real, it was worth it. I might have to get it.

"Until I get to the bottom of this, I'm going to give you girls the benefit of the doubt that you haven't plundered my evidence locker. This is kind of morbid." Rex pointed at a poisoned inhaler from the class reunion murders. "Is anyone really going to pay a thousand dollars for that?"

Betty nodded. "We've done extensive research. People love this true crime junk."

Ava chastised her petite, Darth lieutenant. "*Memorabilia*. The donor said we shouldn't call it junk. Then they'll think it isn't authentic."

Rex looked like his head was about to explode. I decided to back him up.

"This stuff is pretty morbid. You think it will sell?"

Ava pointed to Betty, who was getting out the llama fur for Hilly.

"I'll take it! The actual fur from an animal assassin! Tinkles is like me!" She paused for a bit. "Only…a llama."

A whirring behind me made me look up. The drone seemed to be waiting for a reaction.

"This is kind of crazy…" I started to say.

"*I'm not crazy!*" the drone shrieked. "Why does everyone think I'm crazy?"

We all stood there, shocked into silence by the drone's admission. This was proof, I thought, that it was Sheldon McBride behind it all. Critics had called him crazy when he launched the ethanol drone idea. It had to be him!

"Sorry about that," the drone said when it realized we were all staring at him. "I don't know whatever came over me. Of course no one has ever called me crazy. There must have been some weird glitch in the program."

"Are you going to be here all the time?" I asked.

"Of course! I will be here at the museum 24/7 to oversee operations, make sure the guests aren't doing anything unsavory. You wouldn't believe the horrible things people do at the Lump of Lard museum in Nebraska." The drone shuddered.

"So," I started, "you'll basically be security for the whole building."

"No, I'm representing the interests of the anonymous donor," the drone replied.

"And what will you do if someone does something against the rules?" Rex wondered.

"I can record them." The drone sounded a bit terse. "I have pepper spray and a stun gun."

"If you have *any* problems," Rex said, "You need to call the police department. We'll take it from there."

"What do people do to the lumps of lard at that museum?" Hilly asked.

The drone shuddered again. "Trust me. You do *not* want to know."

"We should go." Rex placed his hand on my back.

I agreed. We'd seen all we needed to see here, and since I'd literally lived all of the exhibits, I wasn't planning on coming back anytime soon.

CHAPTER EIGHT

It was very hard to fall asleep that night. Between worrying about what the CIA would think, wondering how to prove that the drone was Sheldon McBride, and trying to come up with a way to get that Tinkles pelt from Hilly, my phone rang.

"The drone is gone!" Ava sounded panicked. That wasn't like her.

"What do you mean, the drone is gone?" I looked at the clock next to the bed. "It's two in the morning! Why are you still up?"

"The mayor never sleeps!" Ava shouted. "But seriously, we've looked everywhere, and the donor drone is gone!"

I sat up and rubbed my eyes. "It probably just had to go recharge somewhere. It can't run solely on ethanol." Huh. How did they refill it?

"You don't think we checked the charging station in the office?" Ava's voice was in a shrill pitch now. "It only has to plug in once a day and is scheduled to do that at one forty-five, and it's not there! You have to come over!"

"Fine. I'll be there in seven minutes." I hung up and shook Rex awake, telling him what the girls had said.

This is one of the reasons I loved this man. Without argument, he got up, brushed his teeth and got dressed, and met me downstairs. Five minutes later, we were inside the museum. It only took five minutes to get anywhere in Who's There.

The girls were more upset than I'd ever seen them, and that included the time they found out that badass Girl Scout founder, Juliette Low, wasn't a secret ninja. Kelly still didn't believe that I didn't tell them that.

The Kaitlyns were pacing in perfect synchronization that would make a North Korean parade master proud. Inez and

Lauren were wringing their hands. Ava was frantic. Only Betty was calm as she stuffed various weapons into a tactical vest she was wearing.

"Did you bring any guns?" she asked us. "We should probably have guns."

"For a missing drone?" I shook my head. "Not necessary."

Betty turned to the others. "We should've called Hilly."

I looked around. "She's not here?"

The assassin who wasn't an assassin but totally was usually stayed at my old house across the street. She hadn't said she wanted to stay there, but then again, she could break into any building on the planet, so maybe she didn't want to wake us to let her in.

"Ava," Rex said. "You turn on the lights for the whole place. Take the other girls with you. One of you have your phone ready to call me if you see something."

The girls actually saluted my husband and ran off to do what he asked them to.

"Nicely done." I slapped him on the arm.

"I figured we should distract them with something," he whispered. "Come on. Let's take a look."

Lights came on around us as we headed into the haunted house exhibit.

"It is kind of weird not having it around," I admitted. "I mean, the drone was very annoying, but it was kind of like an eager little kid who can't wait for you to see her artwork."

"I don't see anything," Rex said as we moved quickly through the next three exhibits. "There's nothing out of place."

I imagined what I'd expected. I guess I thought we'd find it on the floor, on its back like a dead bug. As we moved through the high school, Corn Hole, and Clue house exhibits, I didn't see anything out of place. For a moment, I thought I spotted it by the llama. But that was just a fuse box that I hadn't seen earlier.

What were we doing here? I'm sure the drone had a handler who managed it remotely. Probably that guy took it home to give it a tune up or whatever and didn't think they had to call the girls to say the drone had malfunctioned. Our meandering through the museum seemed like a bit of a useless errand at this point.

Still, the troop was upset, and I didn't like it when they were. It didn't happen often, but when it did, I got protective. The least I could do was check it out then send them home.

In the last exhibit, I couldn't resist checking out my mannequin. I didn't really have a chance before to do so without looking like I was vain.

After looking around to make sure Rex wouldn't notice, I reached up and poked myself in the shoulder. The other me was standing on a "road" in front of my car as it screamed in horror at the scene. I recognized Carlos the Armadillo as he lay on his back in front of my car.

The mannequin they had for Carlos, while not looking that much like him, was surprisingly lifelike. I bent down and pressed my index finger against his cheek.

I shot up to a standing position. What the hell? That wasn't firm plastic I'd touched! It was human skin! And the man lying in front of me wasn't a mannequin. He was real and very, very dead.

Rex crouched down and took a picture of the man's face. He noticed a wallet half underneath the corpse's shoulder and pulled it out. After locating the driver's license, he stood up. "I was afraid of this. I think you know who this is."

His comment startled me into realization. No wonder the drone wasn't there. Because the dead guy was none other than Sheldon McBride.

"I knew it! He was here the whole time!" I took the ID from my husband.

So this was the face of the famous, reclusive inventor! I looked down at the body to realize he hadn't been dressed like Carlos at all. The dead man was wearing a Hawaiian Aloha shirt, with a dark-red cardigan over it, khaki pants, and canvas tennis shoes. His sandy brown hair was parted on one side. A pair of square, black glasses were in the front pocket of his pants.

Rex nodded. "He probably had to control the drone from somewhere nearby. He must've been at the town hall meeting too. We were so distracted by the drone, we didn't see him."

The girls started to file into the room. Rex gave me a look, and I herded them back into the gift shop. What was I going to tell them? That the mystery donor was dead and unlikely to fund anything else in Who's There?

"You found a body," Ava said. "Again."

"It's him, isn't it?" Betty nodded toward the doorway. "You couldn't stand it," she accused. "You had to kill somebody to lend legitimacy to the museum."

The four Kaitlyns nodded.

"What? No!" I protested. "I didn't do anything. You guys were here the whole time I was!"

Ava closed her eyes for a second. When she opened them, I could see she'd regained control. "It's the donor, isn't it? He's dead, which is why the drone isn't flying around."

"We think so," I agreed.

The door opened, and Soo Jin and Officer Troy Wallace came in, wearing matching penguin pajamas. I looked at the medical examiner and her beau.

"Hi Merry! Hi girls!" Soo Jin called out brightly.

"Why are you both in pajamas?" Betty narrowed her eyes.

"We were at a pajama party," Soo Jin said without missing a beat.

Troy, at least, had the good grace to blush.

The girls bought it hook, line, and sinker.

"Makes sense," Inez said with a nod. "That's good because we didn't get you out of bed."

"We would've felt bad about that," Lauren said as the others agreed.

"You didn't mind getting Rex and me out of bed," I groused.

"That's different." Betty rolled her eyes.

After distracting the girls by suggesting they check the gift shop in case the murderer robbed the place, I slipped back to the exhibit, where Soo Jin was running her hands over the body.

"Nice jammies," Rex said casually to his officer.

"We were in…" Troy started to say before his eyes darted to the doorway. "A pajama party."

Rex shrugged. "It's your night off. Still, try to slip on your uniform next time."

"I didn't have my uniform," Troy started to say. He paused. "Because we were at a pajama party."

Soo Jin had ignored the conversation. She sat back on her heels then looked at the car. After a beat, she moved over to it and pulling out a pair of tweezers, extracted a hair from the bumper.

"I won't know for sure until I get him to the morgue, but I think he was hit by a car," she said finally.

Rex and I looked at each other. That was exactly how Carlos the Armadillo was killed. He was hit with my car.

"This car, I think," she added.

"That car?" Rex frowned. "Are you sure?"

She nodded. "There's fresh blood spatter, and this is one of the victim's hairs." She held up the tweezers before slipping the hair into a bag and handing it over to Troy.

"He was hit by this car, here in the museum?" I gasped. "But that's impossible! This is a model of my old car!" I walked over and opened the driver's side.

Okay, it was a real car. But it wasn't my old one. That had been sold to a little old lady from Winterset, years ago. She hadn't even minded that I'd accidentally killed a Colombian drug lord with it.

Then I saw the long scratch across the glove compartment. I'd made that scratch with a knife, trying to show the girls how to fight in close quarters. Unless someone had that exact same car and made that exact same scratch in that exact same place, that meant…

It might really be my car.

"I need to dust the wheel for prints," Soo Jin said as she stood next to me. "Sorry, Merry."

My thoughts were spinning as I got out of the car and she sat in the driver's seat and opened her case.

"It really is my car," I mumbled to Rex.

He nodded. "I know. While you were in there, I checked the VIN." He held up his phone to reveal a number in the old case file. "It's the same."

"You have your files digitized?"

He shook his head. "I did that when we got married. I figured it was better to be safe than sorry."

Most people might be mad about that. "I get it. At least we don't have to wait to go to the office to look up the number."

Rex studied my face. "You're not a suspect. You were with me all night, from the moment that we came here until right now."

I shrugged. I was used to being a suspect. "At least that's something. Another thing would be that I haven't had the keys to this car since I sold it."

"Soo Jin," Rex called out. "Are the keys in there?"

The medical examiner looked in the ignition, checked the floor and the driver's side visor. She shook her head. "We will need to impound this car so I can go over it thoroughly, though."

Troy came over to us, looking confused. "I'm sorry, but did you say this was your wife's car?"

Rex nodded. "We actually met when she ran over Carlos the Armadillo in this car."

Troy blanched and stared at me. "You ran someone else over in this car?"

"Rex will fill you in later." I turned to my husband. "I don't see any tire marks on the floor. It's a white tile floor. The car would have to have been traveling at some speed in order to kill McBride, right?"

Rex and Troy followed me to behind the car. The tile was clean. But then, the killer could've cleaned that up, right?

The men paced off the distance between the car and the doorway from the last exhibit. There was enough room to get up the speed, but it would've burned rubber to do so, and that would leave a mark.

I ran to the gift shop and asked Betty, "How did you get the car inside the room with the exhibit?"

She cocked her head to one side. "I don't know. Huh. I probably should know that."

"The exhibits were put together by the donor," Inez added. "We weren't here."

Ava squinted at her phone. "Crap. We gotta go, guys. Mom doesn't want to stay up any longer, so she's coming to get us."

"You're having a sleepover at Ava's?" I asked.

The girls nodded.

"It seemed like a good idea…" one of the Kaitlyns said.

"Since today's Saturday and all that," said two more.

Lauren perked up. "Hey! Guys! There's a real murder at the Museum of Murder! We can use that!"

The girls got excited, and Betty handed me the keys before they went outside to meet Ava's mom. I thought I heard one of them say "marketing strategy," just before they drove away, but I was tired and probably heard something else.

"We've got the keys to the building," I called out as I re-entered the real crime scene inside the depiction of a crime scene.

Rex finished a few quiet words to Soo Jin before joining me. I offered the keys, and he took them.

"I didn't ask," he started to say. "But are there any adult staff for the museum?"

The question startled me, mainly because I hadn't thought to ask it.

"There have to be, right?" I took a risk in texting Ava, figuring the teen cabal was working on a marketing campaign that included the recent murder.

Yeah. Drew Phillips. Starts in a few hours. And he's Conrad's dad, Ava wrote.

Betty's boyfriend's dad?

CHAPTER NINE

Out of curiosity, or what I suggested to Rex was *professional* courtesy, we met up with Drew Phillips later in the morning when the director arrived at work. What would the man who raised the kind of boy Betty became obsessed with be like? If you'd asked me a year ago, I'd say a grizzled, ex–French Foreign Legion mercenary named Huey Long, with questionable international connections who listed "being a ninja" as a life goal—or Hilly.

What I wasn't expecting was a balding, out-of-shape, middle-aged man with glasses and a bow tie. I squinted, trying to picture him in sweaty combat fatigues, poring over battlefield intel with a group of freedom fighters. For a moment, it kind of worked…until he opened his mouth.

"Hello," he greeted us in high-pitched voice. "I'm Drew Phillips, Executive Director. Can I help you?"

The man sounded like Mickey Mouse on a helium bender.

I introduced myself and Rex and asked if we could sit down somewhere and talk. He looked around for a moment before leading us into the lobby, down a hallway, and into the first room on the right. It was a nicely appointed office, with plush carpet, good furniture, and a window to the alley.

"This is my first day." Drew ran a hand over his bald scalp. "I was surprised when I got here and the museum was already set up. That doesn't really happen in my field."

"Have you ever worked for a museum as…"—my mind searched for the right word—"…different as this one?"

It seemed like small talk would be the best way to ease this guy into the news that a murder had just happened in the Museum of Murder. I was a little worried how he would take it.

"Yes, well, I knew about the museum, but I didn't know Who's There was so dangerous…" His voice trailed off as he looked out a window that opened onto Main Street. "It doesn't matter, at any rate. My son, Conrad, really likes it here. He's friends with a strange girl, who says it isn't dangerous here as long as we avoid people who murder other people."

The girl *was* strange, but I felt I should make known my connection. "That's Betty. She's in my Girl Scout troop."

"The Girl Scouts let someone who's around murder all the time work with little girls?" He blushed as soon as he said it. "Again, I'm sorry. I'm just a little shocked by the whole thing. And I lived in Chicago my whole life."

I waved him off. "It's okay. Happens a lot, actually."

Philips smiled. "So to what do I owe the honor of your visit on my first day?"

I left it to Rex because he was far more tactful than I was. I tended to just blurt things out, but Rex would be delicate and professional and say something to make it easier to take.

"There's been a murder in one of the exhibit halls," my husband said.

Then again, sometimes I was wrong…

Drew laughed. Then he realized we weren't laughing. "You're serious?"

"Have you seen the exhibits?" I wondered.

He shook his head and swallowed hard. "No. This is literally my first day. I've worked at museums my whole life, but I've never had a murder in any of them!"

"Well, there's a first time for everything," I joked.

The museum director didn't laugh.

Rex told him what had happened and explained that Who's There was actually a very safe place to live, since all murders were by people the victim knew. There weren't any outbursts of violence, no street crime of any kind. As long as you didn't know someone who wanted you dead, you were safe.

"And almost all the victims are pretty bad people," I added with a wink, as if that would help. Granted, I wasn't sure if Sheldon was a bad person or not. The man was insanely wealthy, so there was probably some larceny in his life somewhere. Most of the super-rich people I'd known in my spy days were jerks.

Then again, that was probably due to the fact they were Russian oligarchs, members of the Yakuza, or Colombian drug lords.

I felt a little sorry for the new guy as he leaned back in his chair and took a few deep breaths. Then Phillips got to his feet and buttoned his suit jacket. "I guess I'd better check out the exhibit. I thought being here before the grand opening would be restful." He hesitated. "The body isn't still here, is it?"

"No," Rex assured him. "The body has been removed to the morgue."

"Oh, well, I guess that's alright, then," Drew said in a tone that implied it was not alright.

We led him to the lobby and started the tour. I was a little more relaxed this time and kind of looking forward to seeing the exhibits without a drone hovering nearby, waiting for my reaction, or the dead body of the one person from Who's There who'd hit the big time.

"Normally, I guess, the drone would be a docent and lead people through the exhibits," I said.

Drew looked startled. "Drone? What drone?"

"The drone Sheldon McBride, the anonymous donor, was operating."

Phillips stood very still at the news while Rex slowly shook his head at me. I mouthed *What?* He didn't answer. Maybe I'd overshared.

Rex explained as we started through the museum.

"This is the most recent case." I pointed at the body on the floor surrounded by zombies. "That took place at a haunted house my troop did to raise money for the zoo. The killer made it look like he was being eaten by zombies. Clever, right?"

"Oh, er, right." Drew chewed his lip. "And you say this is the most recent?"

"Oh wait. I forgot about the guy who died a month ago during the Christmas lights festival. I guess that was too recent to fabricate." I wondered if they were going to make it look like the outside of my house? That would be pretty cool. Maybe I could consult on that one.

A loud snort came from the next room, and we ran in there. Iago waddled up to me happily, and I scratched his head.

Drew jumped backward. "Why is there a pig here?"

"This is Iago, the stage pig," I explained. "He's a good boy." I looked at the pig. "Aren't you, Iago?"

Iago squeaked his assent.

"Who's going to take care of him? Who's going to feed him and clean up after him?" Drew sounded panicked.

Rex and I looked at each other. No one had told us that, and it hadn't occurred to us to ask.

"He lives with one of my officers," Rex said finally. "I'm sure he goes home with Officer Dooley at night. But you bring up a good point. You might want to ask the mayor about it."

Every time the CEO saw my mannequin as we moved through the exhibits, he grimaced. I felt a little bad about that, although to be fair, I hadn't known about this either.

"Hold on, back up." Drew held up his hands. "Are you telling me that our donor, who is also Sheldon McBride—hermit genius—is now dead? Here?"

Rex nodded. "I am sorry. This must be a terrible way to start a job."

The director nodded. "It's certainly not my best first day."

"You will not be able to open today, I'm afraid," Rex added.

"Okay?" Drew said as if it were a question. "I'll have to write up a statement to post on the door, our website, and Facebook page."

The executive director must have come to terms with it, because by now he was walking through the exhibits as if it was something he'd seen every day. He stopped in the island murders room.

"Now this is pretty interesting!" He wandered over to the mannequin at the bottom of the stairs and read the panel. "I've always liked the board game. *And Then There Were None* is my favorite Agatha Christie book."

"This was a very creepy case," I said. "Six people died before I could figure out who the murderer was."

He turned to me. "You were at this one too? You were at all of these?"

I nodded. "Yeah, I'm not thrilled about it either, but there you go!"

Drew seemed to lose interest in the exhibit and walked into the next one. He froze when he saw Tinkles, the llama—or the animal's statue—standing next to the elaborate pulley system that resulted in Mehitable Peters, one hundred years ago.

"This one is pretty cool!" I walked over and demonstrated how the device that drove an axe into the eccentric woman's skull worked. "It's actually from the town's history too! The last one took place outside of Who's There, but the victim's family were the founders of this town!"

Drew's mouth fell open. "Are you saying that the llama did it?"

Rex nudged me and pointed to a sign on the far wall that said, *Coming Soon! Kids will have the chance to interact with the exhibit by setting off the mechanism as if they were Tinkles themselves! Fee required. Not legal in the State of Oregon for some dumb reason.*

I was about to say that it was nice the girls were thinking of making the exhibits interactive, but Rex had a stern look on his face, so I said, "Right. That's bad. I'll talk to Betty and Ava."

Drew came over and studied the sign. "I wonder why they'd mention it being illegal in Oregon, since we're in Iowa?"

"Must be her legal team," I said without having any idea if Ava had one.

Finally, we came to the last exhibit and Rex pointed out where Sheldon's body had been found. Troy had marked the spots that needed to be investigated and planned to return any minute in his uniform. The car was still there because we still hadn't figured out how to get it out.

"You haven't been here before now?" Rex asked.

The man shook his head. "I mean, I was here for the interview before the exhibition was installed and the gift shop set up. That's how I knew where the office was. But other than that, I had no idea what to expect."

"Did you know Sheldon McBride or that he was the anonymous donor?" Rex asked.

"Not at all! I only had contact with the mayor's office, and the intern had explained that everything was under control and I was only needed the first day." Drew stared at the spot where the body had been, as if it was still there. "This is the strangest first day I've ever had."

I felt sorry for him. He'd eventually get used to things like this, but it seemed unfair that he was new and hit with a body the first day. There should at least be a week or two before being faced with that.

Rex excused him, suggesting he go work on that statement as Troy and Joanna—the other officer on Rex's police force—joined us. I liked them both a lot. Joanna was smart and friendly, and Troy was competent and adored by Soo Jin. And if she liked him, I liked him.

"Hey!" I looked around. "We never did find the drone! Maybe it recorded what happened!"

Rex nodded and turned to his officers. "Search the museum. Look everywhere. The drone should be here somewhere."

Joanna's eyebrows went up. "Is it really Sheldon McBride?"

"We're waiting for confirmation from Dr. Body," Rex sighed. "The picture on the driver's license in his wallet was of the deceased."

Joanna whistled. "No one has ever gotten a picture of him. This will be huge news."

Rex agreed. "We'll have to send a statement to the press. We can use the license photo, I suppose. Let me know if you find the drone."

Troy and Joanna split up to explore the rest of the museum.

Rex squeezed my hand. "That was a good idea. If the drone captured what happened, this could be wrapped up by lunch."

I rolled my eyes. "Oh right. When has that ever happened? It's more likely we'll spend the whole week following up every clue. Then we'll have a big reveal here in this room and nab the killer."

Rex stifled a grin. "Just because that's how it's always worked out doesn't mean it will this time."

"Hello, little sister and brother!" Ron shouted as he walked into the room, followed by Ivan.

"We are here to work!" Ivan said with a doofy grin.

"No one will touch exhibits, or we will break the fingers they touch with!" Ron smacked his fist into the palm of his other hand.

"No finger breaking," Rex said.

The Chechens looked disappointed.

"And the museum won't be open today after all," I added. "There's been a murder."

"Of course there has been murder!" Ron scoffed. "Is murder museum!" He looked at Ivan, who twirled his right index finger at the side of his head as if I was losing it.

"When did you guys leave here?" Rex asked them.

The men looked at each other and began silently counting on their fingers. It seemed like they were somehow communicating with each other. And maybe they were. These two had been together since childhood.

"We do not know," Ron said finally.

"Is that good answer?" Ivan asked eagerly.

I pressed my fingers to the bridge of my nose and closed my eyes. "Did you leave before, after, or with the girls?"

"Yes!" Ron said. "We did all the things!"

"And we locked up!" Ivan added.

"So you guys were the last to leave," Rex said with no trace of annoyance in his voice. "Did you see the drone?"

"It was on other side of door after we locked up," Ron said.

"So did the girls come back and see that the drone was gone?" I wondered. "Why would they do that?"

"Girls were still here," Ron interjected.

I stared at them. "You locked the girls in here?"

"They have key." Ivan shrugged.

I didn't have time for this. I called Ava. Inez answered.

"Had you guys left and come back to find the drone gone, or were you here when it went missing?"

Inez sighed. "We left. Then Betty remembered that she'd left her nun-chunks, so we came back. The drone didn't meet us at the door. We checked to see if it was charging but couldn't find it anywhere."

Rex nodded. He'd heard the explanation.

There was some mumbling on the other end of the call before Inez asked, "Did Iago get dropped off?"

Rex leaned forward. "The pig is here, but we didn't see anyone drop him off."

"That's okay, as long as he was," the girl responded.

"Mr. Phillips," I asked, "wanted to know who is taking care of feeding and cleaning up after the pig?"

We heard Inez ask the other girls. "I guess we didn't think of that." There was some more chatter in the background. "Betty's going to send Ava's interns over to figure that out."

I hoped Pantu and Bal were up to the challenge. I had one more question.

"Why are you answering Ava's phone?"

"Ava had like a bazillion Pixy Stix. She's doing laps around the house. Bye!" Inez ended the call.

"I wondered how she stayed awake when she doesn't like coffee," I muttered, putting my phone away. "So we know that the guys left and then the girls left. The drone was here when they were here but gone when they returned."

"We need to find that drone," Rex said.

"Can we help?" Ivan asked. "If nobody can come in, we will have no fingers to break, and we do not have anything else to do."

I looked at Rex, and he said, "Yes, but you can't touch it if you find it. You let Merry or me know, okay?"

The men ran off without acknowledging. We were about to go on our own search when Philips came in, looking stunned.

"We've sold ten thousand tickets for just this weekend alone!" He looked like he might be sick. "And we can't open today! Can we open tomorrow?"

I turned to Rex. "If we can't find it here, can't they open tomorrow?"

Rex held his hands up. "Fine. As long as we either find the drone or prove beyond a shadow of a doubt that it isn't here."

Drew slouched, as if he'd been holding his breath all morning. "That's a relief. I'll try to spread the tickets for today over the course of the next two weeks to accommodate people."

He fled, presumably back to his office.

"That's twice the size of Who's There!" I cried out. "They sold enough tickets to double the population!"

My phone buzzed, and I answered Betty's call.

"You're trending on social media," she said without greeting.

"I am?" That didn't sound too bad. I only had a Facebook account for the troop because the girls said I was a dinosaur. "You mean my name is trending?"

"In a bad way," she said. "People think it's your fault the museum can't open today."

How was this my fault? "I had nothing to do with it. Is there a way to clear this up?"

It was like I could see the girl calculating on the other end of the call. "Okay. But it'll cost you." She ended the call before I could reply.

Some days it just doesn't pay to be the one who stumbles over a body.

CHAPTER TEN

As the police searched, I went back to the scene of the murder and sat down on the floor. The moment swept me back to when I first moved back home and I felt that old familiar guilt. Oh sure, it had later been decided that I hadn't *technically* killed Carlos. But that didn't erase the look on his face when he fell in front of my car. I'd be willing to bet his last thoughts were *What the hell am I doing in Iowa, and hey…is that Maria about to run me over?*

Carlos the Armadillo had gotten his nickname for an unfortunate incident as a teen. When he was startled, he jumped three feet in the air, as armadillos do when they are spooked. The Colombian drug lord hated the nickname and told everyone it was really because he had a tough outer shell—figuratively. I think people believed him because he had eczema, which wasn't quite what he meant.

And now, Sheldon McBride, the most famous person to come out of Who's There, was dead and it was made to look like it was my fault. At least, that's how I assumed people would take it. That couldn't be good, right? Killing the town's claim to fame.

Okay, so *I* didn't kill him. But would people think that? In my experience with dictators and advertising professionals (who, in some cases, were the same thing) was that perception is reality. An excellent example was the fact that Betty had just told me that I was trending negatively on social media as the reason the museum wasn't opening.

Did that mean word had gotten out about Sheldon's murder? I texted Ava to join me.

"What do you want?" Ava said less than one minute later, flanked by Lauren and Betty. I hadn't realized they'd arrived. "Inez is working on the press release."

Betty held up her hands as if presenting a headline. "We're thinking something like Hometown Genius Murdered at Museum of Murder and Mrs. Wrath Absolutely Not Involved."

The girls looked at me expectantly, waiting to see what I thought. I was impressed. They usually didn't run things like this past me.

"Did Rex give you the go-ahead to post that?" I hedged, avoiding having to comment on the headline.

Ava looked at me blankly. "I'm the mayor. This museum falls under the city, which is basically me anyway."

"I think the city council might disagree," I murmured.

"No, they're cool with it," Ava argued. "Or at least they will be when I put it on the agenda for the next meeting." She turned to Betty, who was typing on her phone.

"Already done," the kid said. "But we might have to cut something to make room. Like the formal proclamation making pet bunnies official, voting citizens."

Upon seeing the confusion on my face, Lauren explained, "Rabbits are very civic minded and do best in entry-level public sanitation jobs." She scowled. "They do not like parks and recreation or administration. Especially mini lops. They hate everything."

"Of course," I said. "Goes without saying, really. But back to the other thing. Check with Rex and take my name out of the headline for the press release."

"Fine," Ava said, stamping her foot, implying it was anything but. "We have to get this out soon though. Rumors are already starting to spread, and Betty doesn't like that if she didn't spread them herself."

Betty nodded but said nothing.

The girls left the exhibit, and I realized that Rex would probably approve it. Too many people knew about the murder now for it to be kept quiet.

My phone buzzed in my pocket, and I looked at it.

I see you've murdered again! my sister-in-law Ronni wrote.

I sat in the room for a while longer, alone with my thoughts. It was pretty interesting that someone had murdered Sheldon in this particular exhibit. There were easier ones to do it in, like the knife to the heart in the theater, Druid Con, or dumpster. Huh, a lot of people of people who were murdered here died from being stabbed in the heart.

Why would the killer go so far as to hit Sheldon with the car? Seemed like a lot of work. The other exhibits rolled through my mind. There were strangulations, poisonings, electrocution, axe murders, and broken necks. Why did people get so creative when a gun was all you needed to do the trick?

The girls left after letting Rex review the press release. I wandered around the exhibits again to see if I might find something the others had overlooked. In the theater exhibit, I spent some time scratching Iago's head. He didn't follow me out. How did they keep him confined to the one exhibit?

At lunchtime, I ordered pizza for everyone. When I went outside to meet the delivery guy, Medea Jones and Lucinda Schwartz were there, barking out questions at him. When I showed up, the pizza guy shoved the pizzas into my hands and, without waiting for payment, jumped into his car and ran away.

Medea turned her endless fury on me. "Rumor has it that Sheldon McBride was murdered inside the Museum of Murder!"

"Is that a question?" I shifted my hands because the pizza was hot.

"You don't deny it?" Lucinda held a mic in my face. The cameraman zoomed in.

I changed the subject. "No drone today?"

Lucinda looked at the cameraman as if she hoped he'd turn into the drone. "I miss it. I know Frank here wouldn't want his job replaced by a machine, but it was really cool."

"Hey!" Frank complained. "I'm better than a drone! Can a drone do this?"

He dropped to the ground and began doing pushups with one hand while filming Lucinda's boots with the other. He got up and grinned as Lucinda glared at him.

"Uh, Frank? My expertly made-up face and lustrous hair are up here!"

"You didn't answer my question..." Medea started, "...that wasn't a question!"

"The city is releasing a press release at any moment now" was all I said before going inside and locking the door.

"Pizza!" I called out to the others. "In the break room!"

We all met up in a break room that had been decorated with crime scene tape. At least the chairs were comfy. Nobody looked very happy.

"Where's Ron and Ivan?" I asked. "I ordered them anchovy pizzas."

Rex shook his head. "They said they had to go home for some reason, and I told them it was okay."

"I'm guessing you haven't found the drone?" I asked.

Joanna picked up a slice of pepperoni. "We looked everywhere. Troy and I even went over each other's areas again, but we found nothing."

"Maybe the killer took it with them," Hilly offered as she loaded a plate and sat down next to me.

I jumped a little in my seat. "When did you get here?"

I could tell by the looks on the others' faces that they were wondering the same thing.

"I've been here all night," she said before taking a bite.

We all stared at her.

"What?" Hilly seemed surprised. "There's a nice cot in the basement. I just slept down there."

"Then you were here during the murder!" I nearly dropped my piece of pizza. "Did you see anything?"

Hilly laughed. Then she realized we weren't laughing. "There are multiple murders in the exhibits. Wait…did something else happen?"

Rex turned to his officers. "You didn't check the basement?"

"There's a basement?" Troy frowned.

Joanna shook her head. "We didn't see any way to get into a basement."

Drew raised his hand, "I didn't know there was a basement either."

We all turned back to Hilly.

She held up one finger until she finished her slice. Then she got up, brushed off her lap, and said, "I'll show you."

We followed her to the women's restroom. Troy and Drew hesitated about going in until they saw Rex do it. At the last sink, Hilly turned on the spigots then proceeded to wash her hands. We waited until she dried them and then followed her out of the bathroom.

"Why did you all follow me in there?" she asked. "Weird."

"We didn't realize you weren't leading us to the basement," I said wryly.

Hilly rolled her eyes. "I *had* to wash my hands first! It's like you guys aren't into hygiene."

"Can you show us now, please?" Rex asked patiently.

The assassin broke into a wide grin. "Sure! It's not far!"

We followed her into the gift shop and exhibit hall where Sheldon died. She walked into the mockup of my kitchen and opened the door that went down to the basement in my house. Then she disappeared.

I walked over and checked it out. "She's not kidding!"

We followed her down a staircase that led to a basement that looked like a cell in most third-world countries. The cinderblock walls and cement floor made it a bit chilly. In one corner was a cot with a sleeping bag and pillow. A duffel bag sat next to it. There wasn't anything else in the room.

"How did you find this place?" I looked around. It was a pretty normal basement, as far as basements go.

Hilly stared at me as if I had two heads. "Duh. It's the door that goes into the basement in your house."

"I thought it was a fake door," Drew said, and the rest of us agreed.

Imagine putting a basement door where the mockup of a basement door was. It was kind of genius. And it was the last thing anyone would think of.

"This could be where the killer hid out at some point." Joanna went and looked under the cot.

"I doubt it," Hilly snorted. "I was here all night. I'm a pretty sound sleeper, but I'd notice if someone else was down here."

"What time did you go to bed?" I pressed her.

Hilly cocked her head to one side for a moment. "Midnight, I think. Passed out the minute my head hit the pillow."

So she could've slept through someone being down here. Hilly might think she'd know if someone else was here, but she wasn't wrong about being a sound sleeper. Once in Ulaan Baatar, she slept through two earthquakes and an explosion. I had to wake her up. And even then it wasn't until she'd had two cups of coffee that she agreed to get moving.

Rex was testing all the walls, as if looking for a secret way in. Joanna and Troy were doing the same.

"There's no other way in here," Hilly said. She thought for a moment. "Actually, I don't know if that's true or not. I just came down here to crash." She looked at me. "Can I stay at your old house?"

"Absolutely," I confirmed. It was better to have her there than here. "Did the girls know this was down here?"

"No, I don't think so." The assassin cocked her head to one side. "I remember I was excited when I found it and couldn't wait to tell them."

"Did you hear anything upstairs in the early hours?" I asked. "Like a car driving and hitting someone?"

Hilly considered this. "No," she replied with more confidence than she should've had.

Rex pulled me aside. "This could be how the killer hid, waiting for the museum to close."

I wasn't so sure. "The only problem is Hilly. She really is a very sound sleeper. It's possible she didn't notice anything. But someone down here with her?"

We went back upstairs and found the girls eating the last few pieces of pizza. Great. I'd only had one slice.

"Did you guys know about the basement?" Rex asked before I could.

"*There's a basement?*" Ava shouted.

Hilly bounced on the balls of her feet. "Yeah! It's really cool! Wanna see?"

They swarmed to the doorway and out of the room. I found a pizza crust and started gnawing on it as my stomach growled.

"I think we can call it," Rex sighed. "The drone is not here. If it were, we would've found it." He turned to Joanna and Troy. "Head back to the office. I'll be there shortly."

"I'm going to stay," Drew said as if he wasn't sure he believed it. "It's my first day. I'd like to put in a full one before the onslaught tomorrow."

Rex and I cleaned up the crime scene tape and replaced the Carlos mannequin—the one thing he had found in a janitor's closet.

"I wonder why the boys cut out so quickly," I thought out loud as Rex looked at his vibrating phone.

He froze. "Randi and Ronni have gone into labor!"

CHAPTER ELEVEN

I guess I knew this day was coming—it just seemed so unreal. I was going to be an aunt! As an only child, it was something I never dreamed I'd be. Of course, if you'd asked me years ago if I ever thought Ron and Ivan would be parents, I would've laughed until I hyperventilated. Don't get me wrong, I was happy for them, but I didn't really see them as the fatherly sort. Then again, I didn't think Ronni was the motherly sort, unless you consider obsessive, seething hostility to be a solid parenting style.

This was going to be great for Rex because he loved kids. It was probably why he often looked the other way or refused to press charges against my troop. Now we were going to have a couple of babies in the family who wouldn't be able to do anything dubious for a few years yet. What was the age kids started becoming hooligans? Three? Four? Five? I made a mental note to look that up so I'd be prepared when Blasto and Blasto launched their criminal careers. I would be there to cover for them because that's what aunts did, right?

These thoughts coursed through my mind as we raced to the hospital and ran inside. Rex was so stunned, he almost used his police lights to get there, but since everything in Who's There is five minutes away, he decided not to…in spite of me insisting it would be really fun.

I beat him to the admission desk, but he wasn't even out of breath, so while I was doubled over and panting, he asked the receptionist where the twins were. Turned out, we didn't need to ask.

"I hate every last one of you!" Ronni's voice screamed as we neared the room.

"No she doesn't," Randi spoke calmly.

We found the right door, and Rex asked if we could come in, and upon getting permission, we entered. I've seen the births of two babies over my lifetime, so I was prepared for anything. The first time was on a film in health class in high school, and that counted even if I did faint at the end (I was a bit squeamish then). The second time was when I had to help a Russian oligarch's wife give birth in the back of a Yugo. When I say *helped*, I meant that I held her hand while a startled, passing dentist delivered the baby. I did faint that time, and despite what Aleksi said, I was sure it was from blood loss from his wife holding my hand so tightly. Olga even named the baby after me, which was nice even though my real name wasn't really Oksana. I think it counts.

"They're not far along," a nurse told us. "It'll be a while."

Ron sat at Ronni's bedside, holding her hand, while Ivan sat with his wife, Randi. Rex's sisters looked so much alike that the only way I could tell who was who was because of which husband they had.

"I'm going to kill you for doing this to me!" Randi shrieked at Ivan, who looked terrified.

"No you aren't," Ronni said calmly. "Just think how happy we will be once the boys arrive!"

My jaw dropped open. Had the men switched places for some strange reason? I wouldn't put it past them to come up with a goofy reason like *in Chechnya is bad luck to comfort own wife during birth of child.* Ah. That must be it.

Or at least, I thought so until I saw Rex's expression.

Ivan looked at us pitifully. "Wives have exchanged brains!"

Ron nodded but said nothing.

"They did?" was all I could think to say.

"Aiiieeeeeeee!" Randi shrieked. "Get this thing out of me, or I will kill each and every one of you! Slowly! With a stuffed otter!"

"That's possible," I told my husband. "There was a guy in Okinawa who killed two Yakuza members with a stuffed weasel. You wouldn't believe how much blood there was."

Rex recovered quickly. "Can we do anything to help?"

Ron and Ivan jumped to their feet.

"Yes! Thank you!" Ron said before the two of them ran out of the room, leaving us to comfort the sisters.

I was torn. Randi loved me, but right now she was looking like she wanted to murder me with an otter. Ronni hated me, but it could be a trap. In the end, Rex solved the problem by going over and holding Randi's hand. That was smart. The twins doted on Rex, so she was unlikely to kill him, with the bonus being that there were no taxidermied animals in the room.

I closed the door to see I was wrong. Behind the door were two stuffed chickens, each cradling eggs wrapped in blue blankets. Maybe they brought these for luck. I slowly walked over to sit next to the person who hated me more than anything in the world.

Ronni smiled at me as I sat down. "Thank you, Merry. The boys really needed a break." She closed her eyes and clenched her teeth. Randi screamed in the bed next to her. After a moment, it passed. "These contractions are a bit harder on my sister."

"Um, okay," I said as I took her hand in mine. "You really are Ronni, right?"

Ronni laughed. "Of course I am, silly! Who else would I be?"

Rex had a grimace on his face that told me Randi was crushing his hand. If he was surprised how his sisters were acting, he didn't show it.

"It's just that…" I bit my lip, not sure if I should say the rest out loud. "You don't normally like me."

"*I* hate you!" Randi shouted. "If it helps!"

Ronni giggled. I'd never heard her giggle before. This was getting weird. "I don't hate you, Merry! You're my sister-in-law! I love you!"

"Are Mom and Dad on the way?" Rex asked Randi.

His sister unleashed fury. "Those bastards are on a cruise to Greece! They should've been here!"

I didn't know that, and it looked like Rex didn't know that either.

Ronni nodded. "Now, Randi, you know they've waited a long time for this trip. I'm happy for them celebrating their anniversary in Crete!"

"I'm not!" Randi shouted. "I hope they get eaten by a minotaur!"

Ronni's face broke into a big grin. "Hey! That's a good idea! We've never done a minotaur before!" She looked at me hopefully. "Merry, be a darling and write that down for me!"

"Um, sure." I ruffled through my purse until I found a Girl Scout permission slip that Betty had filled out with *The bearer of this note can have anything they want*' signed *The Mayor* (I'd been meaning to talk to her about that) and a broken orange crayon. "Got it!"

Rex asked, "Can I get you some water, or ice chips, or something?"

"How about a flamethrower so I can burn this place down?" Randi shouted with rage in her eyes.

Ronni turned to me and gave me a small smile. "She really doesn't mean it, you know. My sister's never had much tolerance for pain, I'm afraid. It'll be fine when the babies come."

"Will you be like this when the babies are here?" I asked a bit hopefully.

She patted my hand. "Probably not. Unless I'm in pain for a while afterward. In that case, yes."

This was how the twins reacted to pain? If just Ronni was in pain and Randi wasn't, then wouldn't my life be a lot easier? That wasn't helpful thinking, and I felt a little bad about my thoughts of using thumbscrews on my usually angry sister-in-law. But still, this seemed like a solution to my usual issues, even if it was a smidge unethical.

Another contraction came through, and while Ronni seemed to only be meditating, Randi started swearing at Rex. He took it like a champ.

The nurse popped back into the room. "Everything alright here? We have had requests from some of the other expectant mothers for you to please keep it down a little." She smiled amiably.

"Just try to stop me!" Randi shrieked and threw her phone at the door.

"Alrighty, then," the nurse said. "We'll just keep this door closed." Which she did.

"She's very nice," Ronni said. "I'll have to bake her some cookies. Or maybe we can do a diorama for her of this moment. I've got a whole shipment of rats I've been meaning to use."

"She gets nothing! We hate her!" Randi shouted.

Rex attempted to calm his sister down and was rewarded with a string of some very obscene expletives.

Now I knew why the guys fled. The nurse said it might be a while, so I was starting to worry how long they were going to be gone.

"I heard you had an unfortunate incident at the museum," Ronni tut tutted.

"Another body! You probably killed him!" Randi glared at me.

The nurse popped in to let us know that screaming about murder wasn't conducive to the peaceful and calming atmosphere they were trying to create. Randi hurled a bed pan that slammed into the door just after the nurse closed it again.

"Randi!" Rex had a sternness in his voice that surprised me. "You could hurt somebody! Do you want me to have to write you up on assault charges?"

Nobody said anything for a moment. My husband's normally cool demeanor was gone. I'd never seen him like this.

"Whatever, jerk!" Randi rolled her eyes but didn't say anything more.

"Thank you!" the nurse called cheerfully from the other side of the door.

Rex didn't respond but told his sister, "We are here for you. If there's anything we can do to make you comfortable, just let us know. But throwing things around isn't helpful. Okay?"

Randi narrowed her eyes but nodded.

"She really doesn't mean it," Ronni whispered to me. "In fact, she'll be mortified once this is over. Poor thing!"

"Are you getting excited about the babies?" I tried to change the subject.

"Oh yes!" She beamed. "We're working on middle names right now. What works best with Blasto: Orel, Emil, or Ira, do you think?"

Sensing a trap, I said, "They all sound good. Are they family names?"

Ronni nodded. "From our family. Ron and Ivan want Wally or Azlan, but since they picked the first name, they don't have a say in the second."

"That seems fair," I agreed. It occurred to me that the men both had Chechen last names, but I didn't know what they were. "Will they go with the surnames?"

Ronni shook her head. "They took our names when we got married. They said it would be better to have American last names."

"Oh! I guess I didn't know that." Why didn't I know that?

"Son of a newt!" Randi shouted. "Here comes another contraction!"

Ronni closed her eyes and took deep breaths. It seemed like the contractions were coming regularly now. I volunteered to get the nurse and go on a lengthy search to find Ron and Ivan.

Rex rejected that. "I'll just text the men. We shouldn't call the nurse until absolutely necessary, and I don't want to bother her."

Thwarted! To be fair, I shouldn't be thinking of abandoning him. We probably had hours before they were even close to…

"They're coming!" Randi shouted.

Rex hit the button. I'd never seen anyone move so fast.

The nurse came in and checked the women as Rex went and stood in a corner. I stayed where I was, paralyzed by the fear that Randi would throw something at me.

"Well I'll be! She's right!" the nurse said. "I'll go get the doctors!"

I pulled out my phone and called Ivan. He didn't respond. It went into voicemail. "Ivan is not here. Not near phone, I mean. Phone is probably in other room or is lost. Leave message, and if Ivan finds, he will call back. Unless phone is broken. Then Ivan will go to nice little phone store to get another. This will take a long time. In this case, Ivan will call back tomorrow. Good-bye."

Two doctors, flanked by four nurses, barreled into the room. I joined Rex, and we flattened ourselves against the wall.

"What should we do?" I asked, a little panicked.

"Randi, Ronni," Rex called out. "We'll be in the waiting room…"

"You're not going anywhere!" Randi roared. "Those idiot husbands are missing! You're filling in for them whether you like it or not, or I will hate you forever!"

"That's odd," one of the doctors said. "They're both going to deliver at the same time. I've never seen that before."

"Merry?" Ronni beamed. "Would you come and hold my hand, please?"

Without hesitation, I joined her, standing behind her bent knees where I hopefully wouldn't see much.

"Rex is cutting the cord!" Randi shouted.

"We don't really do that anymore," the doctor said. "Too many fathers fainting and all that…"

Ronni's face fell. "Oh no! And the boys were so looking forward to it! I'm sad that they'll be disappointed."

"I'll wrap it around their scrawny necks for not being here!" Randi screamed.

"Here they come!" one of the nurses said as the doctors took up positions, and Randi began screaming in a way that I thought a priest or exorcist would better suit our needs.

Ron and Ivan ran in and over to their wives. The men had a look of fear I'd never seen on them before. Wait…that wasn't entirely true. There was that one time back in Chechnya when their boss thought of replacing the two bone breakers with younger bone breakers. And they were only twenty-five. Fortunately I was able to convince Wally that experience was more important than youth when it came to precision bone busting. I don't know if that was true or not, but his fifteen-year-old nephews were very disappointed. He had to buy them two goats each and a flock of wizened chickens to placate them.

"Rex and Merry, dears," Ronni said in a soft voice. "Could you please stay? I would love for you both to be here when the boys arrive!"

We fled back to our corner, staying out of sightlines of what was going on.

"Are we supposed to, you know," I whispered. "Do anything?"

"Like what?" Rex whispered back.

"I don't know what the protocol is in this situation," I admitted. "Take pictures or chant or do some sort of prayer circle?"

"I thought you'd been through this before," my husband murmured.

"We were in a Yugo," I scoffed. "There wasn't room to do anything."

"Merry?" Ronni called out. "Could you give us some words of encouragement?"

"Okay." My mind went blank for a moment. Then I started chanting, "Larak tarath! Larak tarath! Larak…"

Rex silenced me. "What are you doing?"

"The Mak Tar strength chant," I hissed. "The troop watched *Galaxy Quest* at our last sleepover, and it's all I can think of. You don't think it's appropriate?"

Rex called out in a soothing voice. "You're doing great! Soon this will all be over and the babies will be here!"

I patted him on the shoulder. "Good call. The Mak Tar strength chant was getting a little repetitive."

"It was a nice idea." He smiled then continued to praise his sisters.

Ron and Ivan continued to hold their wives' hands, but I did notice they were starting to swear in Chechen. Hopefully no one else would notice.

"Here comes little…!" Ronni's doctor paused, looking at her intently.

"Blasto." Ronni smiled sweetly.

"Blasto?" The doctor seemed confused, like he was being teased. "Okay, here comes little Blasto!"

"Same here," Randi's doctor shouted.

"Also Blasto, you moron!" Randi shouted.

Her doctor stared at her. "Seriously? The boys are named Blasto and Blasto?"

Ron stood up and walked around behind the doctor. One look, and he fainted.

"Ron!" Ivan screamed and ran over. He took one glance between Ronni's knees and fainted, landing on top of Ron.

"Can someone deal with this?" Ronni's doctor shouted after stepping on one of the conked-out Chechens.

Rex and I ran over and dragged the two men out of the way. I began slapping Ivan hard across the face to rouse him. I may have used a bit more force than necessary, but it was satisfying.

"You're going to miss this!" I shouted in his ear. There was no response.

Randi's final wail left us both deaf as the twins made their final, simultaneous push...

CHAPTER TWELVE

"That was weird," my husband said as he collapsed on the couch next to me.

"Yeah. At least Ron and Ivan came to at the end. What did you say to Ron that made him jump up like that?"

Rex stretched his legs. "I told him if he wasn't there for the birth, he couldn't name the baby, and Ronni was thinking of Egbert. How did you get Ivan up?"

"When the slapping didn't work, I twisted his ear. Ivan has always had very sensitive ears."

"At least they were there for Blasto's and Blasto's births. I've never seen such big babies before. And all that black hair!"

He wasn't wrong. The boys looked like small sumo wrestlers. "I am glad you were able to stop Ron from attacking the doctor for not letting him cut the cord."

Rex sighed. "It was the second time in a couple of hours that I had to warn my family off assaulting medical workers. That was new."

"At least I didn't faint!" I was really proud of that. Of course, I didn't look at what was happening either.

We slouched on the couch as if we had run a marathon. Instead, we'd gotten to be there when our nephews, Blasto and Blasto, entered the world. That was cool.

"They were kind of cute," I admitted.

Rex turned his head. "I'm happy to have babies in the family, and I fully intend to spoil them rotten."

For the briefest moment, I worried that he was dropping a hint. Then I put that out of my mind. I didn't want kids. I already had eight girls. Now we had two boys. And I could barely manage my cats.

As if on cue, Philby trotted into the room and laid two dead mice at our feet. She sat expectantly, waiting for praise.

"Since when do we have mice?" Rex frowned. "We've never had mice before."

I patted the fat feline führer on the head. "I think they're gifts for the babies. I'll get a bag."

"You think our cat knows that my sisters had babies, escaped to somewhere where there are mice, and brought the mice as a gift for them to taxidermy?" Rex called out.

"Of course! Philby probably heard us talking." I came into the living room and scooped up the mice, bagging them. I frowned. "What do we do with them now?"

Rex sighed. "Put them in the fridge. That's what my sisters say we're supposed to do."

We made dinner and went to bed earlier than usual.

The next morning, Troy from the station called. Kevin insisted that the Officers Hamlet learn how to answer 9-1-1 calls, and it was causing problems because the people calling couldn't understand the hamsters, and the hamsters apparently had atrocious handwriting and no one could decipher the messages. The good thing was that the calls weren't real emergencies and Troy was able to call people back due to caller ID, but someone named Helen Burken threatened to sue because the officers didn't come quick enough to find her lost cat.

Rex fled to the station to sort things out, and I promised to pick up some sort of gifts for the babies while he was out. I was just grabbing my coat when the doorbell rang.

I opened it to find five men on the porch, all grinning expectantly at me.

"Who are you?" That was a bit rude, but I was looking forward to shopping.

The five men on my doorstep looked at each other for a moment, as if they weren't entirely sure and hoped one of the others would know the answer. They were all dressed like Sheldon McBride—with sandy-colored hair in a side part, large, black, square-shaped glasses, an Aloha shirt with a brick red cardigan, and khaki pants. A pair of red Keds completed the outfit, and every single one of them was dressed this way.

One of the guys in back asked the others, "May I?"

They all did a sort of *by all means motion* with their arms that you don't usually see in movies after 1959, and he stepped forward.

As he pushed the heavy glasses up on his nose, I realized there weren't any lenses in them.

"I'm Simon McBride," he said simply and waited for me to respond.

"You're related to Sheldon McBride?" I wondered out loud. And if they were, did they know he was on a slab in the morgue?

The group laughed louder than they should have.

"I wish!" Simon gushed. "No relation. McBride isn't my real last name. It's Cakeman. But I changed it…" He paused and then waved his arms. "We all changed it to McBride to honor the legend."

I looked at each one. "You all changed your last names to McBride? Why not go all the way and change your first names to Sheldon?" To be honest, I was curious.

A collective gasp filled the air.

"We would never do that!" one said.

"There's only *one* Sheldon McBride!" gasped another.

"That and," one in the back said, "we found it too confusing."

I blinked at them. "Okay, so you're a bit obsessed." They were *a lot* obsessed. "Why are you here on my doorstep?"

Had they heard about Sheldon? With all the chaos around the twins' deliveries, I had no idea if the press release went out or if it had exploded on social media.

"Well?" I did not invite them in.

I should say that this is not the Iowa way to behave. Normally I would've let them all in and offered refreshments. Oh, I know, women alone shouldn't do that. But I was pretty good at sizing people up, and I was fairly certain I could take all five without breaking a sweat.

Simon the spokesman looked around. "It's kind of personal. Can we come in? It's cold out here."

"Alright," I sighed. "But the rest of you need to tell me your first names before I do."

They were very happy to do this. Besides Simon, there was Sandy, Sebastian, Stan, and Sam. I stepped back and ushered them inside, telling them to head to the dining room. Once we were all seated, I asked if they wanted anything to drink.

Simon looked at the others, who nodded their assent to whatever this was.

"Do you have any Irn Bru? It's the only thing Sheldon drinks!"

Well...*drank*. I wondered if I should tell them what happened. On the other hand, if they knew I was somehow involved, they might not leave me alone.

"The Scottish soda that tastes like bubblegum?" I was a bit taken aback. "No, and I don't think you can buy it anywhere around here. I have sparkling water, Diet Coke, regular water, and lemonade."

They seemed disappointed and passed on the drinks.

"What are you doing here?" I asked again, but slowly this time in case they needed a reminder.

"Oh! Sorry!" Simon said. "We heard that Sheldon McBride may be the anonymous donor behind the Museum of Murder and came here to see him!"

"We've never seen him!" Stan said.

"This might be our big chance!" Sam cried out.

I really should tell them. But something held me back. "So...you guys are his fan club?"

All five of them laughed in a way that made me feel a little stupid.

"We are *not* a fan club," Simon snickered. "Fans are simpering, star-struck losers! We are *followers*. There's a huge difference."

My eyebrows went up. "Oh? Really? In what way?"

Again with the snarky laughter.

"We live our lives the Sheldon McBride Way," Simon said after a moment.

Stan nodded, "It's a lifestyle."

Sam added, "It's not for everyone."

Simon continued, "We dress like him, only eat what we've heard he eats, and are now experimenting with drone technology. We've been to every museum he's sponsored and anyplace where there's been a sighting of him."

I narrowed my eyes. "For the third time...why are you here, at my house? You will not be asked a fourth time. Instead,

I'll drag you outside by the hair and toss you onto the pavement. Understand?"

They nodded, but I thought Sebastian and Sam had dreamy looks in their eyes as if they hoped I would do it.

"Because the museum is about you and Sheldon is sponsoring it." Simon shrugged. "It's an obvious connection. And he's also from here. So we're guessing you two are close, personal friends."

Stan's eyes glazed over in a swoony way. "We've never met anyone who was a close personal friend!"

Sebastian nodded but said nothing.

"Or even anyone who has seen him!" Sam added.

"Guys…" I held out my hands. "We aren't close personal friends. We aren't even acquaintances." But I did find his body. This was the moment to tell these guys…

The five looked at each other a moment.

"That's good enough for us!" Simon grinned. "Obviously Sheldon is obsessed with you! Which means that we are now obsessed with you!"

"What's your favorite color?" Stan shouted.

"What book are you reading right now?" Sam produced a notepad and pen and was poised to write down my answer.

"Have you ever had Irn Bru with Sheldon?" Sandy wondered.

"You can't be serious," I sighed.

"Very serious." Simon's face turned to stone. "Sheldon doesn't do anything without reason, and for some reason he picked you."

I heard the front door open and close. Rex walked in and stopped in his tracks upon spotting me at the head of a table filled with Sheldon McBride clones. If he was startled, he didn't show it.

He walked over to Sam, who was sitting closest to my husband, and held out his hand. "Hello, gentlemen. I'm Rex, Merry's husband."

Sam's eyes grew wide as he very carefully reached out and grasped Rex's hand. He shook it vigorously and then let go, turning to the others. "I touched the hand of the man who's married to the woman Sheldon is obsessed with!"

The others all gasped and held out their hands. I wondered how they managed to get through life with so obviously few brain cells in their heads. It made sense that someone like Sheldon McBride would avoid these clowns.

Rex shook all their hands, perhaps a bit curious that they never introduced themselves.

"These are the McBrides," I told him. "They are followers of Sheldon McBride and are here to see me because I have some sort of connection to the man due to the museum going up."

Rex nodded as if this made perfect sense. "Nice to meet you, gentlemen. Did Merry offer you anything to drink?"

"They turned me down because we don't have Irn Bru," I said drily.

Rex thought about this for a moment. "I'm sorry we can't oblige you. And I'm sorry I can't stay. I just had to run home and pick up something. Nice meeting you all."

Why didn't he tell them about Sheldon's murder? Perhaps he summed them up and decided they weren't a threat. Or maybe the press release hadn't gone out yet. Either way, my husband had decided he had no problem abandoning me to these guys. Rex disappeared into the kitchen and then waved as he walked past us on the way out. I heard the door open and close again. And once more, I was alone with Sheldon McBride's followers.

"Why do you think Sheldon made the museum in your honor?" Simon asked.

"I don't think he did." I was about to tell them that I'd never met the man…well, alive anyway, when an idea formed in my mind. "Hey, I do know one thing. Sheldon loved…loves Girl Scout cookies, and my troop is getting ready to sell. I might have an order form around here somewhere…"

This seemed to energize the group.

"Do you know what his favorite is?" Sam asked.

"Thin Mints," I said quickly. "We're not supposed to start taking orders yet, but since you're all friends of Sheldon"—I winked—"and he's already given me his order, I can make an exception."

Before they finally left, they'd ordered five hundred cases of Thin Mints. At least that was something. They told me they were staying at the Radisson. I made a note to let the girls know there were some new suckers in town.

And I'd tell them not to let the guys know Sheldon McBride was dead. Not yet, anyway.

CHAPTER THIRTEEN

After the Sheldon McBride Followers left, I started thinking about Sheldon's murder. Was it possible these guys did it? They could've come over here to see if they could find out who the suspects were. It wouldn't be hard to find out that my husband was the town's detective.

But were they that smart? They wouldn't be the first people to act ignorant in order to get intel. In Colombia, there'd been three guys in Carlos's team who pretended to be ignorant muscle. They acted the part by pretending to not understand simple words, letting howler monkeys get the best of them, and pretending not to know what eggs were.

I'd almost believed it until I caught them playing chess in the jungle one day while discussing the physics that were required for a multiverse to exist. Turned out they were Interpol and hadn't known that the CIA had me embedded here. I had to pretend to kill them so they could escape. They let me keep the chess set as a thank-you, but I don't really play. I should dig it out and give it to the girls. Betty would like that.

Were these guys trying to play me? And what was up with changing their last names to McBride? And I know they did because all of their credit cards had that surname when I scammed them into buying cookies.

After deciding that I should probably tell Rex about this, I fed the animals, grabbed my coat and bag, and drove to the police station.

As I passed through downtown, I saw what looked like a Soviet bread line forming and going for two blocks down the street. It was at the museum! Huh. It really was going to be popular. At the head of the line, I expected to see the girls, but instead there were the red velvet ropes with Ron and Ivan standing there, arms folded across their chests. Their expressions appeared to be menacing a middle-aged couple, who looked like they wondered if they'd made the right decision to come here.

"I can't believe the line outside the museum!" I said as I plopped down in a chair opposite Rex. "You allowed it to open?"

My husband ran his hands through his hair. "It didn't seem fair not to. Drew was losing his mind, trying to figure out how he'd make up one day's lost tickets. By the way, what was up with your visitors?"

We talked for a bit about my visitors earlier. The McBride Followers were pretty weird. But were they killer weird?

"You think they may be involved?" Rex scratched his chin. "I was wondering the same thing. Looks like they're staying at the hotel. I should talk to them."

I leaned forward and snagged a piece of candy from his candy dish. "How do you know that?" I hadn't told him that!

"One of them had a keycard sticking out of his shirt pocket. Spotted it when I shook hands with him."

Now he knew. Hopefully I wouldn't get in trouble for not telling him myself. "I didn't tell them about the murder. I wasn't sure if the news had gone out yet."

Rex turned his monitor toward me, and I saw the headline. "It went out an hour ago."

I sat back and chewed. "Do we have any suspects?"

"You mean, do I have any suspects?" Rex corrected.

"You always say that, but it doesn't stop me," I pointed out.

Rex sat forward, resting his elbows on his desk. "There's Hilly, of course. She has the background for it and was staying underneath the crime scene. Ron and Ivan could've come back and killed him. But I don't really suspect those three. The McBrides are on my radar. And I'm not ruling out Drew Phillips. Granted, he appeared to be horrified and didn't like closing the museum on opening day."

"And he's Conrad's dad. The boy Betty is into," I added. "If he is the killer, then we risk Betty's wrath, or meltdown, and neither one is something I want to be around for. I'm sure Sheldon had lots of enemies over the years. Any one of them could've hired a professional to kill him."

Rex's right eyebrow went up. "You assume it's a professional?"

"I don't assume anything, but it's a possibility. Whoever it was had to break into the museum without being caught and ran over and killed Sheldon while Hilly slept below that same room."

My husband considered this. "And it's likely that McBride has rich enemies. Any of them could've hired someone." He sat back in his chair and sighed. "If that's the case, the assassin came in for this one thing, killed McBride, and left town forever. That would be impossible to solve."

An idea popped into my head. "Not necessarily. I think I know who to ask to find out if there were any contracts out in the area."

Rex groaned. "Grigori? You're going to see that guy?"

I shrugged. "He likes me. And you'd better not go. It wouldn't do for you to be seen with a Russian mob leader."

Rex was silent for a few minutes. "Tell you what. I'll go see the McBrides, and you can talk to Grigori. But take someone with you. I don't want you going alone."

It was really hard not to roll my eyes. Rex knew about my past. I was certainly capable of going to see Grigori without incident.

"He has a lot of armed men," Rex reminded me, as if he could read my thoughts.

It wasn't worth arguing about, even if he was wrong.

"Hilly can go. They're afraid of her." And me, but I didn't say that.

Rex sighed as if giving in to something he didn't want me to do. After a quick kiss goodbye, I left his office.

The main area was humming with activity. Joanna and Troy were concentrating on their computers, and Kevin was talking to the Hamlets, who were sitting at tiny desks on top of his desk. I wondered if he really thought that by adding the hamsters, he'd doubled the workforce.

"What's going on, Kevin?" I stopped at his desk—something I never did.

He looked up at me slowly with hooded eyes. "Officers Hamlet need to work on their penmanship."

Sure enough, the hamsters were holding tiny pencils and scribbling on tiny sheets of paper. I squinted at what they were writing, but it was just scribbles. Like a lot of things Kevin did, this seemed like an exercise in futility.

"That's nice," I said. "Hey, I was wondering why you loaned Iago to the museum?"

"No, Hamlet," he chastised the one closest to me. "That's not how you spell…" He looked back at me. "How do you spell 'fireball?'"

I spelled it out for the man and his rodent and asked him my question again.

"Oh," he replied as he slouched in his chair. "That. Iago is his own pig. He likes going to the museum, so I let him."

"Who feeds him and looks after him?" I pressed.

"I don't know. Somebody else?" He pulled a tiny sheet of paper off another hamster's desk and asked him to do it again.

I left him to it and headed out to my car. My question about Iago was barely answered, but someone must be taking care of the pig, so I decided not to worry about it. It was most likely Lauren.

I called Hilly.

"Hey, are you still at the museum or at my old house?"

"I moved into your house. There's no shower at the museum. You should really put a shower in the basement because it's not a great guestroom."

"It's not a guest room," I insisted.

"That's not how I see it." The assassin paused. "Are you picking me up? I'll be ready in two minutes."

As I drove to pick up Hilly, I wondered about Rex's fears. It seemed to me that someone would have to have knowledge about my accidental killing of Carlos in order to stage Sheldon's murder the same way. It seemed unlikely that the killer could do this as an outsider. Still, it didn't hurt to check. If any contracts had been issued, Grigori would probably know about it. He was the first one to find out about the contract on me last year.

Hilly bounded out to the van and got in. "Hey, I heard Ron and Ivan had their babies!"

Hilly was close to the Chechens, and my sisters-in-law liked her.

"The twins had the babies, and yes, both Blasto and Blasto are here."

"Yay!" She bounced up and down in her seat. "I'm so excited! I'll have to get them each a present. Do you think a garrote or switchblade is more appropriate?"

"Neither. They're one day old," I said as if it would dissuade her.

Hilly went on as if I'd never said anything. "I'll get switchblades engraved with their names and birth dates…so they can tell whose is whose."

"It'll be the same name and date on both," I replied. "It's unlikely that they would be able to tell them apart." I described the babies to her. "It's as if the babies are twins too."

"Oh sure, that can happen," Hilly said. "Do you know anywhere that could engrave them for me in town?"

"Switchblades are illegal, so probably not," I sighed. "Why don't you get them something traditional? Like engraved baby spoons…"

Hilly beamed. "That they can fashion into shivs when they get older! Great idea!"

I gave up. Instead I explained what we were going to do.

"Okay." She sat back in the seat. "But I still don't think he was killed by anyone. I would've heard."

"Who do you think killed him? A ghost?" The idea made me laugh until I saw her face.

"Of course it was a ghost! What else would it be?"

I looked at her as we left town and headed out into the country. "You're joking."

She shook her head. "I'm not! It happens all the time! Especially in San Marino!"

In spite of myself, I asked the obvious question. "Why San Marino?"

She shrugged. "How would I know? You should ask the ghosts there. I've lost a couple of targets to them over the years."

For a moment, I thought about going there. Instead, I decided to prep her on what we were about to do.

"You think there's a contract on the dead guy?" She didn't look convinced. "I guess technically, that could be true. I just think I'd have heard of it."

I stared at her. "You're plugged into the *private* market?"

"Of course! I have to think about retirement. I don't want to be bored. I can't just sit around and do nothing like you do!"

I took some offence to that. "I don't do nothing! I have a Girl Scout troop, I'm married, and I solve murders sometimes," I grumbled.

Hilly's face beamed. "I could get married! That's a great idea!"

"You can't just get married," I snorted. "It doesn't work that way."

"Why not?" The assassin studied my expression from four inches away, which was unnerving. "I just find a guy, and voila!"

There was no point in arguing with her. "Yeah, but that'll be forty some years from now."

It looked like she was doing the math in her head. "Not if I retire before then. I could retire tomorrow if I want to."

I said a silent prayer that Hilly would not retire tomorrow.

She continued. "And then I'll move here and get a guy to marry me and have a house with a couple of pets, and I could kill people for fun now and then."

I tried to keep a straight face. "You should find a financial advisor and start talking to them..."

I didn't finish because she pulled out her phone and tapped some numbers on the screen.

"Hello? Phyllis?"

I mouthed the words, *Who's Phyllis?*

"My financial advisor." She returned to her call. "Yeah, Phyllis, I could retire tomorrow if I wanted to, right?"

After two seconds, she turned to me. "Phyllis said I can!" Hilly turned back to her call. "Thanks, Phyllis! I'll let you know!"

That as all I needed, Hilly living here, killing people right and left and stalking some guy to make him marry her.

"Don't worry." She patted me on the arm. "I'm not ready. Maybe in a month or two. Okay?"

We pulled up the long drive to Grigori's adorable bungalow. If you didn't know better, you'd think you were driving up to a charming cottage where a little old lady who loved flowers and fairy tales lived. Unfortunately, you'd be wrong, because Grigori was a stone-cold killer. But he was a stone-cold killer who had adorable basset hounds, a delightful garden, and looked like Santa.

In the front yard, four men armed with assault rifles were sitting on a bench working on various latch hook rugs. Upon seeing us, they carefully set down their craft and picked up the rifles. I parked, and we got out.

"Oh, it's just you," the lead man said.

He and the others went back to their rugs.

Grigori burst through the front door like a genial killer Santa. "Merry! And Hilly! What a lovely surprise!" His thick accent produced flowery words. "Come in! We can have tea and scones on the back porch!"

We followed him into his gorgeous hideaway, past the bookshelves full of regency romance novels, through the magazine-worthy kitchen, to a three-season room on the back porch. In the summer, the garden was ablaze with beautiful flowers and filled with butterflies. In the winter, it still managed to be pretty somehow.

"Sit, please! I'll get the tea tray!" He went inside.

Hilly looked around. "Where's Jerry?"

I stared at her. Jerry, Grigori's former right-hand man, would've killed to have Hilly interested in his whereabouts. "In prison in Colorado."

She gaped back at me. "He is?"

"You knew that. And I don't think you should bring it up in front of Grigori."

The Amazon chewed her lip. "Okay. But you really should have told me!"

"Here we are!" Grigori brought out a tray that held hot cups of tea and a three-tiered cake stand filled with petit fours, scones and Devonshire cream, and finger sandwiches.

My stomach growled. You always ate well at Grigori's, and even if he killed you afterwards, it was worth it.

"Yay!" Hilly said as she filled a plate.

The food was, of course, amazing. Once you got past the idea that Grigori was a Russian mob boss who did bad things, you had to admire him as a host. While we ate, two basset hounds wearing brightly colored sweaters rambled into the room and presented themselves for attention. I scratched Cuddles and Fluff behind the ears, and they melted to the floor with a harrumph.

"You must see the rug I am working on now!" Grigori handed me a partially done rug featuring a dozen kittens in sunbonnets, leaping into the air. "This one will be a masterpiece!"

I agreed, although I had a different definition of masterpiece.

"How are Ron and Ivan?" Grigori asked as I helped myself to my third scone.

"They just had babies!" Hilly squealed. "Two boys, one to each!"

Grigori clapped his hands and beamed. "Bravo! Congratulations to them both! I will make them rugs for their nursery!"

I swallowed the last of the scone. "I'm sure they'll love it. But really, Grigori, I'm here on business."

Lines of disappointment etched themselves into the old man's face. "This is not just a social visit?"

"Well…no." Now I felt bad. I should've just lied and said yes.

He looked at me over his wire-rimmed glasses. "Can we please call it a social visit? It would make me happy!"

Why not? "Sure. But I do have a business question for you." I told him about Sheldon McBride and asked if he knew of any contracts out on him.

"Hmmm…" He tapped his chin thoughtfully. "I know who you are talking about. I don't think I've heard of anything. Hold on."

He left the room and returned with a bright-pink laptop covered in daisy stickers. A piece of paper was sticking out of the closed computer. In big red letters, it said: *KILL ORDER—NO MERCY ALLOWED EVEN IF HE IS FAMILY*. Grigori opened it and set the piece of paper facedown on the sideboard.

He tapped on the keyboard and, after a few minutes, said, "Ah. There is one request. No one had officially taken it on, however. But it is there."

I leaned forward and snagged a chicken salad finger sandwich. Grigori made a sublime chicken salad. "What does it say?"

"They didn't ask me?" Hilly gasped.

Grigori looked at her. "Are you taking contracts on the side now?"

"No." She pointed at me. "But Merry and I were just talking about my retirement, and I might do it then!"

"Good. I will have a use for you." Grigori nodded before turning back to the screen. "It says here that someone in Who's There offered half a million dollars for the hit." His fingers returned to typing.

"Someone in Who's There has $500,000 they can just blow on a hit job?" I asked.

"But it was never confirmed." Grigori waved his hand at the screen. "If they killed him and didn't follow the appropriate procedure, I weep for the future."

"That does seem unprofessional," Hilly agreed.

"Is there any way to find out who put it out?" I asked. "That might lead us to the killer."

Grigori shook his head. "I don't know. No one requested information either. I am surprised, as this would be an easy one."

Hilly agreed. "And I was right there!"

"But it wasn't you," I said in a way that made me sound doubtful.

Hilly looked wounded. "Of course not! I would've thrown him in Wally's dumpster if I did. I do have a reputation to protect, you know."

"Grigori," I asked. "Would you be able to track down who hired the hit?"

He shook his head. "I am afraid I'm not much of a hacker. Do you know someone who is?"

I did. But I wasn't sure I wanted Betty involved. "Could I log into whatever database this is and try?"

Grigori nodded. "You just need to set up a username and password. I can also reach out to my Killer Hookers group on Facebook to see if anyone knows anything."

That sounded promising. "Let's do that now."

"Okay!" The crime boss smiled broadly. "What should we have as your username? Something that is not obvious, I think."

"Beetle Dork!" Hilly cried out.

"Too obvious." I glared at her. I had the nickname Beetle Dork because Hilly once made me the star of a graphic novel where a loser spy with that name got into misadventures. And a lot of people in town knew I was BD. So that wouldn't work. Thankfully.

"CIA Girl Scout!" Hilly decided.

"Again...too obvious," I snapped. "It has to be something that wouldn't connect me to anything."

Hilly kept shouting out suggestions that would all ID me to anyone on the site. I was getting annoyed until she came up with Must Love Bagels. That seemed like it would work. We picked a password that I'm not going to tell you. Grigori wrote down the website, and after another half hour of stuffing ourselves, we said goodbye.

Rex would be happy to know that the killer might be local.

Someone in Who's There wanted Sheldon McBride dead...and they got their wish.

CHAPTER FOURTEEN

"What do we do now?" Hilly wondered as I drove home. "Can we go see the babies at the hospital?"

That seemed like a good idea. "Maybe the gift shop has something we can get for the boys," I agreed.

Ron and Ivan were working at the museum, so maybe the twins would like having visitors. Besides, I could get used to Ronni being nice to me. Her kindness during delivery meant we'd turned a corner in our relationship, and I was excited to have both twins like me.

In the gift shop, we found two blue teddy bears and two gorgeous floral arrangements for the new moms. They were going to love this stuff...and me!

"What the hell are *you* doing here?" Ronni shouted at me as she cradled a huge baby.

"Ronni!" Randi rebuked softly. "Not in front of Blasto and Blasto!" She smiled at me. "I'm so glad you guys came to see us! The boys are working today. Terrible about that body they found!"

"I'm sure she did it!" Ronni jutted her chin at me, although she did do it in a softer voice. "She's always killing somebody! Why don't they lock her up?"

I guess we were back to normal.

The twins loved the bears and flowers, and I felt good about that, even after Ronni announced that they were obviously from Hilly.

"Want to hold Blasto?" Randi asked. Ronni, as if afraid I might want to hold her son, held him away from me.

Hilly waved them off. "I'm not so good with babies."

I reached out and took the baby from Randi. He was huge! I smiled and fussed over him, and even though he was asleep, I was rewarded with what I thought was a smile. I guess I could get used to being an aunt! My heart melted a little. Hopefully they wouldn't need me to be a den leader in Boy Scouts. Rex could handle that.

"So cute!" I cooed.

"And they came at the same time and look alike!" Randi leaned back against the pillow and closed her eyes.

"So Blasto and Blasto?" Hilly asked. "I like it! It's like Bora Bora or New York, New York!"

"How are we going to tell them apart?" I wondered out loud.

"It's obvious!" Ronni groused.

Randi opened her eyes. "We're going to call them by their middle names."

"Don't tell her!" Ronni snapped. The baby on her lap never woke up.

Randi ignored her twin. "My baby will be Blasto Wally and Ronni's will be Blasto Azlan!"

"Oh good! Now we will sort of be able to tell them apart," I breathed out. Then I froze. "I'm sorry, I didn't mean it like that…"

Randi laughed and waved me off. "It's okay, dear! I totally understand."

"I don't!" Ronni snapped.

Randi ignored her. "The doctor says the babies are so similar in every way from their blood type to doing everything at the same time in the same way. He says that technically, they are probably more like siblings than cousins. Isn't that nice?"

Hilly looked confused. "Wait…Wally Azlan? Like the guy in the dumpster?"

If the twins were offended, they didn't show it.

"Yes! Exactly!" Randi said.

The boys both made a loud noise simultaneously that made me think it was time to change them.

"See?" Randi beamed. "Everything at the same time!" She reached for a button and called the nurse, who came in right away.

I handed Wally to the nurse and made our excuses to go. The twins seemed tired, and I didn't want to stress them out. In the hallway, we heard the nurse shout, "Dear Lord in heaven! I think we need bigger diapers!"

"Well, how do you like that?" Hilly said as we got back in my van. "They named them after one of my hits. They must really like me!"

"Technically, you helped Wally kill himself," I pointed out.

Hilly ignored me because she was thinking. "Hey! If I have kids someday, I could do the same thing!" She frowned. "But that means I'd have to have like seventy kids. Or I could name one kid all the names! Let's see, his name would be Hector Oleg Francisco Barry…"

The list continued until I dropped her off back at my house.

"…Toby Ito Chia Rodrigo Max Curtis…"

As I drove away, she was still listing names. Did she really remember the name of every hit, in order? For anyone else, I'd say no.

I sat in my driveway for a few moments, thinking back on what Grigori said. He'd told us that someone from Who's There had put out the hit. Which meant someone here in town might have killed Sheldon themselves when no one else picked up the assignment. It would have to be someone who knew that assassination market existed. Someone like…

"Hey Merry!" Teo answered on the first ring. "What's up, my friend?"

Teo the Tapir and I had known each other in Colombia. He'd since retired to Who's There, looking for friends, since most drug lords didn't have many…alive. And even though he'd helped me when I'd had a contract out on me, he still knew about the business and often hung out with Grigori.

"Are you in town?" I asked carefully. No point in tipping him off if he was the killer.

"Sadly, no! Elena and I are on a father-daughter cruise to the Aleutian Islands. We've been gone a week already and won't be back until next week!"

There was some shouting in the background.

"Okay! Be right there, buttercup! Hey, Merry? We'll have to get together when I get back. Right now I'm in the middle of a shuffleboard tournament. Adios!"

He ended the call before I could breathe a sigh of relief that it wasn't him.

I'd have to look into Sheldon's past in town and see if he had any enemies. Someone from Who's There wanted him dead, but who? Why? Was it something from when he grew up here? Someone he left behind? Or maybe someone he ripped off? Where could I find out?

I reached over to check my bag for the scones I'd smuggled out of Grigori's, when my wallet fell open and my library card fell out. Unfortunately, I didn't find the scones. Hilly must've taken them. But I did get an idea.

The library! They had yearbooks from every year! A quick check on Wikipedia told me Sheldon had graduated from Who's There High in 1998. That was the yearbook I needed!

The Who's There Public Library was an old Carnegie Library, built in 1907 with money granted from the Andrew Carnegie Corporation. I didn't get over here as much as I liked, but I knew the girls had borrowed a bunch of books on Iceland for our Thinking Day project.

Genevieve, the elderly librarian, came to greet me when I came in. She was probably as old as the library itself. I asked if I could see Who's There high school yearbooks.

The woman directed me to the section where the yearbooks were stored, and I found the books starting with 1995, when he would have been a freshman, to 1998, when he graduated. I started with the last one, and because there were one hundred students at the time, I found Sheldon McBride quickly. For some reason, it was a blank spot that said *Photo Not Available*. I leafed through the other seniors and saw the same thing a few times. It must not have been a big deal back then.

Even with no photo, there was a blurb under his name. Sheldon had been voted most likely to succeed, which wasn't that surprising. I went back to the beginning to go through each page to see who his friends were, hoping I'd be able to find those people again in the class photos.

"You're looking for Sheldon McBride?" Genevieve appeared over my shoulder. "I remember him. He was always in here on weekends and throughout the summer. Always wanted science books. I knew he'd amount to something." She paused. "I just didn't think he'd be murdered back here."

I sat back in my seat. "What was he like?"

The librarian tucked some hair behind her ear. "Oh, he was quiet. Always buried in books. I had to send him home at closing nearly every time he was here. I wouldn't know much about him outside of this place because I'm always here and never go anywhere."

That might be a problem. Genevieve didn't mention him hanging around with anyone.

"Do you remember him coming in here with friends?"

"There was someone..." Her index finger tapped her glasses. "He came in with Sheldon in the beginning. But I could tell this kid didn't think hanging out in libraries was fun. Who was it?" Her voice trailed off as she thought. After a moment, she shook her head. "I'll think of it. Maybe not today, but it'll come to me."

I pointed to the blank spot where his photo should've been. "Is this normal?"

"Oh yes." The librarian scowled. "The high school makes people pay a photographer for the senior photos. Some families can't afford it, so they don't have a photo. Sad, really. She patted my shoulder. "Just shout if you need me. We're the only ones here." With a brief smile, she vanished.

It would probably be better to start at the beginning, so I went back to the first one and opened the book. Freshmen didn't usually get much attention in yearbooks. There was a photo of him this time, but he had long hair and bangs that covered his eyes. The photo wasn't very good quality. None of them were, I realized. I leafed through the book to see if I could find his name elsewhere, and I just spotted his name in a group photo of the Library Club. He was in the back row behind a very tall girl. All I could make out was the top of his head. Maybe I'd have more luck in the others.

Moving on to the sophomore yearbook, I found him again in the Library Club (again in the back row), but also in the Science Club. He was sideways, bent over a microscope, hair covering his face, with three other kids—a girl and a boy in profile, and a boy with his back to the camera. In the class photos, his picture was once again missing. There was no way to tell if the other kids were friends of his or not.

The junior yearbook offered up some interesting stuff. As usual, his class photo was missing, but the same kids, I think, were in the Science Club that year, and it looked like they were in Library Club, where they were listed. Audra O'Malley was the girl. Brian Atkins was one of the boys, and the other was Matt Bronson. I took some photos on my phone. Audra and Matt could be seen clearly, but like Sheldon, who was still looking into that same microscope, Brian's partial back was to us. It was almost like the two boys didn't want their photos taken.

Sheldon appeared in one other picture—a sort of composite of the junior class at the end of the book. In this one, he appeared to be Audra O'Malley's prom date. At least, I think it was him. The photos were from a distance and were a bit blurry and dark. There were no other photos of him with the boys.

With all this information, I returned to the senior yearbook. Brian's photo was missing from the class pages. Audra and Matt weren't in either the Library Club or Science Club. Brian still was, but this time both boys were looking through microscopes.

After all this, I wasn't sure if I had anything useful or not.

"Genevieve?" I called out as I approached the front desk. "Do you know if any of these kids were in here with him?" I held out the phone and scrolled through the photos.

"That one." She pointed at Brian. "I never saw the other two kids. You might ask Mr. Fowler. He was the science teacher around that time."

I didn't recognize the name. Obviously Mr. Fowler had retired before I got there. "Does he still live in town?" I asked.

"Oh sure." The librarian pulled out a phone book, looked him up, and wrote down an address and phone number. "Here you go. He ran the Science Club. Nice man. He can tell you more about Sheldon and the other kids."

I thanked her and left the library. Sitting in my van, I was lost in my thoughts. Audra and Matt looked somewhat familiar. Then again, this was a small town, so I'd probably seen them in public many times over, but because I didn't know them, it didn't register.

I called Mr. Fowler, and he agreed to meet me for coffee the next day. I decided to head over to the museum. Something was bothering me, but I didn't know what it was. Maybe immersing myself in murder would help.

CHAPTER FIFTEEN

The line was shorter. Ron and Ivan let me in without a word. I stood in the lobby and looked around. This was the first day the exhibit was open. Hey! This could be a good idea! What if the killer or killers came back to the scene of the crime?

In order to stay incognito, I first went into the gift shop and bought a black baseball hat with the logo on it. Stuffing my short blonde hair into it and pulling the brim down low, I wouldn't get a second glance.

There were a lot of people here. I pretended to look at the exhibits but actually studied the people around me. As folks poked around and took selfies with the deceased mannequins, I surreptitiously checked them out.

Most of them I knew from one thing or another. There were teachers from the elementary school where we'd held our meetings until this year, when the girls went to the middle school. There were staff members from the Girl Scout Council, who waved when they spotted me. My mechanic, grocery store clerks, and bankers were there. It was a hodge podge of the whole town.

Who's There wasn't very big. At just over five thousand, it was still possible to see perfect strangers and pass people you knew. For years as a spy, I'd lived all over the world. For the past seven—or was it eight—years, I'd lived here.

When I was younger, I'd wanted to be a secret agent and travel everywhere. I never thought I'd find myself back here, married, with baby nephews and a troop that could someday overthrow and run a small country.

"Hey!" Riley Andrews said quietly in my ear. "Interesting place you have here."

I pulled him into a corner near the statue of the vulture in the haunted house exhibit.

"Where have you been?" I badgered, even though I hadn't even thought about him since this whole mess started.

"I was on a ski trip with *someone*." His eyebrows went up. "I just got back into town and saw that the museum was open. I thought I'd check it out."

Riley had been my handler when we were both with the CIA. The drop-dead-gorgeous womanizer and I had a romantic fling that had the shelf life of a banana. He'd retired from the CIA and FBI to open a private investigation firm in town. Kelly had left her job as an emergency room nurse to work for him. She was on the cusp of becoming a real private investigator, and I was very proud of her.

"I understand this is all about you." He grinned. "Typical."

"I guess you didn't see your handiwork in the last exhibit," I pointed out.

Riley had killed Midori Ito and dumped her in my kitchen in my very first case here. Her mannequin was in my fake kitchen.

His perfect smile froze. "Really? The CIA won't be happy about that."

"I don't think they can do much about it. Sheldon, the donor, hired some serious legal muscle to make sure the museum wouldn't get in trouble." I hoped that even though McBride was dead, his lawyers would still come through for this place.

"Did I hear that Ron and Ivan had their babies?" He clapped me hard on the back. "Congratulations, Auntie!"

I filled him in on the whole thing, including Hilly's and my recent visit. "But the real news is that Sheldon McBride was murdered here."

A few people looked at me with interest. I dragged Riley into the corner and lowered my voice. "It happened yesterday."

"Maybe that's why everyone is here?" He held up his phone, where CNN had a story on it.

Ah. "I hadn't looked at the news. I'm still surprised the McBrides didn't say anything."

Riley's eyebrows went up. "His family?"

"They wish!" I started to say more when the five men appeared in the doorway, all wearing black from head to toe with devasted expressions.

"Them," I whispered before explaining who they were.

They walked through the haunted house exhibit, not seeming very interested in what was going on. Then they headed into the next exhibit.

"Are they prime suspects?" Riley asked.

"I think so. Rex went to see them. Either they heard from him or saw CNN." My eyebrows went up. "I wonder how they got black clothing so quickly?"

It didn't seem like something they would anticipate. Sheldon was too young to die. For a moment I wondered what this would do to the group. Would they disband or form some sort of cult like…

"Bird Goddess!" Stewie, the dred demi demon Odious, and his sidekick Mike—who, as far as I knew, was just Mike—appeared at my side, dressed in dark black robes.

"I see the Cult of NicoDerm is represented," Riley said.

"Of course!" Stewie scowled at the thought that they wouldn't be. "The dred demi demon Odious is a harbinger of doom!" He raised his hands over his head and wiggled his fingers in a move he called Demon Fingers. "All in his presence shall despair, and…and…" He dropped his arms and turned to Mike. "Line!"

Mike swallowed hard, his Adam's apple bobbing nervously. "Um…I can't remember."

"Mike!" Stewie stomped his foot. Any passerby might look at his short rotund stature, red hair, and freckles and think he was a petulant child. "You have one job! See, this is why you don't have a title yet!"

The cult had adopted me years ago. They called me Bird Goddess and thought I had the mystical ability to talk to birds. It seemed silly to mention that anyone could talk to birds. Getting them to answer back was the real trick. And even I hadn't mastered that yet.

"I think Mike should have a title," I decided.

Stewie looked at me with what appeared to be betrayal. Mike's hooded eyes opened a little bit more as he looked hopeful.

"Yes!" Mike said. "I've been telling you that for years. The Bird Goddess is right!" He turned to me and pressed his hands together as if he was praying. "Oh Bird Goddess, can you bestow a demony title upon me, your humble servant?"

"Don't do it," Stewie groused. "He hasn't earned it."

Mike, who never contradicted Stewie and actually never said much of anything, gave a monologue. "I have been with the cult from the beginning…even before the girls! I should have a title too! You wouldn't be anywhere without me! The Cult of NicoDerm would be a cult of one dude!"

Stewie drew back his arm and gave the most telegraphed punch in the history of punches. There seemed to be no force to it at all. It didn't even dent the fabric of Mike's robes.

"Ow!" Stewie whined. "See what you made me do? Now I have to discipline you!"

"How would you do that, exactly?" Riley asked.

"I dunno." Stewie rubbed his fist. "We need a dungeon with chains and a rack!"

"Or…" I held up one finger. "You could treat him equally and give him what he wants."

This was, like all cult business, starting to infringe on my time where I'd rather be doing something else. I walked into the next exhibit and pulled the fake dagger out of the dead mannequin's chest. A couple of people gasped. I returned and placed the blade on Mike's shoulder, ignoring some of the cries of alarm around me.

"I, Bird Goddess of the Cult of NicoDerm, with the power vested in me, dub you, Mike the Menacing Monk of Moroseness! Congratulations! Go forth and be, um, whatever!"

Mike beamed. It was more expression than I'd ever seen from him before. I then gave him the knife and asked him to put it back in the fake body. He literally skipped away.

"You shouldn't have done that!" Stewie stamped his foot again. "You've overstepped your powers, Bird Goddess! This could get you kicked out of the cult…" He raised both ends of his robe in the air, "Forever!"

I shrugged. "Okay." I grabbed Riley's hand. "Come on, I'll show you what happened to Sheldon."

CHAPTER SIXTEEN

Instead of going through eight more exhibits, I dragged Riley back into the lobby and through the gift shop. I wasn't prepared for what I found in the exhibit hall where Sheldon McBride was murdered.

Betty stood on a box and had a megaphone. "And this is where they found the body!"

The crowd looked down at Carlos's mannequin and gasped.

"Now, for only $50 more," the kid continued. "You can buy this one-of-a-kind commemorative travel mug that keeps hot drinks hot and cold drinks cold!" She held up a long, gray tumbler with Sheldon McBride's image doctored to look like his last moments on earth in terror. How did they get that, when Rex had the driver's license at the station?

The crowd went wild and stampeded past us to the gift shop. I ran over to Betty.

"What in the world do you think you're doing?"

The child looked at me as if I was an idiot. "Capitalizing on his death, duh!"

I snatched the tumbler from her hands. "I can't believe people will pay $50 for this crap."

Betty snatched it back. "Uh, commemorative travel mug."

From the angle she was holding it, I could see a small banner that said, VOTE FOR AVE.

"Vote for Avenue?" I asked.

"It was supposed to be AVA," Betty sighed. "But we had to get these here quickly, so there wasn't much quality control. The Kaitlyns are on it."

We followed her finger to the doorway, where the four Kaitlyns were drawing an *A* over the *E* with Sharpies. People were literally screaming for them.

"And you've turned it into a piece of political campaign propaganda?" I said that with a bit more admiration than chastising. It was brilliant. At this rate, half the town would have them.

"We've sold four thousand already today," Betty added. "Ava's going to win the next election."

"It's three years away!" Riley said, again with more admiration.

"It's good to get a jump on these things. Hopefully anyone thinking of running will see it and decide not to." She looked at me. "What? Ava is mayor and helped get this deal done. The museum is here because of her. Why not exploit that?"

"Did you just say you've made $200,000 on these already?" Riley whistled.

"Sort of. Because we needed this batch overnight, the cost was pretty high. Vladimir gets sixty percent. The next batch, however, will not only be spelled right, but will also only give him a thirty percent cut because they've already done whatever to the machine that makes these."

"I don't suppose you could sell Girl Scout cookies through the gift shop?" I mused out loud.

"Of course!" Betty said. "We just don't have any until next week."

"Next week?" I asked. "We don't get them for almost a month."

"Pretend you didn't hear that, then," Betty said. "I'd better go help the others."

Riley and I stood staring at the whole scene. It was like throwing gasoline onto a bonfire. I might have been a little proud that I had some hand in teaching them that.

Meanwhile, the exhibit was empty. I walked Riley through what we'd found and was even able to get him into the basement unseen.

"And Hilly heard nothing? That doesn't seem like her." Riley frowned. "You never found the drone either?"

I shook my head. "If it hasn't shown up by now, I'm guessing the killer took it and destroyed it."

"It was only yesterday," Riley said. "But I see what you mean. Besides, half the town will be looking for it now. It's more likely to be a souvenir."

"Which makes me suspect the McBrides even more." I bit my lip. "We'd better get back up there before the room fills up for Betty's next sales pitch."

While their actions were almost always questionable, I would never worry about my troop and money. They made more money as kids than I'd made in my whole life. These kids could pay for college easily. Actually, they were more likely to hack into financial aid and hide the money in shell corporations. My heart swelled with pride. I think I'd taught them that.

Hopefully, Kelly would never find out. She was more into doing things the right way. I understood her point. She was worried we were turning out criminals more than entrepreneurs. But I thought she was wrong. I thought it was a bit of both actually.

I called Rex on my way home to tell him my concerns about news trucks all over town. The murder of one of the most famous inventors in the US would be a huge story.

"I know," Rex sighed. "I've been fielding calls all day from major media outlets. I've told all of them that coming here won't change the way we investigate. But I have a plan."

I turned into the driveway. "What's that?"

"I've set up a phone number the media can call 24/7," he said.

"What sucker is going to be stuck with that duty?" I wondered.

"The Officers Hamlet," he said. "If they can get a story out of them, it'll be worth reading."

I spent the entire night looking up people, from Sheldon's classmates to his family. His parents died in a car accident on I-80 when a truck full of feed jackknifed to avoid a runaway cow. The McBrides hadn't stood a chance.

Most of what I found was that the McBrides were a poor family and that Sheldon struggled against the odds to become the genius of a generation. In interviews, which were few and always over the phone, he mentioned his family and his hardships as if he was reading a press release from the McBride Corporation. He probably was. Most of those interviews were word for word, exactly the same.

Sheldon's past was as mysterious as the lack of photos in his yearbooks. I also looked into Audra, Matt, and Brian on social media. Audra was the only one with a presence there—and just on Facebook, where she posted maybe once a year. It was always about cats.

I thought about Rex's plan to handle the media. It wouldn't stop them if they wanted to show up, although I doubted that the press could find out more about Sheldon than I had.

Still, the urgent need was that I needed to find out what happened to Sheldon before we started getting cable news trucks all over Main Street. The girls would most certainly go rogue with the attention. Forget throwing gasoline on a bonfire. The access those girls would have to international media would be like dropping an atomic bomb into a volcano.

CHAPTER SEVENTEEN

The next morning, I met up with Ted Fowler at Martha's Café. It wasn't my favorite place, but Fowler had insisted. Martha was the owner and a real terror who had some bad habits, like bringing you coffee with her thumb in it. She had one rule, and that was whatever she says goes. There were stories all over town of people who'd gotten booted from Martha's for various infractions, from complaining about her thumb being in their coffee, to asking for changes to anything on the menu or requesting extra stuff. She once threw me out for asking about extra ice in my water. She told me if I didn't like the way she made a glass of water, to go someplace else. Fortunately that was a long time ago, and she's since forgotten my overstep of the power dynamic.

After making sure Fowler wasn't already waiting for me, I took a table in the window and waited.

"What'll ya have?" Martha loomed over me like a giant, angry pigeon.

"Hot tea. And I'm waiting for someone."

Martha didn't move. "Hot tea? You think this is England or something? We have coffee, pop, and water."

"Fine." I hesitated a moment, sizing up the risk. "I'll have water, then." Yeesh! It wasn't like tea was only something the rest of the world drank.

"You have to order something," Martha said in a bored voice. "I can't just give you water, you leech."

"A cinnamon roll, served warm with melted butter on top," I said breezily. I wasn't going to make it easy for her.

Martha rolled her eyes and walked slowly away.

The door opened, and a man who looked to be in his sixties came in. He was tall, handsome, and had gray hair. It must be Ted Fowler. I waved him over, and he broke into a huge smile.

"It's so nice to meet you, Ms. Ferguson!" Ted said after shaking my hand and taking a seat. "I've heard a lot about you."

Uh-oh.

"Really? From who?" I asked. "And it's Merry, please."

"Linda Willard," he explained.

Linda Willard had been my fourth-grade teacher. She'd helped me with a case or two. But after becoming a champion crossword puzzle designer, she'd moved to Chicago.

"You two were teaching at the same time? I thought you taught high school?"

He nodded. "I did. She was assigned to be my mentor when I started here. She said you're very sharp."

I almost dropped my napkin. "She did?" That was nice to hear!

"And your father did a couple of online meetings with my students over scientific matters."

Now I was really confused. My dad was one of two senators from Iowa, and a high-ranking one. But as far as I knew, he didn't dabble in science.

The confusion must have been noticeable because Ted held up his hands. "He had some connections to the Smithsonian. He introduced the head of the museum to the kids. He was very inspirational."

"You know more about me than I do about you," I said with a touch of envy.

In the spy world, it was your business to know more than your contact did. You didn't have to let him know that, but it was very helpful to over-prepare. Obviously, I hadn't.

Martha trudged over and dropped my cinnamon roll in front of me before plunking down a glass of water with one ice cube. Fowler ordered a cup of coffee and a donut. Martha gave me a look before stalking back to the kitchen.

"So, what's this about? I was flattered when our town celebrity wanted to meet with me. Over the past few years, I've heard about your leaving the CIA and the murders you come across now and then."

"Well, if you talked to my dad, you probably know it wasn't my choice to leave the CIA," I replied. "And I can't help the murder thing. Bodies just have a way of popping up around me."

His face fell. "Like Sheldon McBride."

I nodded. "Like Sheldon McBride."

"Let me guess… You want to know a little more about him because I was his advisor."

This guy was smart. I liked him.

I picked up my fork and cut into my cinnamon roll. "That's right. I'm working to help the museum stay open. McBride donated the money for it. I'm hoping the town can keep it going."

Fowler didn't say anything as Martha dropped off his coffee and donut. I waited as he poured sugar into his mug and stirred.

"It's too bad about Sheldon. He was a misunderstood kid. Geniuses usually are. I've taught a lot of smart kids, but no one at his level. It's a big loss." Ted sighed and stared off into space for a moment.

"I'm sorry," I said. "I can find next to nothing about the man. Did you stay in touch?"

"We did. Oh, it was only a few times a year, but Sheldon always sent a birthday card and called every now and then to bounce ideas off of me. He once said I was the only one he trusted because I knew him before he was famous." His smile faded into a sad expression, and I felt bad for him.

"That seems a little sad, that you were the only friend he trusted," I murmured.

Ted agreed with me. "It was. He had a few friends in high school but later told me he never had friends like that again. I think something happened either in college or right after that put him off relationships."

"Sounds lonely. But harder to make enemies that way. Do you have any idea who'd want to kill him?"

Fowler regarded me as if wondering whether he could trust me. Finally, he spoke. "I'm sure he had enemies in the industry. But I think you should look closer to home."

I looked around. "Like here?"

"Like closer to his home." For a moment, it seemed like he wasn't sure to tell me more. "He was married, albeit very briefly…"

"He was married?" I gaped. Wikipedia hadn't said anything about that!

"Sheldon got married right out of college. They were only married six months. I was a witness at the courthouse. I didn't like her, myself. Sandy didn't seem equal to him. I thought he deserved better."

A murderous ex-wife makes a great suspect! "Who is Sandy? Why isn't there any mention of her online?"

Fowler shrugged. "Now that I can't help you with. When they split up, Sheldon never mentioned her to me again."

I wondered if the McBrides knew? There was a Sandy in the group. It's possible he took the name as a nod to this woman. If anyone knew, it would be fanatic followers.

"Do you have a maiden name?" I asked hopefully.

Fowler shook his head. "I'm sorry. I only met her on her wedding day, and she was tight-lipped. Didn't say a word to me."

This sounded like a good job for Riley the PI.

"You said he didn't have friends after high school. So he had friends *in* high school?" I wasn't going to let him know I'd already perused the yearbooks.

"He did have a few." He chuckled softly. "Nice kids. A girl and two boys. They were close until their senior year. Sheldon never explained why he only hung out with Brian after that. I didn't pry, thinking he or the others would tell me when they were ready. But they never did."

That made sense. In spite of what teachers think, kids don't often think they're buddies.

"Can you tell me about them? I want to get a picture of who he was before he left here."

Ted sighed and stared into space. "Let's see. There's Brian Adkins. He's a CPA, I think. And Audra O'Malley and Matt…" He tapped his fingers on the table. "Matt Bronson. That's it. I know they still live around here because I see them out and about sometimes, but we never talk."

Ted must've realized what I was thinking because he added, "It's nothing like that. I get along with all of my former students. Audra, Matt, and I always say hi, but that's about it."

Museum of Murder | 121

At least I wouldn't have to go far to find them. It didn't seem likely that they would have killed him if they hadn't talked since high school. I was still friends with Kelly, and I saw other people I went to school with from time to time. Kevin for one. But I didn't stay in touch with anyone else.

Ted spoke up again. "Sheldon is a real loss to the world. I was fascinated with his ethanol drone. The kid had great ideas. I remember thinking he had more than he could ever make good on. Now I guess they're all lost."

Fowler's voice cracked on the last word. He was really feeling the loss. I felt bad about pumping him for intel.

He looked at me for a moment. "I hope you catch whoever did this. I really do. Sheldon could've made the world a better place. And now he won't have the chance."

"Did you talk to him recently?" I asked gently.

He sighed heavily. "Last week. He'd told me about the museum, and I was at the big announcement at city hall. I have a ticket for this afternoon. But I don't think I can do it. I don't know if I could handle seeing where he died."

"He told you about the museum?" I suppose it wasn't odd, since they'd stayed in touch.

He gave a wan smile. "He was so proud of it. Felt like he was giving back to Who's There. It's kind of a weird way to do it, but Sheldon was wired differently. We talked about him endowing a scholarship for one high school senior each year to study science in college. I hope he put it in place before he died. It would have been a huge boon to the town."

"That would've been great," I agreed. "Can you think of anything else he told you?"

Ted rubbed his chin thoughtfully. "Now that you mention it, there was something. He said he was working on an old idea from high school that he thought could be big. It was just in the early stages, however. I'm sure it never got off the drawing board."

I wasn't sure if it was relevant or not. "What kind of ideas did he have in high school?"

Ted spread his hands wide. "I tried to recall when he said that. I have had so many students over the years that I can't remember everything. I remember something about a flying car, a pill you could eat that would be a whole meal…like in *Willy*

Wonka. But they were ideas a kid would come up with. I can't see him inventing those things now."

That didn't sound like something he would be killed over. Unless he really was close to inventing a flying car. That would be awesome. "If you remember, will you call me? It might be nothing, but it could be a clue of some sort."

"Absolutely," he agreed. "I'd like to see whoever did this behind bars."

Fowler got kind of quiet. I felt bad for him. One of his students made it big, and he was so proud of Sheldon. To have him murdered in his prime would be devastating.

We made small talk for a few minutes. I guess when you have a heady discussion on the murder of someone you cared about, you have to cleanse the palate with talk about the weather.

After he left, I paid Martha and thought about what my next move should be. I decided it was time to get some real research in.

And I knew just the man to do it for me.

CHAPTER EIGHTEEN

I blew into Riley's office bearing lunch. Kelly was at her desk, typing on her keyboard. Riley was staring at his screen. I dumped the bags of hamburgers and fries from Oleo's on the table, earning surprised looks from the two of them.

"Lunch?" Kelly came over. "You read my mind!"

Riley slowly approached the table, leery of the smell from the bags until I produced a salad for him. Someday, that man was going to lose his mind and go on a junk food bender. I only hoped I'd be there to see him do it.

"Riley told me about Betty and the girls," Kelly said as she unwrapped the best burger in the State of Iowa.

Crap. Now she'd be mad at me for not telling her or stopping it. I shot a warning glance at Riley, who ignored it.

"And I think it's great!" my best friend finished.

My burger paused halfway to my mouth. "You do?"

She rolled her eyes. "Of course I do! The girls inviting other troops to host cookie booths at the museum is unselfish and inspired!"

I looked at Riley, who pretended to be fascinated with a tomato.

"Oh. That. Right." I took a bite. I wasn't sure if that was true or if Riley just said that for Kelly's benefit.

Kelly cocked her head to one side. "What did you think I meant?"

"I thought you were talking about the girls promoting Ava's campaign so early," I lied easily.

Kelly looked at her boss. "He didn't tell me about that. Oh well. I guess it was bound to happen sometime."

She wasn't mad! Riley must have left off the more serious infractions. For a man who didn't like kids, it was pretty cool that he was covering for mine.

"So what's with lunch?" Riley asked.

"I need you to do some research," I said between bites of my fries. "Sheldon was married to some woman named Sandy for a short time. She could be a viable suspect." I filled them in on my coffee break with Ted.

"That seems like a long time to hold a grudge," Kelly muttered. "Do you think she would come back and murder him out of the blue?"

"You don't have a maiden name?" Riley frowned. "That won't make it easy."

"I have great faith in you," I lied again. "This woman was married to one of the most famous reclusive inventors in recent history! You can find something."

"And I suppose you want me to do it pro bono." Riley shook his head.

Huh. I did kind of do that to him a lot. I also paid him sometimes, but since he was paying my best friend, I figured he needed to get paid.

"Tell you what," I decided. "I'll see if Rex can give you a contractor deal. If not, I'll pay for it."

Kelly eyed me warily. "Why are you so keen on this? You hated the idea of the museum."

"I did," I agreed. "But you should see the lines for that place. It's putting Who's There on the map!" The murder map, but that counted. I placed my hand over my heart. "And I'm nothing if not very civic minded."

Kelly snorted but didn't disagree. "We know where he went to college and when he graduated. If they got married right after college, then he probably met her there. I'll see what I can find."

"That's the spirit!" A thought occurred to me. "Hey, has anyone seen Hilly today? I always wonder what she's doing if she's not with me."

The two shook their heads.

"Maybe she's gone home?" Kelly suggested with a bit of hope in her voice.

"Maybe..." I said. "I won't worry about it yet." Another thought occurred to me. "See if you can find out something on a group of Sheldon McBride Followers."

Riley grinned. "I started looking into them. They don't have much of a trail online. But I found a nonprofit under the name of Simon McBride. I'll keep digging."

The two worked while I cleaned up the food and ran out to pick up ice cream for dessert from Feeling Lucky's House of Delights. The afternoon passed with me bouncing suggestions off of Kelly and Riley for research ideas. At one point I called Rex and talked him into considering paying Riley a contractor fee for doing the work. My husband said he'd get back to me, which meant I should find my checkbook when I got home.

It was late in the afternoon when the door opened and Betty and Conrad walked in. Kelly and I looked at each other.

"And this is where Mrs. Wrath and Mrs. Albers hang out to solve murders." Betty waved her arm around the room. She spotted Riley. "Oh, right. That's Mr. Andrews. He used to be in the CIA and FBI but now just sits there while the women do all the work."

Riley's eyebrows went up, but he said nothing.

"What are you two doing here?" I asked.

But Betty was now staring at Conrad as if he were a unicorn who loved black bag drops and wet work.

Conrad turned to her and, realizing the girl wasn't going to say anything, spoke instead. "Betty's taking me on a tour of town where all the murders and mysteries have happened."

Betty nodded but said nothing. That's when I realized she was wearing a dress. I almost fainted. It was winter! And she was...Betty!

"How do you like it here, Conrad?" I ventured.

"It's pretty cool," Conrad said casually. "I like how it's murdery but not really dangerous because it's always someone who knows the victim. I only know Betty and my dad here, so I'm probably okay."

"That's...mostly true," I agreed.

"And Betty's pretty cool," Conrad added.

Betty turned an alarming shade of red, and for a moment I thought she'd stopped breathing. I whacked her on the back, and her skin tone went back to normal.

"Thanks," Betty said. "I needed that."

"Are you alright?" I whispered so Conrad wouldn't hear.

She looked at me in surprise. "Of course I am. Why would you think I wasn't?"

"She does that sometimes," Conrad said. "I think she needs more Vitamin C."

Betty pulled a notepad out of her pocket and wrote that down. Hmmm… Conrad could prove useful should I need Betty to pay attention to something. I knew girls could join Boy Scouts, but could boys join Girl Scouts? He'd make a valuable addition to the troop.

"How do you like Who's There?" Kelly regained her voice. "I hear your dad runs the new museum?"

"I like it so far. Chicago was scary. I spent a lot of my time at the library. I like to read. Now I can do it outside without getting mugged or picked on."

Betty had moved closer, and I saw her write, *read actual books*, and *defend Conrad* in her notebook.

Conrad walked over to Riley. "Were you really in the CIA and FBI?"

Riley gave his most charming smile—one that used to melt the panties off even the most dour prison matron. Not sure what he was going for here with Conrad, but the kid's pupils didn't dilate, so I guessed he was immune to Riley's charms.

"That's right." He pointed at me. "I was her handler back in the CIA. And Betty misrepresented me a little."

I looked at Betty, who looked furious that Riley would contradict her. I'd have to watch her in the future to make sure she didn't exact revenge on him.

Riley handed Conrad his card. "I'm a private investigator now. This is my firm. Mrs. Albers works for me. And Mrs. Ferguson doesn't solve my cases."

"Yes she does," Betty argued.

I nodded in solidarity because the girl was right.

"Anyway…" Conrad looked at the card. "That's pretty cool. I've never met a private eye or former FBI agent before."

"We've gotta go," Betty said. "It's dinnertime, and I thought I'd treat him to Oleo's."

"Your parents aren't waiting for you to have dinner at home?" Kelly asked.

Was this a date? I wondered.

"No," Betty said. "I told them Ava needed me for a thing. Bye!"

"Nice to see you again!" Conrad nodded before they both went out the door.

"He seems nice," Riley said before going back to his computer.

My phone rang. It was Ava.

There were no pleasantries. The kid dove right in. "Some lawyer named Britta Almondine is here from McBride Corp to talk to you about the drone."

"Define *here*," I asked.

"At the museum," Ava said. "I've gotta go. We've got a meeting with all the city staff to blackmail them into buying Girl Scout cookies. Bye!"

She hung up before I could warn her not to threaten anyone.

"She's going to use extortion, isn't she?" Kelly sighed and pulled out her phone. "I'll call her."

Kelly got a voicemail recording, so she left a message explaining how extortion wasn't the Girl Scout way.

"I'm going with you," she said after. "I've been wanting to see the museum without having to get on a waiting list for a ticket."

"Okay." I shrugged. "She's just going to give me something to help track down the drone. It could be boring stuff."

Kelly brightened. "Then I can roam the museum while you talk about boring stuff! Win-win!"

CHAPTER NINETEEN

"So what ever happened to the drone?" Kelly asked as she got into the car.

"It's still missing in action," I said.

It really bothered me that we'd never found the drone. At this point, I was certain the killer must have taken it. Rex had contacted Sheldon McBride's company—the originally named McBride Corporation—for any information on how to locate the drone. They said they were sending someone out. That was yesterday. And now someone named Britta Almondine was here.

Knowing McBride, he probably had an overly elaborate technology that made it possible to track down the drone. I was hopeful but not optimistic that they could locate the equipment. Still, whoever took it was my main suspect for the murder.

I wasn't ruling out the McBride Followers to have killed him and taken the drone as a trophy. Still, why would they kill their hero? Then again, there was that true adage that you should never meet your heroes because they most often turned out to be not very heroic.

Case in point, the CIA had a spy I'd admired from the moment I joined up. Karine Baker had been a masterful agent in the Cold War. She'd evaded capture in East Germany for ten years, scored massive troves of intel, and even fought off three attackers in a Berlin alley, wearing high heels and a dress.

About four years into my tenure at Langley, the CIA honored her with a dinner party. Riley, knowing how I felt about Karine, managed to score me a seat at her table (by sleeping with the special assistant), and I was over the moon. I had all kinds of questions to ask but decided it wouldn't be a good idea to overwhelm the older woman. Besides, I was at a table for eight. Monopolizing the legend would just be rude.

The magic night came, and it turned out I was sitting right next to Karine! I was so excited as I sat down. The elder spy was dressed in an elegant black caftan and was sipping a glass of red wine. No one else had joined us yet! I had her all to myself!

"Excuse me, Ms. Baker," I gasped after introducing myself. "I'm a huge fan of yours!"

The woman turned her head and regarded me coolly but said nothing. Then she turned back to her drink and even started looking around. I'd been a bore! Oh no! I decided to try to impress her.

"The Red Schnauzer gambit was a masterpiece." I was referring to an incident where Karine had fooled a group of menacing Stazi agents who were approaching one night as she was walking down the street. The East German police had begun to suspect the woman and were on the lookout to arrest her. Karine feigned tripping and falling and lay on the ground, clutching her head. She even opened a bottle of red nail polish and rubbed it on the side of her face.

The men finally surrounded her.

"Oh thank goodness you're here!" She clutched her ankle while making sure they could see the red nail polish on her face. "I tripped on something, hurt my head, and I think twisted my ankle! I feel so foolish because I'm late for a dinner with the chancellor!"

The men paused, unsure what to do. I'm sure they were wondering if they were wrong about her. This lady spoke perfect German with the right accent. She claimed to be late for dinner with the chancellor. If they arrested her, would they be the ones in a gulag next week?

One man stepped forward. His name was Gunter Friederich. A coldhearted bastard who enjoyed torturing women and children. He asked for Karine's papers, and she happily supplied them. The other men dropped back. If Gunter was going down, they weren't keen to go down with him. Fortunately they stepped out of range.

"Everything looks like it is in order," Gunter sneered. "But I don't believe you. I think you're a spy."

Karine laughed. "Well that's just ridiculous!" She lowered her voice. "If I was a spy, I'd know that your code name with the West Germans is Red Schnauzer, and you'd be taken in by those men over there!" She gave them a friendly wave, and they waved back.

The fact that she'd known Gunter was a double agent made him hostile, but he had the men carry her back to her apartment. With her cover blown, she crossed the border into West Germany later that night. Without incident.

And that was just one of many harrowing tales about her! And at the moment, the woman was behaving as if I wasn't there. I decided to brave another attempt before someone she wanted to talk to sat down and I never got another chance.

"Well, it's an honor just to sit at the same table as you," I said.

Karine's head snapped toward me, and she grimaced. "Who the hell are you? I didn't risk my life over and over for this country just to sit with some stupid nobody!"

I was so shocked, I got up and excused myself. Later, Riley told me she had a horrible reputation with people. She may have been a great spy, but she actually loathed other people and was especially jealous of other women spies. I never asked him for another favor. This was also one of the reasons I didn't really mind when Hilly pranked him.

Kelly and I drove to the museum to meet Britta Almondine.

Fortunately it was after hours, so there wasn't a line of people waiting to get in. Instead, two of the Kaitlyns stood there, waiting for me.

"Conrad's dad went home for the night," one of them said.

"We agreed to wait for you," said the other.

"Is anyone else here?" I asked.

The girls shook their heads before opening the door.

"Here's the keys." One of the girls held out her hand. "We have to get over to city hall to help Ava. You haven't seen Betty, have you?"

That caught me off guard. My troop always knew where every other member of the troop was at any time.

"She went to dinner with Conrad," Kelly replied.

The two girls looked at each other, communicating silently, before taking off. We went inside, locking the door after us.

"Hello?" I shouted. "Ms. Almondine?"

There was no answer. I guess I should've asked the girls where she was.

"I'll bet she's in the office," Kelly suggested.

We tried it, but no one was there. I suggested that maybe the lawyer wanted to see the exhibits. Kelly thought this sounded like a good idea, and we went back to the lobby.

"It's kind of creepy here at night," my co-leader said as she looked at the shadows on the walls.

She wasn't wrong. It was dark, and the mannequins cast weird shadows on the floor. "At least the exhibit lights are on. She probably just wants to see what Sheldon spent all that money on. Come on!"

We called out her name as we entered the haunted house exhibit. Louise Lutkin's dining room was empty of people…well, living ones that is, too. As we stepped into the Druid Con exhibit, my spydy senses began to tingle.

"I've got a bad feeling about this," Kelly echoed my suspicions.

"You feel it too?" I whispered.

She nodded. "It's like this whole place is one bad feeling."

We approached the crowd of mannequins that surrounded the fake corpse of cable scream queen Deliria. Only, it wasn't Deliria. Lying there, on the floor, a knife sticking out of her chest, was a woman we'd never seen before.

"She's breathing!" Kelly screamed and dove to a kneeling position beside her.

I called 9-1-1 as Kelly held the woman's hand and spoke quietly to her.

Once the ambulance was on the way, I knelt down on the other side of her. "They'll be here in five minutes or less," I encouraged her.

The woman's eyes went from the ceiling to me. "Sheldon!" She gasped. "Killer is here!"

A shaky hand clasped mine. There was something in it. The woman had passed me a note or something, but I kept hold of her hand. Was this Britta Almondine? She was very elegant-looking and appeared to be around Sheldon's age, with shoulder-

Museum of Murder | 133

length blonde hair, blue eyes, and a trim figure in a very expensive suit. Was this the lawyer?

The sirens roared outside, and I let go of her hand, shoved the note into my pocket, and ran to let the EMTs in. By the time we got to the woman, she was dead. Kelly shook her head and told them not to touch the body until Soo Jin got here.

"You okay?" I asked.

Kelly nodded. "Did she give you something?"

That's right! I pulled it out of my pocket. It was Britta alright. This was her business card, listing her as VP of Legal Affairs for the McBride Corporation. I turned it over, but there was nothing else besides her contact information. Why did she hand me this? Did it mean something, or was she just identifying herself? I stuffed the card back into my pocket, and it hit me.

"The killer is still here!" I said before running off toward the next exhibit.

No one followed me. Kelly shouted that she'd go the other way. I couldn't stop her, but maybe Rex would arrive before she could do much. Kelly was the most efficient and capable person I knew. But even with her PI training, she was no match for a killer who would be desperate to get out.

I searched the hiding spots in every single exhibit until I met up with Kelly and Rex, who'd just arrived, in the gift shop.

"Britta told me the killer is here!" I said quickly.

Rex excused himself and returned moments later. "Troy and Joanna are checking the office area and basement, but it's possible the killer got out the front door between the EMTs arriving and our turning up."

He was right. It was exactly what I would've done. Not that I'd stabbed many people in museums. Usually I just used a gun. It was so much simpler.

Troy and Joanna turned up and shook their heads.

We joined Soo Jin's examination back in the exhibit hall after I locked the doors again.

"Stabbed in the heart," the medical examiner said. "Death would've been quick."

"She was alive for a few moments." Kelly shook her head sadly. "She said something to Merry."

Everyone turned to look at me. "She said the killer is here. But I think they escaped while we were trying to save her." I looked around for a purse or briefcase. "She's Britta Almondine, Sheldon's lawyer."

I handed my husband the business card as the EMTs zipped Britta into a body bag and onto a cart, wheeling her away. Joanna and Troy decided to give the exhibits another search. Kelly went with them.

"The killer clearly doesn't want us to find that drone," I said. "They killed Britta and took whatever she had to find the drone with them."

"I should close down the museum," Rex sighed.

"That's what the killer wants you to do!" I said.

My husband's eyebrows went up. "Why do you think that?"

I shrugged. "It's what they always say in movies. It could be true."

The others came back and told us they found nothing, again. That left only one place to search.

Rex looked at me. "The basement."

I was on the run before he could tell me not to, but he beat me to the door and got between it and me.

"My officers and I will check it out," he said firmly before drawing his gun.

Troy and Joanna drew theirs and followed their boss down into the secret basement. After a few moments, they came back up empty-handed.

"You can't close the museum again," I said. "Both killings weren't necessarily tied to the museum. I think they were tied to Sheldon McBride and he happened to be here."

Rex gave me that look that said he disagreed. "Both murders were staged like exhibits. If they weren't connected and were just crimes of opportunity, the killer would've just dumped them in the lobby."

I thought about that for a moment. He had a point, and I didn't like it. But why didn't I like it? I didn't want the museum to open in the first place. Somewhere along the line, it had grown on me. Also, I didn't want Drew to leave and take Conrad with him because that would upset Betty, which seemed way worse than the two murders we'd just had.

I'd often wondered...or make that, worried, what would happen should Betty become emotionally unstable. That girl was the coolest cucumber of anyone I've ever known. I always imagined that she'd grow to the size of Godzilla and take out most of Iowa if something ever upset her.

"We have to keep the museum here," I insisted. "If Conrad moves away, we could have a Godzilla moment."

"Godzilla?" Rex's jaw dropped.

"Oh sure. You think that sounds crazy. But don't come crying to me when she grows to sixty feet and lurches"—I held my arms in front of me and demonstrated—"and takes down power lines and stomps on Boy Scouts. Consider yourself warned." I walked away.

Kelly joined me. "I've worried about that myself," she admitted. "I just hoped we'd get her to college and she'd kind of normalize from there."

"Rex wants to shut down the museum," I sighed.

Kelly nodded. "I heard. And despite the chance that it would send the director fleeing back to the safety of Chicago, I think he might be a little right." She saw me reacting and held up her hands. "Just temporarily, that is. After all, Sheldon put a lot into this."

"Let's go get a drink," I said. "I need to sort things out in my head."

CHAPTER TWENTY

Kelly picked up her glass of wine and took a swig. "You never suggest just going out for a drink." She looked around The Tavern. "This place hasn't changed since we were in high school."

I was pretty sure it hadn't changed since the 1950s. The faded décor, crumbling wood paneling, posters for Olympia Beer, chipped tile floor, and cash register were the same. Even the board that said *Beer—10 cents* had the price crossed out and changed twenty times. And the jar of pickles on the counter looked like a biohazard.

A drink was what I needed, and this was the closest place. Or maybe it was just getting out of that museum. I didn't want to go home and sit around, doing nothing but waiting for Rex to come home.

"One theory," I said slowly, as if testing out the words. "Is that Britta was murdered to keep whatever device they used to find their drones out of our hands, right?"

Kelly thought for a moment. "I don't know. Why not just send the drone to the bottom of the reservoir at the quarry? Even if they had something to find it, it could be damaged beyond repair." She swallowed a sip of wine. "At least, that's what I'd do."

I always wondered what they'd find in that quarry if it ever dried up. "Okay…that makes sense. So why kill Britta, then? Why not just knock her out and take the device? And why wouldn't they think the McBride Corporation would just send another one?"

Kelly threw her hands up. "Maybe the killer is an idiot? That shouldn't come as a surprise. Most of them are. Most killers get caught."

She wasn't wrong. I'd heard Rex say that for years. "So let's say the killer isn't very bright and thinks that killing Britta and taking the technology is the end of that. Why kill her and leave her like Deliria? Why go to all the trouble of killing Sheldon just like Carlos was killed? We still don't know how he managed it with Hilly sleeping downstairs."

Kelly snorted. "Yeah, well, for all we know, Hilly isn't the light sleeper she thinks she is."

I sat back on the bar stool, and it wobbled. "I'm just saying that it seems like the killer is going to a lot of trouble to make things seem like one thing."

"But you think it's something else." Kelly nodded. "Misdirection of some sort."

I ticked off on my fingers. "First, the drone goes missing. Then the technology for the drone goes missing. We could be dealing with something else. Foreign spies are always looking for intel on the latest technology. Why couldn't it be something like that? They don't even care if someone else comes out with another device—they're already in Beijing with both the drone and the technology to find it."

"You think this might be international espionage?" Kelly asked. "Huh. I guess I didn't think of that. You may be right."

I continued. "And if that's the case, then the killer is going to be difficult to unmask."

"But they just left here within the hour," Kelly suggested. "They didn't leave after killing Sheldon. Or they had a comrade here to get the device." She shook her head. "I hadn't thought of the target being the drone. Then why kill Sheldon and Britta?"

I shrugged. "Maybe they fought back? Maybe they wanted to put an end to Sheldon's inventions? Maybe the killer didn't want to leave behind loose ends? The possibilities are endless."

We sat in silence for a few minutes, each lost in our own thoughts. In spite of myself, I kind of wanted it to be an international incident so I wouldn't have to deal with it. Rex wouldn't have to deal with it. We could just move on.

And leave it unsolved in a town where there were never any unsolved cases. The thought grated on me.

"There are three kinds of possibilities here," I reasoned. "Number one is that it's someone local, for whatever reason.

Number two is that it's something personal against Sheldon that may be outside of Who's There."

"Which is very likely," Kelly said. "You don't get that successful and not have any enemies to show for it."

"And three, it's corporate espionage—either domestic or international—by a person or nation that wanted the technology."

"All three of those could mean that the Museum of Murder was just an opportunistic staging place that could be a red herring in and of itself," Kelly concluded.

"In all of those three scenarios, that would be true. Which means there's a good reason not to shut down the museum at all."

"Right." Kelly clinked her glass on mine. "You just explained three ways that the museum isn't involved. We just needed a drink to get that sorted out."

It made sense. Not the drinks part…but the part about the museum just being an unrelated accessory to the crime. But would it be enough to convince Rex of that? I wasn't sure. That guy was smart. I knew because it was one of the reasons I married him.

But I was smart too. I could do this.

After some sleep, in the cold light of day, I felt a little more hopeful. Well, not in the idea that the Chinese were behind this because that would make solving this nearly impossible. Still, there were things I could do to at least check suspects off of my list.

Rex had been called to Bladdersly to consult on some drug issues they were having there and would be gone all day. And while that didn't mean I had carte blanche to investigate, he hadn't told me *not* to investigate.

A quick call to Riley told me they were still working on finding answers. I asked Riley to use his CIA contacts to find out if there were any foreign spies in the area, and he said he'd get on it.

In the meantime, I called Simon McBride and asked if I could talk to them. He invited me to their suite at the Radisson. After mulling over what I wanted to know, I got in the van and drove the five minutes to the hotel.

To my surprise, there was a Sheldon McBride Suite. The hotel must have decided to give things a local flavor. As I approached the door, I noticed it was swathed in black fabric. I pulled back a bit of the material and knocked.

The door was answered by a very somber Simon, who was dressed in a black turtleneck sweater, black pants, and black shoes. A black arm band was practically unnoticeable and, in fact, seemed redundant. Simon looked depressed as he led me into the large living area with four sofas arranged in a square. Four different closed doors must have been bedrooms and bathrooms. A small kitchenette was in the corner.

To my surprise, the place was remarkably clean.

Sam, Sebastian, Stan, and Sandy all said a somber hello. All were dressed in black clothing.

I sat down on one of the couches. "How are you guys holding up?"

Stan and Sam burst into tears, and Sebastian ran out of the room, slamming one of the doors behind him.

"Is he going to be alright?" I pointed to the door.

Simon shrugged and sat down. "We're all pretty shaken. You should've told us when we came to your house the other day."

The other three nodded.

"Sorry about that too. But since my husband is the lead detective and we'd just discovered the body, Rex didn't want me to share that information with anyone. It might have jeopardized the investigation."

None of that was particularly true...but they didn't know that.

The men all nodded, which was a relief. I didn't want them clamming up or turning on me. I had a few things I needed to know.

"It was such a shock," Simon said. "He was too young to die."

"I'm impressed with your group," I said. "You had a passion and followed it. That's great."

"Well, Sheldon was an impressive person. Now we'll never know what he could've done for the world," Stan sniffed.

"You guys must know more than anyone about him," I said carefully. "I'm helping my husband with his enquiries. We want to get a picture of the man so we can find the monster who did this."

That seemed to hit a positive note. The guys perked up a little. Whether it was from my silly fawning or the idea that they could contribute to catching the murderer, I wasn't sure.

"We know everything there is to know about him!" Stan said proudly.

"Yeah!" Sam exclaimed. "No one knows more about him than us!"

"That's perfect." I smiled. "I met with his high school teacher yesterday, and he said he'd kept in touch over the years, but didn't know a lot about what was currently going on in his life."

The four men leaned forward.

"You met Ted Fowler?" Simon gasped. "Can we meet him too?"

"You have to set that up for us!" Stan whined.

Sam wrung his hands. "Please?"

I waved him off like it was no big thing. "Of course. No problem. So you know about him?"

"Uh, yeah!" Simon snorted. "He was only the first major influence on Sheldon's life! We know he advised him in high school, encouraged him in college, and got a birthday card from him every year!" His face lit up. "I would have loved to have gotten a birthday card from Sheldon McBride!"

I nodded. "And was a witness at his wedding."

The men froze, staring at me as if in horror. The door opened, and Sebastian stuck his head out. "Wedding?"

"Well, as you know, it wasn't really a wedding. More like a justice of the peace thing," I chuckled. "I am curious about his ex-wife, Sandy."

Four of them turned to their friend, Sandy, as if he held the key to this information.

"We didn't know about a marriage," Stan said slowly. "Are you sure about that?"

I could've played this by gasping in shock that they didn't know this, but it seemed pretty obvious that they didn't. Instead I went for curiosity. "That's what Ted Fowler said. It was right after college, and it didn't last long before they got divorced."

"Did you know about this?" Simon poked a finger into Sandy's chest.

The young man was stunned. "What? No! Of course I didn't."

"Because it was weird you chose the name Sandy," Stan added.

"Because it's my actual name!" Sandy squeaked. "I didn't know!" He thought for a moment. "But I suppose on some level, it does make me a little closer to Sheldon than you guys."

The others slumped in their seats. Sam and Stan actually nodded.

"You didn't know about the wife, then?" I repeated.

Simon, once again, took the lead. "We didn't know about it at all. Wait a minute…" He disappeared into the same room Sebastian had come out of.

"He's going to get the college yearbook," Sam confided.

"Since he married right out of college," Stan said, "it's most likely he knew this Sandy in college."

Looks like I came to the right place. "I knew if anyone could figure it out, you would."

They beamed and high-fived each other as Simon returned with one yearbook.

"She'd have to be in his senior yearbook," he explained as he turned to the first tabbed page. "His picture isn't in here, but maybe we can find a Sandy."

"What else did Fowler say?" Stan asked me.

"He barely knew her, but he didn't think the marriage would last long…and it didn't."

"Guys," Sam said, "this is like high school when he broke off from his friends."

"Audra O'Malley?" I asked.

They stared at me.

"You really did your homework!" Sebastian said admiringly. "Sheldon was friends with Audra, Matt, and Brian. But we think, from looking at his high school yearbooks, that he had a falling out with Audra and Matt by senior year."

They'd done what I'd done. That was encouraging.

"Do you know what happened?" I leaned forward.

"No." Stan shook his head. "We think it was some sort of love triangle and Matt won Audra over. But we aren't sure."

"Found something!" Simon shouted.

We crowded around him as he pointed to a picture of a guy in an Aloha shirt with his back to the camera, hugging a girl. We could only see the back of her head and the photo was black and white, so we had no idea what color her hair was. The caption said *Seniors at the Spring Fling Dance.*

I pulled the book toward me. "How do you know this is Sheldon? I've never found any other photos of him."

"It's the shirt," Simon said confidently. "People didn't really wear them back then. He was a trailblazer in fashion too."

I wasn't convinced.

"There's a girl with hair like that in one other picture." Simon leafed through the book. "Here! She's not hugging him, but their arms are touching in a way that they might be holding hands!"

Once again, we saw the back of the same guy, and the girl was looking over his shoulder at the cameraman and laughing. It did look like their arms were touching. But there was something else about this photo.

"This picture was taken at the Spring graduation picnic," Simon added. "Which makes her a prime candidate for Sandy!"

"Except," I said with a sigh. "Her name isn't Sandy. That's Audra O'Malley."

Three of the McBrides fainted. I took a picture of the photo with my phone.

Was there a Sandy, or did Sheldon McBride marry Audra O'Malley?

CHAPTER TWENTY-ONE

"Oh yeah!" Stan said slowly. "It is her!"

"But she's not Sandy!" Sandy complained, maybe feeling like his special connection wasn't special anymore.

"Could've been a rebound," Sam suggested. "Maybe Audra dumped him, and he met Sandy around that time and had a quickie marriage."

Sandy brightened a little at the prospect.

"Maybe you're right," I mused. "I mean, Ted Fowler would certainly have known that it was Audra who Sheldon married, if he was the witness."

"Guys who are brokenhearted sometimes fall for another girl right away," Stan man-splained to me. "Not that any of us would know what that's like."

That seemed surprisingly honest of him.

Simon nodded. "Our lives have been devoted to all things Sheldon. Like nuns, sorta."

He must have seen the strange expression on my face because he hastily excused it. "We are worshipping Sheldon and his brain. We don't have time for distractions."

"Which"—Sam held up one finger—"is why I've always advocated for a reverse harem."

The others stared wistfully into space.

"A reverse harem?" I asked.

Sam gave a short nod. "I read a book about it once. It's where one woman has a harem of boyfriends. I thought we could give it a shot."

It seemed unlikely.

"I'm sure there's a woman out there who does the same thing we are doing," he continued. "Only she calls herself Shelly or something like that."

There was a general consensus that the woman may possibly exist. I left it alone, tempting as it was.

"Let's back up a bit." I held my hands up. "So the idea is that Audra dated Sheldon in high school. Then she left him to be with Matt. Then she started dating him his senior year in college but dumped him and this other woman married him. Is that what we're thinking?"

"Yes!" the five of them shouted simultaneously.

"I have another question for you. Have there been any attempts by foreign governments to try to steal Sheldon's technology?"

The five men thought for a moment.

"Sheldon was always afraid of that," Simon admitted. "Many people think that's why he went the recluse route. You couldn't even get into his company without a serious background check, and visitors were screened and fingerprinted."

"The Chinese were interested," Stan said. "I remember reading about it in *Iowa Ethanol Today Magazine*. The writer said that the Chinese were sending spies to every tech company in the country, and they speculated that Sheldon's company was one of them."

I'd really hoped the foreign espionage theory wouldn't be true. Finding a Chinese spy would be difficult. Then I remembered that hit order coming from Who's There.

My thoughts were interrupted by a knock on the door.

Simon went to answer it, and Hilly bounced in.

"Hi! What's going on?" the assassin asked.

The five men stared at her in shock.

"Your name wouldn't happen to be Shelly, would it?" Stan asked.

"No, why? Is yours?" Hilly replied before sitting next to me on the couch. "So, what are we doing here?"

What was *she* doing here? "Guys, this is my, um, colleague, Hilly." I introduced the men to the assassin.

"Why do you all have the same names?" she asked. "And why are you all in black? Who died?"

I turned back to the guys. "One more question before we go. Do you know anything about Britta Almondine?"

Simon took his eyes off of Hilly and regained his senses. "Yeah! She's Sheldon's lawyer. She's been with him forever.

Rumor has it they met in college and even went to grad school at the same school."

An idea formed in my mind. "Could she be Sandy?"

The five men shrugged then returned their attention to Hilly.

"What do you think about reverse harems?" Sam asked her.

"What's that?" Hilly seemed interested.

I took the yearbook from Simon and found a class photo of Britta. I took a picture of that too. Seeing that I wasn't going to get anything more out of the guys with Hilly here, I said my goodbyes and dragged the assassin out to my van.

"What was that all about?" I asked her.

"I followed you" was her reply.

"Where have you been?"

"I went shopping in Omaha. I got some neat stuff! Want to see? I found this giant machete! I'm thinking of making it my new signature weapon!"

"No, I don't. Let me ask you something… Do you know if there are any Chinese operatives in the area?"

Hilly frowned. "I don't know. They usually don't introduce themselves to me because I'd kill them." She perked up. "Hey! I could use that new machete then!"

I texted Kelly to remind her to have Riley to check for any spies in the area. Then I sat back and closed my eyes to think about where things stood in the case.

"I hear you had a dead lawyer at the museum." Hilly studied my face closely. "Are you killing people without me again?"

"Again?" I opened one eye and looked at her. "When did I ever do that in the first place?"

Hilly shrugged. "I was just trying to trick you into admitting that you had done that without me."

I threw my arms in the air. "Hilly! Why would I do that?"

She nodded. "I know. It's silly to think you wouldn't want me to join in on the fun."

"No, I mean why would I let you know in the first place?"

She looked wounded. "Are you saying you wouldn't?"

I felt a little bad and patted her on the arm. "My killing days are over, and it wasn't something I set out to do. I'm not like you. It isn't the only thing on my job description."

She pouted. "It isn't the only thing on my job description. There's also 'other duties as assigned.' Granted, that's almost always killing more people, but it isn't specifically assassination, you know! I have depth!"

"Sure you do," I said as I started up the van. "What time is it?"

Hilly looked at her wrist. Where there wasn't a watch. "Noon, why?"

Because I'd forgotten something. "We need to eat. Because we have a troop meeting at one."

"During the school day?" asked the assassin who didn't even know what a school day was.

"Out early today. Come on. Let's get some lunch and get over to my old house—where you're currently staying."

CHAPTER TWENTY-TWO

"Where's Betty?" Kelly looked around. "Everyone's here but Betty!"

"That seems like a red flag." I walked around the room.

There were seven girls. We had eight. And the one who was missing never, ever, ever missed a meeting.

"She'll be here," Ava said. "She doesn't miss meetings. But can we start?"

"Okay," I said. "Thinking Day is coming up fast and so are cookie sales. We have a lot to do before then."

The door opened and in walked Betty and Conrad. The girls waved before turning back to me. The fact that there was a boy in the meeting didn't seem to faze them. It fazed me. We have never, ever had a boy in a meeting, and I was fighting an overwhelming urge to kick him out.

"Conrad lived in Iceland for two years," Betty said before steering him to a seat.

The kid nodded. "That's right. My mom is Icelandic and still lives there. I know a lot about it."

"We're lucky to have an expert," Ava said. "Conrad knows all kinds of stuff."

"Instead of rotting shark," Conrad spoke up. "You should have Icelandic chocolate. They have really good chocolate there. And they eat chocolate bars for breakfast sometimes."

I liked Iceland even more after hearing that! I elbowed Kelly and wiggled my eyebrows.

"You can find the chocolate bars online," he continued. "Fifty-six percent bittersweet is my favorite."

Kelly wrote that down. "What else?"

"Seafood," Inez said after an annoyed glance at Conrad. Was there a rivalry there? "They eat a lot of fish."

"I don't think we can have seafood samples." Kelly shook her head. "They might go bad over the three hours of the event. We can't make everyone sick. They won't let us do a booth again."

"They eat hot dogs a lot," Conrad said. "Icelanders love hot dogs. And skyr yogurt."

Betty piped up. "We can do little cups of skyr yogurt to hand out."

The other girls seemed to like this idea.

"Yogurt and chocolate," I agreed. "That sounds good."

Inez nodded grudgingly but said nothing. I didn't want a rift in the troop. Conrad wasn't pressing his expertise, which was nice. But Inez did seem a bit upset.

I held up my hands to get their attention. "Let's form teams. The four Kaitlyns, and the other four girls. Conrad, you sit this out. I'll need your help in a minute. We need cultural ideas. Like a folk dance, or music, something like that. You have fifteen minutes."

I pulled Conrad into the kitchen. "Can you show me where to order this chocolate?"

He nodded and took over my laptop. "My mom works for a food wholesaler in Reykjavik. She can probably cut us a deal. I'll go to her website and pick out a few things." He looked up at me. "It's very nice of you to let me stay. I didn't want to intrude. Girl Scouts are pretty awesome. I never wanted to do Boy Scouts. So thank you."

I left him to it and joined Kelly in the living room. "He has very nice manners," I said. "Even thanked me for letting him stay and said he never wanted to be a Boy Scout and that Girl Scouts are cool."

Kelly's eyebrows went up. "That's nice to know. I never would've pegged Betty as one who'd pick a nice, quiet, bookish boy with good manners."

Me neither. "They say opposites attract. And maybe he'll rub off on her."

"And then they had these things called necropants that the witches used to make money," I heard Betty say. "They'd skin a dead guy's legs and wear them like leggings. It made them rich because money appeared in a little bag in front."

Maybe I spoke too soon.

"Here's a picture!" Lauren called out, and the girls crowded around her.

"Cool! We can make them!" Inez, seemingly over the slight, was enthusiastic.

"Try to find something more current," Kelly encouraged.

I would've backed her up, but I was looking up "necropants." When I found them, I showed them to Kelly, who immediately announced that we would not be doing anything like that. I guess using a dead man's scrotum to collect magic money was too over the top for her.

Conrad came back into the living room with a printout. "I emailed Mom. She thinks this is a great idea. Her company is going to sponsor us and send the yogurt and chocolate for free. Is that okay?"

"That's awesome!" Conrad was seriously growing on me. Maybe he could join the troop in some way?

The thought crashed as soon as I thought of it. The last thing I needed was for Betty and Conrad to break up down the line and spend the rest of the troop's years keeping her from killing him.

Kelly recruited Conrad to help get the snack ready—which was samples of the cookies that would be for sale and chocolate milk. Meanwhile, I sat in a chair and checked my messages. There was one from Randi, asking if Rex and I could babysit. One from Ronni saying that I was never allowed to ever babysit the boys. One from Soo Jin asking me to call her, and one from Simon McBride asking if there would be a memorial to Sheldon at the museum and could he say a few words since he had the same last name.

All of these could be dealt with later because Kelly and Conrad appeared with the snack and the feeding frenzy began.

"He really was a good helper," Kelly enthused as the kids ate. She lowered her voice, "I asked him about his friendship with Betty."

I dragged her to a corner of the room. "And?"

"He considers her his best friend here." Kelly risked a glance at the troop. "I think Betty's feelings run stronger."

I looked over, and Betty had some kind of contraption where she was watching Conrad without looking directly at him. The boy sat next to her and quietly ate his cookies.

"It might not be a bad thing," I reasoned. "She hasn't really acted out this whole meeting. Well, except for suggesting the necropants."

Kelly shuddered. We took a few moments to snag what was left of the cookie tray. My troop were like locusts when it came to Girl Scout cookies, and I was no different.

We started the presentation of ideas with the Kaitlyns, who focused, it seemed, exclusively on puffins.

"Puffins are cute birds whose babies are called pufflings," one of the Kaitlyns started.

"Thousands of them live on the island during the summer," another said.

"We think we should do an exhibit with real puffins," the other two said simultaneously.

"And Icelandic ponies!" Lauren suggested.

I raised my hand. "Why don't we just use the Shetland pony and call it an Icelandic pony?" I asked.

The girls didn't need another pony. They already had a pony that they got as a gift from the sister city of Who Dat, Louisiana.

Lauren looked at me as if I was an idiot in a way that made me wonder if I was.

"Icelandic ponies and Shetland ponies are completely different animals! People will be able to tell."

The other girls nodded in agreement.

I pulled up the two on my phone and compared them. "They look similar enough to me. Besides, the kids attending Thinking Day won't care."

"That's beside the point!" Lauren said. "As a junior zookeeper, I have a reputation to protect. If I say it's an Icelandic pony, it has to be one!"

Huh. Her tirade didn't include some bizarre fact that most likely wasn't a fact, like Icelandic ponies sharing 99% of their DNA with lizards or being fluent in German.

"Did you know," Betty read off her phone, "that the first Basque language dictionary was created in Iceland by an Icelander?" Her face was almost smiling, and it was a somewhat terrifying thing to see. The Basque people were her favorite cause. "He learned it from sailors."

Conrad nodded. "He was my great-great-great-second cousin or something. And I'm part Basque on my dad's side."

The room grew silent as a hushed awe descended. He might as well have proposed and been done with it. Betty froze up, blinking at him.

"I don't think we can get a puffin," Kelly said, breaking the tension. "They don't have any at our zoo. And I think using the pony as a representation of the Icelandic pony is a good idea, if we can get permission to have a pen for him. Now, we have food and the pony. We need a craft and costume."

"Lopapeysa sweaters," Hilly shouted from the back room. She'd been in there since before the meeting started but declined to join us so she could sharpen her machete.

The girls nodded as if they'd known she was there all along.

The door in the hallway opened, and Hilly joined us. She saw Conrad and pointed to him while looking at me. "That's a boy. I think you've got a spy. Should I *de-flea the bonobo* for you?"

Betty recovered. "That's Conrad. He's with me."

Hilly looked questioningly at the girl but, when she got no response, said, "Okay."

"What was this lopapeysa thing?" Kelly asked.

"Lopapeysa sweaters." Hilly pulled up a picture on her phone. "Knitting is big there. These might be easier to do than the dresses they have as their national costume."

"I don't know," Kelly said as she studied her own phone. "It would take some time to get them, and they're very expensive."

Hilly waved her off. "No problem. I can knit them in time."

We all stared at her.

"What?" she asked. "I spent a couple of months in Iceland for something, and they taught me to knit."

"And after only a couple of months," I asked, "you can knit complicated sweaters? For all of us?"

"Maybe not for the adults," Hilly admitted.

Conrad was typing on his phone. "No problem. I'll have Mom send some for you and Mrs. Albers. You both look like size medium. Mom's got a friend who knits them."

I waved at him. "Make mine black."

"Already done," he said.

"What about a craft?" I asked.

"How about knitting?" Ava asked.

"We can't teach kids how to knit in a couple of minutes," I protested.

Hilly raised her hand. "I can!"

I looked at Kelly in hopes she would come up with something better. She didn't.

"Okay," I agreed. "But you have to teach the girls. If you can teach them, you can teach others. And you need a small project," I decided.

"Yay!" Hilly cried out. "I'll order needles and yarn. This is going to be fun!"

Conrad nodded. "Knitting was such an important part of Icelandic industry that they invented the Yule Cat—a giant cat who, on Christmas Eve, eats kids who don't get clothes for Christmas."

It was as if the room exploded as the girls started squealing.

As if anticipating my incredulity, Conrad continued. "The idea is that if they didn't get new clothes, the kids were lazy and didn't help their families with the wool production to make those clothes. Knitting was too important to the economy, so they invented the Yule Cat to scare kids into helping card wool, spin wool and knit. At least, that's what my gran told me when I didn't help her wind yarn."

"We should make a giant Yule Cat!" the four Kaitlyns screamed with excitement.

As the girls spiraled into a frenzy of googling, I told Kelly, "At least that's all handled."

"Do you think Hilly can knit eight sweaters in a month?" Kelly asked.

"I've already got two," Conrad said. "Betty can wear one."

Betty, perhaps faced with the prospect of Conrad giving her a sweater—which, for all I knew, was the equivalent to an Icelandic proposal—stopped breathing for a moment. Then she fainted.

All activity ended as we looked at the normally tough girl, unconscious on the floor.

"She'll be alright," Conrad said. "She does this whenever I talk about giving her something."

It was then I knew I had to find a way to harness the power of Conrad to keep Betty in line.

CHAPTER TWENTY-THREE

It took the rest of the meeting to hammer out the logistics. Finally, the girls were picked up. Conrad asked me to take him to the museum, where his dad was. Betty seemed a little out of joint with this request but got in the car with her parents anyway.

After Kelly left to go back to work, Hilly and I took Conrad to the museum.

"So, Conrad," Hilly started after we'd parked the car. "What are your intentions with Betty?"

Conrad pushed his glasses up on his nose. "My intentions are strictly honorable, I assure you."

Hilly looked questioningly at me.

"He said he's going to be nice to her," I translated.

"Good," Hilly said. "Because if you don't, I will *float the wombat*. And wombats can't float. They can't even swim. Got it?"

The kid nodded. "Sounds fair." He opened the door to the van and got out. "Thanks for the ride, Mrs. Ferguson."

I watched as he went inside the museum. "Actually, wombats are good swimmers," I said. "Lauren had us watch a documentary on it once."

It had been a documentary on how all of the world's most dangerous critters lived in Australia, and immediately, my troop wanted to go. Wombats weren't especially dangerous. I suspected the documentarian threw in that scene to break up all the violence from the scary kangaroos, spiders, and cassowaries.

Hilly grinned. "Yeah, but he doesn't know that, does he?"

I'd be willing to bet a fight with a Yule Cat that he did. But Hilly looked like she had accomplished something, so I let it go.

"Hey," she said. "Let's go inside. I want to get the make and model on that dumpster. I'm thinking of buying one just like it."

The museum was open for another half hour, so we headed inside. Traffic was a bit light, and I wondered if the novelty had worn off a bit. Hilly skipped through the gift shop, diving into the exhibits. I followed at a more leisurely pace.

I paused for a moment to look at the replacement of the car that took out Carlos and Sheldon. I still didn't know how that had been done. There wasn't enough room to back the car up and really get enough speed.

"Hey Merry!" Hilly hollered from up ahead. "Can you come here and see this?"

Moments later, I joined her at the dumpster.

"You've got to be kidding me! I just asked Rex not to shut down the museum, and there's another murder?"

Hilly looked closely at the man in the dumpster. "I didn't do it!"

"I didn't say you did!"

She studied my expression. "You were thinking it, though."

"I wasn't. Okay, so I have in the past and this is your usual MO, but I don't think you did this."

The man in the dumpster had long brown hair and a heavy mustache and beard. I had no idea who he was, but I knew it wasn't Wally. Rex was definitely going to shut the museum down now. And Drew would pack up Conrad and take him home. This was bad.

I kicked the dumpster. "Rex is going to close this place down now. There's no way he'd keep it open after three murders took place here."

Hilly cocked her head to one side. "Why not?"

Seriously? "Because it invites murders!"

"Because it's a museum of murder, duh!" She rolled her eyes. "Where else are you supposed to do it? If you ask me, it makes total sense to have murders here."

"Hilly, it doesn't make sense to have murders *anywhere*. And if they keep popping up in one place, then you shut the place down."

"Well that's just ridiculous!" The assassin snorted. "I think he should leave it open. It's far more convenient this way. You'd always know where the murders were. No more joggers stumbling over bodies. No more missing bodies. They'd all be in one location. Easy!"

Arguing with an assassin over the convenience of a centralized murder place probably wasn't a good idea.

Drew walked in, frowning at a clipboard. "Merry, I wonder if you..." His voice trailed away as he noticed that the legs coming out of the dumpster weren't straight, but bent and wearing different shoes.

"Oh crap," he sighed. Then he turned around and walked out of the exhibit.

I texted Rex the information. I really didn't want to hear him say *I told you so*.

"I told you so," Rex sighed. "Now we have to close this place down before there are any more murders."

"At least this isn't a used dumpster, filled with garbage!" Soo Jin called out from inside the thing. She stood up. "Stabbed in the heart. Just like the exhibit." Her eyes darted to the exhibit hall two rooms away. "I really hope we don't get an axe murder next. Those are so messy."

"Closing it down doesn't necessarily mean the killer will stop dumping bodies here," I argued. "In fact, maybe we should have it open 24/7 and have guards posted so the killer doesn't have an opportunity to dump another body here."

Ava appeared with Lauren and Inez in tow. "Why is Mr. Phillips updating his resume?" She noticed Rex and Soo Jin. "Another one? Hey! Maybe this will take us up to 20% of the murders in the state!" Ava punched her fist in the air. "Suck it, other mayors!"

"That's probably not the best attitude," I muttered.

Hilly bounced up and down, clapping. "I think it's great! Ava's showing ambition! Who wouldn't want to be the best in the state?"

"Not helping," I said. "Girls, you should go. Find something else to do, like talking Phillips out of moving away."

Ava blanched. "You don't think he would take Conrad, do you?"

Inez and Lauren looked at each other and gasped.

"Come on, guys," I said. "Betty was fine before Conrad moved here. She'll be fine if he has to leave."

The three girls shook their heads.

"It'll be like an apocalypse," Lauren whispered. "But instead of koala biker gangs, it'll be worse!"

Inez seemed to agree. "Maybe we should all move now? What's a place that would be safe?"

"You guys are overreacting." I tried to sound casual. "If Conrad moves, Betty will be fine. There will be other boys."

Ava gave me an expression that somehow resembled pity. "You have no clue, do you?"

And with that, the three of them fled the room.

Hilly walked over to the dumpster and helped Soo Jin out of it. "Hey, if the museum closes, can I have the dumpster?"

"If we solve these murders," I decided, "there will be no more." I turned to my husband. "Any idea who he is?"

Rex shook his head. "Soo Jin hasn't found a wallet. She'll fingerprint him down at the morgue. Since the first two were tied to Sheldon McBride and his business, I'm going to travel to his headquarters in Nevada and see if HR can help me. I'm also going to ask their security if there've been any threats."

"You're going to be gone? When? How long?" I asked.

"I'll leave tomorrow. Be back in a couple of days. You'll be fine," He squeezed my shoulders. "You've been without me before."

"It's not that! We're supposed to babysit tomorrow night!"

Rex tried to hide his grin. "You just need me to help babysit."

"That's right!" I gasped. "What am I going to do?"

"I'll help," Betty said as she walked in. She must have seen the look on my face, because she added, "No, seriously. I'm an accredited babysitter."

Rex smiled. "There you go! Betty is an expert babysitter. You won't miss me at all."

"It'll be fun," Betty said. "I'll bring snacks. See you at six tomorrow night."

CHAPTER TWENTY-FOUR

After taking Rex to the airport in Des Moines the next morning, I cold called Audra O'Malley and asked if I could meet her for lunch. To my surprise, she said yes without hesitation, and an hour later, I was sitting in Oleo's waiting.

The picture I had of her was from years ago, and I hoped I would be able to recognize the woman. My mind was buzzing with questions, but I had to find a way to ask them in a manner that wasn't threatening. I was surprised that she had agreed to meet me. All I'd said was that I was Merry Ferguson, I was helping the police with their inquiries about Sheldon and wanted to ask her what he was like. She didn't know me from Adam. I wondered why she'd agreed.

I didn't have long to wait. As soon as I'd gotten my drink, a woman in her forties, looking somewhat like her, walked in. I waved, and after looking around, she came over and sat down.

She did not take off her coat. Clearly this woman was here to find out what I wanted before she decided to answer anything.

"Hi, Audra," I said, introducing myself. "I'd like to buy you lunch, if that's okay."

Audra didn't smile. She also didn't agree. "I really didn't want to come. Matt said I shouldn't. But Mr. Fowler had said you were one of the good guys and that I should talk to you. That's the only reason I'm here. And I'm not staying if I don't like what you have to say."

I nodded. "That's fair. And I'm sorry for your loss as far as Sheldon goes. I know you were friends in high school."

She looked at her hands. "That was a long time ago. I haven't seen Sheldon in a long time."

For a moment, I thought I'd cut right to the photo of her with him during his senior year in college, but something made me hold back. Jumping to a direct question like that might make her flee. But I also knew from her posture that getting even the simplest info out of her was going to be difficult.

"Mr. Fowler's really nice." I smiled. "He wasn't at the high school when I was there."

The woman relaxed a little. "Yes. He was a really good teacher. He's the reason I went into chemistry." She hesitated. "I work at the medical lab in town."

"I love it when a teacher inspires you to find your calling. With me it was Mrs. Callahan and political science."

Audra bit her lip but seemed interested. "Oh? Your dad's in politics, right? Did you go into it too?"

"No, I went into government work though." I didn't want to tell her I'd worked for the CIA. Nobody trusted them. It might scare her off.

"Matt...my husband...went into engineering." She didn't say any more. In fact, I got the impression she'd thought she had said too much.

"Is that Matt Atkins? Mr. Fowler told me about all of you. Said you were good friends."

"We were..." Her voice faltered as she looked away. "Look, Sheldon and I went out our junior year in high school. Then we broke up and I started dating Matt. Sheldon didn't like that, and we stopped being friends. That's all I have to say about that."

Basically, she had just filled in the blanks, which was useful. But it didn't explain the picture in the college yearbook.

"And you never saw him again?" I asked. "Still, it must have been a shock to find out he'd been murdered."

Audra's lips were pursed tightly. "It was."

"A lot of years have passed. You didn't get together when he came into town for old time's sake?"

"No. I mean, yes, a lot of years had passed, and Matt and I weren't angry with Sheldon anymore. In fact, we were kind of proud of his success. We didn't meet with him because we didn't know he was even here. If we had known, we probably still wouldn't have seen him because we were...we were embarrassed about how we'd left things back in the day. It seems so silly now.

I mean, we were in high school. Lots of time has passed since then. It would've been nice to catch up and tell him that we were happy for him."

She was loosening up and chatting now. "Why didn't Matt want you to talk to me?"

Audra laughed. "Oh, he's always been a bit paranoid about people knowing we'd been close to Sheldon back in the day. We went to our ten-year high school reunion, and all anyone wanted to talk about was if we were still in touch with Sheldon…could we arrange for them to meet him…invest in their ideas…come to their weddings." She blushed. "It was awful. Not one person asked us how we were doing. We never went back again."

"That would be awful," I said with as much sympathy as I could muster. "I can't imagine how I'd handle that."

I'd been to one reunion, and half the class ended up hallucinating on LSD and three people ended up murdered, and now there was an exhibit in the museum on that.

"What about Brian Atkins? Are you still in touch with him?"

The woman sighed sadly. "No, we're not. We haven't seen him in years. He never forgave us for what he considered a betrayal of Sheldon. I don't even know where he is." Her attitude changed quickly, and she became angry. "But I don't know why he should be so high and mighty! He was always jealous of Sheldon and his ideas! Brian was such a sycophant—but he secretly hated Sheldon."

That was interesting. I'd known plenty of toadies in my time, and a lot of them hated the very person it seemed they'd worshiped. Could Brian be our killer?

Audra looked nervously at her watch. "I really have to go. I only get half an hour for lunch."

We hadn't even ordered!

"I really do appreciate you meeting with me. I just have one question left. I found this in Sheldon's yearbook from college and wondered if you could explain it?"

She looked curious as she took the phone from me. When she saw the picture, she gasped, jumped to her feet, and dropped the phone. Without another word, she ran out the door.

Oh well. I was here, so I ordered a burger and fries and thought about what had just happened. Had Audra recognized herself and fled? Had she been cheating on Matt with Sheldon in college and was afraid I'd jeopardize her marriage? If so, then Sheldon meant more to her than she let on.

My food came, and I ate slowly, still pondering the very brief interview. I felt bad for Audra. She seemed nice enough. It wasn't necessary for her to talk to me, and in fact, her husband had said not to. But she'd listened to her former teacher and come anyway.

Points to Mr. Fowler for still having that influence. I'd have to see him again and show him the photo. I didn't think he was lying about Audra possibly being this Sandy. And it was still possible that the photograph was perfectly innocent. That Sheldon had married someone named Sandy.

I should probably talk to Matt. And Brian. Fowler thought Brian lived in the area, but Audra said she hadn't seen him in years. I'd have Kelly track him down. Brian was a solid suspect as far as I was concerned. Someone jealous of his best friend, who wanted to be his best friend, could very likely kill that same friend.

But it didn't explain Britta Almondine's murder or this mystery man. Which still meant the whole thing could be chalked up to industrial espionage. That would explain the first two murders. Hopefully Rex would find something out on his trip.

Now I had to wonder about talking to Matt. He'd made it clear he wasn't interested in talking to me. Should I just take his wife's word for it that Matt felt the same way she did?

What if this was tied to the old days? It didn't seem like Audra had much interest in Sheldon, aside from her strange reaction to the photo. Maybe she was embarrassed and didn't want Matt to know she'd hung out with Sheldon? We still didn't know for sure if she was Sandy. Sandy could be someone entirely different.

And then there was Brian. He wouldn't be the first toady to pretend to be a loyal friend while waiting for a chance to take him out. Revenge is a dish best served cold, or so they say. Was it possible that he was our killer?

I decided to shrug off Matt...for now. My phone buzzed. Right on time! Kelly sent me Brian's number. Instead of wondering how she was able to read my mind, I called Brian but got voicemail. I left a very short message, just introducing myself and asking if he had a minute sometime.

My mind reeled back to Sheldon's murder. After lunch, I started the car and headed for the hospital. It was time to visit Soo Jin and see what she knew.

CHAPTER TWENTY-FIVE

"Hey Merry!" Soo Jin called out from her desk in the morgue. "What's up?"

Did she really not know? I came here all the time to find out the details on various murders.

"I have some questions about the murders at the museum," I said.

She held up an index finger. "Before I forget, I got something for the twins' babies!" She pulled two gift bags out from under her desk and handed them over. "I called you earlier about it. Can you get them to Randi and Ronni?"

I felt a punch in the gut as I remembered I'd be babysitting tonight. "Sure. I'm going to see them tonight."

Soo Jin clapped her hands in glee. "Great! Thank you! With a triple murder, I'm too busy to do much more than go home and collapse every night. Thankfully, Troy always has dinner and a glass of wine ready for me."

My eyebrows went up. "So you guys are getting serious, huh?"

Soo Jin had the good grace to blush deeply. It only made her more beautiful. "I guess you could say that." She smiled to herself. "Troy's such a great guy. I'm very lucky."

"*He's* the lucky one," I assured her. And no, I wasn't just saying that to butter her up for intel, although that was a good way to do it. Most people reacted very well to flattery.

She got up and closed the door to the office. "He really is amazing. Smart, handsome, and so thoughtful!"

This was good to know because I didn't know Troy that well. "You deserve to be happy!"

"Thanks, Merry." She put her hand on my arm. "You're a good friend! Now, what do you want to know?"

I sat down in a chair opposite the desk. "I just can't really believe that Sheldon was run over in the museum. No matter how I try to work it out, the car just couldn't get that much speed up to pull it off."

She nodded and pulled out a file. "I'm inclined to agree. He was definitely hit by a car, but I'm pretty sure it isn't the one in the exhibit. The blood and hair were added to the car. We can't find any other mark on it. I think Sheldon was run over somewhere and brought to the museum. In order to make it look like he died just like Carlos the Armadillo, they painted on the blood and stuck his hair on the bumper."

I sat up. "He wasn't killed in the museum?"

"I don't think so. I think it was done to make it look like he was killed there. But the blood spatter doesn't correspond to the marks on the body. His injuries are consistent with getting hit by a car, but my gut says it wasn't done with the car in the exhibit."

"Which means he could've been hit anywhere!"

She nodded. "I'd say finding where he was hit is going to be extremely difficult."

I relaxed back in the chair. "What about Britta Almondine? Any news on her?"

Soo Jin shook her head. "That was just a plain old stabbing in the heart. Like the John Doe you and Hilly found yesterday. I haven't found any forensic evidence on the bodies. Whoever did it was very careful.."

"No ID on the latest corpse?" I pressed.

It would be really nice for her to say exactly who it was and why he was killed. But that was expecting too much.

She shook her head. "We're running his fingerprints and DNA, but he may not be in there. Rex has asked me to shave him for a better chance of sending out a notice. He has an unusual amount of facial hair."

"Isn't that convenient?" I mused. It seemed like the perfect way for the killer to cover their tracks. Although I didn't think he had his victim grow an unusual amount of facial hair so he could stab him later.

"I wish I had more for you." Soo Jin sounded disappointed for me. "I'll be shaving him tomorrow. Rex wants a photo of him while he's at Sheldon's offices."

Rex still had at least another hour before he'd be there. I'd have to wait until tonight to see if he found anything.

"This kind of sucks, not knowing who this guy was," I said more out loud than to myself.

"I know. My job is basically done. We are waiting to see if there's any family to claim the bodies, but that's proven tough. Troy can't find any next of kin for Sheldon, and Britta's family is on a six-month scientific survey of Antarctica. Sheldon's parents passed away years ago."

"Right," I said, remembering what I'd found about their accident. "Any other family?"

"I don't know. There's no mention of any aunts, uncles, or siblings."

I got up and headed for the door. "I've got someone I can talk to! Thanks Soo Jin!"

Ted Fowler agreed to let me come to his house. He lived in a modest split-level only four or five blocks from where I lived.

"Come in!" He smiled. "Would you like something to drink?"

Personally, I'd have loved a glass of wine, but since I was babysitting later, I thought better of it. "No thanks. I just have a couple of questions, if you don't mind."

"Not at all! I don't get many visitors!"

Fowler led me to his living room, and we sat down.

"I'll get right to the point. My husband, the detective on the case, is trying to find out if there's any extended family here. We know his parents died years ago. Do you know of anyone else in the area?"

Ted rubbed his chin thoughtfully as he stared into space. "Hmm... I don't recall having another McBride in class. I only met his parents once, but they were older than usual, even then. Sheldon told me once he'd been a surprise baby."

"But there still could be a sibling?" I pressed.

"Oh sure. But if Sheldon was a surprise, later in life, I doubt they were close in age." He got up for a moment and got the phone book.

Why didn't I think of that? Nobody really used phone books anymore, but we still received one every year, left on the doorstep.

"There don't seem to be any McBrides," Ted said. "I'm sorry I can't be more help."

"I completely understand. By the way, thank you for encouraging Audra to meet with me. We had lunch earlier today."

The older teacher smiled. "She's very smart. She and her husband both. They were a pleasure to have in class, and I'm proud that they went into scientific fields."

I thought of something. "Why do you think Matt discouraged his wife from talking to me?"

He looked surprised for a moment. "Did he? Well, I don't know about that. But then, Matt was a quiet kid who kept to himself. It's possible he doesn't like to talk about personal things."

"How about Brian Atkins?" I asked. "Do you think he'll be receptive?"

Fowler nodded. "I think so. I know Brian came back here after college and, as far as I know, doesn't socialize much."

"Why not?" Was that too pushy a question? Oh well, it was out there now.

"Some people just aren't very public. Brian didn't participate in anything in school besides the Science Club. He had a good head for it but pretty much let the others take the lead. He was more an idea man, I think."

My phone buzzed. I ignored it. "Well, thank you for your time. I'll pass that on to my husband."

Fowler walked me out and waved as I got into the van.

My phone buzzed again. I looked at the screen.

Dropping off the boys a little early, Randi's text said. *See you in five minutes!*

At that very moment, I realized I'd forgotten to show Fowler the picture of Audra and Sheldon. Unfortunately, I was out of time.

CHAPTER TWENTY-SIX

It was Ivan and Ron who dropped off the babies in their car seat carriers. Wally and Azlan were fast asleep.

"Thank you for this, but please do not really sit on the babies," Ivan said. "Is good to be going on double date tonight."

"Babies take up wives' time. We need attention too. Ronni did not ask if I worked out this week." Ron flexed his biceps and pouted.

Ivan nodded. "And Randi has not asked to feel my muscles even once!"

"Are you sure about this?" I hoped I didn't sound like begging. "The boys are only a few days old."

The men looked at each other and laughed.

"Oh sure!" Ron said. "Back home we take babies out hunting when one day old."

"To get them used to killing things," Ivan added. "Is good to do when young."

"Um, okay," I bent down to see that my nephews were snugged up with blankets. Maybe they wouldn't even wake up. "And the supplies?"

Betty walked in with two hefty diaper bags in tow. "Got it. Bottles, formula, diapers, the whole thing." She handed the men a business card. "That's my number. I'm available most of the time. This gig is free, but after that, I'll give you the friends and family discount of fifteen percent off of my hourly rate of twenty dollars an hour."

The men shrugged. "Okay. Bye!"

"Betty, I've got a confession to make. I've only babysat one kid, once. And that was Finn when she was older than this. I don't know anything about newborns."

Betty rolled her eyes. "It's easy. Treat them like they break easily. If they cry, it's because they're wet or hungry. That's it. I've done this lots of times."

I relaxed a little. "I didn't know you had so much experience."

"I've been babysitting for two years now. All ages. I even watched a kid who was older than me. This is no sweat. Besides, it gives us some bonding time."

My eyebrows went up. "Bonding time?"

"Well yeah. You usually have to share me with the rest of the troop. Now you have me all to yourself. Great, right?"

Maybe this wasn't such a bad idea. Betty did seem to have more experience than even Rex. The babies were sleeping. Maybe they'd sleep the entire time. I heated up some frozen pizzas, and soon Betty and I sat down on the couch to eat.

Leonard came over and gently sniffed the babies. Then he laid down between the two carriers and went to sleep. Martini climbed up onto little Wally and passed out. Philby walked in and hissed at both babies before climbing onto the coffee table to glare at us.

"So, *boys*, am I right?" Betty wiggled her eyebrows.

"What do you mean?"

She set down her plate. "Conrad is a boy, so…"

I waited for more that didn't come. I had a feeling Betty was trying to get something out of me, but I wasn't sure what that was. Don't get me wrong. I'd always been there for the girls for advice. Of course, they'd never required more than *which pocketknife has the best kill rating*, or *how many matches do you need for your campfire to be seen from space*.

"You like Conrad, like a boyfriend?" I ventured.

Betty punched me in the shoulder and rolled her eyes. "Uh…no! Why would you think that?"

"Because you have a silly grin on your face, you've been glitching since the day you met him, and everyone is terrified what will happen if he moves away because his dad is worried about all the murders."

"Huh." Betty thought for a moment. "So the murders might be a deal-breaker? Conrad doesn't mind."

I handed her a napkin. "Yes, to most people, a murdery town is a deal-breaker. Conrad's dad might not want to stay here."

She threw her arms up. "He works in a Museum of Murder! Why would he think that?"

"Some kids want to raise their kids in safe places." I eyed the boys, who were now awake and staring at me.

"I don't think Conrad would move because of that," she said finally.

"It won't be Conrad's choice. It'll be his dad's. Or his mom's. She could have him move to Iceland."

She thought for a moment. "I could live in Iceland."

The volcanoes weren't as terrifying as Betty. Iceland may not agree.

"Your parents wouldn't want to move to Iceland."

She nodded. "I should get working on that now. Play around with some subliminal mind work, talk about how much aliens love living in Iceland, talk about the high standards of their schools, make the toilets tell them we should move there…" She stared into space for a moment. "Oh yeah, I could totally make that work. Do they have Girl Scouts in Iceland?"

I pulled it up on my phone and showed her. "They do. And with all that gorgeous wilderness, their camps are probably awesome." Wait! What was I saying? I didn't want Betty to move to Iceland!

Wally and Azlan both raised their fists and rubbed their eyes at the same time before staring quietly at me again.

"We should check it out," Betty said. "I can plan a trip for the troop this summer. We've got the money from our various shell companies. I'll make a call."

"Hold on." I held up my hands. "We don't *know* that Conrad is moving there."

"Yeah, but it doesn't hurt to be ready, just in case, right? *Be prepared* is the Girl Scout motto. Although I've always thought it should be *Be Prepared to Destroy Your Enemies*."

"Well…no, I guess it doesn't hurt to be prepared…" Truth was, I'd always planned to travel with my troop when they were old enough. Now that they were in middle school, it might be time to start planning. But by that I meant baby steps.

"There's a lot to do before a trip like that," I started. "For example, the whole troop would need passports. And it takes time to get them."

Betty cut me off. "We've already got them. A year ago. You filled out the form to sponsor our applications."

I shook my head. "I didn't. And I think it's your parents who have to do that…"

She looked seriously into my eyes, and I had the feeling she was trying to hypnotize me. "You did, you just don't remember. And we're all listed as orphans so we didn't need parental…you know what? Forget I said that. Moving on…"

It felt like my heart stopped for a moment. "No, I'd like to double back to that. It seems like fraud against the US government…"

She shook her head. "Not important. Besides, your dad is a senator. He can get us out of any trouble."

"That's not how that works either." I thought about my dad getting in trouble for sponsoring a group of fraudster teens. It made my head spin.

"Should we feed them or something?" I pointed at the babies, whose eyes were still locked on to me. They hadn't even blinked.

Betty settled back on the couch. "No, you don't do anything unless they cry or fuss. If they're sitting there, it means they're comfortable."

I watched them for a whole minute, and they still hadn't blinked or taken their eyes off me. "Have you ever seen babies just sit like that?"

Betty leaned forward for a look. "No, but I read about it once. It's kind of freakish, but if they aren't upset, we don't do anything that might upset them."

I wondered if the boys had inherited this from Ron and Ivan—two men I'd once watched stare into space for two hours, and when I asked them what they'd been thinking about, they seemed confused…about *thinking*.

I finally had to look away from the babies. "Look, let's back up to the boy thing. That's where we started."

"Okay." Betty rolled her eyes. "That's what I'd wanted to talk about in the beginning."

"What is it about Conrad that you like?" I thought this would be an easy question.

Betty grinned, rolled her eyes, and began smacking me in the arm. "You know!"

"No, not really." I was about to ask more when Hilly walked in.

"Okay, don't panic!" She threw her arms out in front of her as if to stop us from doing something. "I'm here. Everything will be alright."

I stared at her. "What, exactly, do you think is wrong that we should panic about?"

She cocked her head to one side. "I don't really know. You just always seem to need me to sort things out."

"No, I don't," I started to say.

"We're talking about boys," Betty said. "And traveling to Iceland."

Hilly grabbed a slice of pizza off my plate and sat cross-legged on the floor. "Boys like those two?" She pointed at the babies.

"No, boys like…*boys*," Betty floundered. "*Boy* boys…that thing."

It was startling to observe her being flustered.

"Betty likes Conrad." I got to my feet so I could go get more pizza. "She thinks if he moves to Iceland, she should move to Iceland."

Betty tossed a half-eaten slice of pizza onto my plate. "You can have that. It's not burned enough." She looked at Hilly. "All I'm saying is you should be prepared in case you suddenly and without warning have to move to Iceland."

I left the room, dumped the half-eaten pizza slice, got another plate and, along with mine, piled them high with pizza before returning.

"…There's no crime in Iceland," Hilly lamented. "If you *puff the puffin*, it's really hard to escape too because it's an island."

Betty wrote down, *Don't kill anyone in Iceland without Hilly.*

I handed Hilly a plate. "No one is going to assassinate anyone in Iceland. Look, we're just talking about guys and crushes and stuff."

Betty narrowed her eyes. "What Conrad and I have is real."

"Have you thought about where you want to get married?" Hilly replied before I could respond. "Iceland's okay, but personally I think Beirut is nice."

"I…" I paused and turned to Hilly. "You've thought about getting married in Beirut?"

"Well sure! If Pakistan isn't available…"

"Who are you planning to marry?" I pressed.

"Manny, of course," Hilly said. "I just need him to drop all the restraining orders he's filed against me…"

The assassin was referring to a bodyguard who had, against my will, protected me recently when a contract had been taken out on my life. Manny was a great guy, and Hilly had really taken to him the moment she laid eyes on him. Unfortunately, the feeling wasn't mutual because Hilly came on so strong. No, that's an understatement. Because Hilly swooped in like Mothra, leaving swathes of scorched earth behind her.

Betty pointed a piece of pizza at her. "You need someone in government who can make those things disappear."

"Why does Manny have any restraining orders against you?" I sat down on the couch and glanced at the babies, who were still staring at me. Martini was now lying on top of Wally's head, like a roadkill hat. Wally didn't even seem to notice.

Hilly stared into space as if she had trouble remembering. "I think it might have something to do with the time he was upset with his mailman, so I delivered him, bound and gagged, to Manny's front porch."

There wasn't much anymore that Hilly could say that stunned me, but my jaw dropped open. "You did what now?"

She threw her hands in the air. "I thought I was *helping*!"

Betty shook her head and sighed. "Some guys are so clueless, am I right?"

The last thing I needed was these two bonding over disturbing ways to impress guys.

"Anyway," Hilly continued. "I thought I got it sorted out. Manny wasn't upset with the mailman. He was upset with the guy who sorts the mail." She paused. "Of course, he didn't seem happy about that either when I showed up with *that* guy unconscious in my trunk."

"Stop wreaking revenge on postal employees!" I shouted.

For a moment, I freaked out, wondering if I'd upset the infants. I looked over to see them still staring at me.

"What's up with that?" I pointed at the babies.

Hilly looked. "Oh that. They either find you fascinating or are plotting your death."

"I find it hard to believe it would be the second option, seeing that they're only a few days old," I said before taking another bite.

"You'd be surprised what babies are thinking!" Hilly said. "I'm reading their minds right now. It's definitely the death plotting thing."

"Makes sense," Betty said.

I considered this a moment. "Well, as long as they aren't crying and are unable to literally operate a weapon, I think that at least for tonight, I'm okay."

Hilly looked at Betty. "She doesn't know anything about boys, does she?"

"Nope," Betty answered.

CHAPTER TWENTY-SEVEN

I walked over to the babies and stood in front of them. Their tiny eyes rose up to my face. I took a step to the right, and their eyes followed. I stepped to the left, with the same results. I started moving all around the room, and no matter what I did, their eyes were fixed on me.

"What's really weird is that they can't see well at this age." Betty had returned from the kitchen, where she'd managed to burn a couple of pieces of pizza in the microwave.

Now I was starting to get worried.

"I definitely think it's the kill thing," she said.

Hilly looked me up and down. "I get it. Sometimes I look at you like that myself."

"Since you two are such experts on babies, I'm going to go to the kitchen and do the dishes." And I went. I even lingered over rinsing the plates before loading them into the dishwasher.

When I was done, I looked to see how much time had passed. Five minutes.

"Shouldn't we feed them or something," I said as I walked into the living room.

Hilly and Betty each had a baby in their laps, who they were feeding with bottles. The boys turned their heads to look at me and stayed that way.

"Maybe they think I'm fascinating," I suggested.

Hilly and Betty laughed.

"That's right," Hilly said. "You just keep thinking that."

The boys never took their eyes off me the whole night. Even when I left the room, I swear I could feel their eyes on me. It was unnerving, and I once spent a weekend at a mime convention in Russia where no one spoke the entire time. I did get some good intel there though. Believe me, it was not easy to do all of my talking with my actions. But by Sunday, my "locked inside an invisible box" performance was perfect, and I had satellite photos of Putin's mystery dacha.

Just when I thought I couldn't take anymore, Rex called. I ran into the kitchen with my phone. I don't know why—I just felt safer there.

"Hey babe! You're missing some bonding time with the boys," I said.

"Sorry about that," Rex said. "It's taken me forever to find Sheldon's offices. Apparently, he paid Google Maps to give multiple false addresses. It was only after I called the director of HR that she told me where to go. When I got there, everyone was gone for the night."

"Sounds weird," I conceded. "Which is nothing like what's happening here."

There was a moment of silence. "What *is* happening there?"

The words came out in a rush of breath. "Hilly dropped by, the boys have been staring at me, without blinking, the whole time, and Betty wants to talk about boys and how she would move to Iceland if Conrad did."

"Iceland?" Rex asked.

"Never mind. By the way, I talked to Soo Jin. She told me about Sheldon being hit by a car somewhere else."

"She texted me that you'd been by," Rex said. "What do you think about Sheldon being killed in another place?"

I heard what sounded like singing in the living room and ignored it. "Soo Jin is so smart, I wouldn't even second-guess that. It doesn't make finding his killer any easier though. By the way, can you ask HR about Sheldon's wife, Sandy?"

"Sheldon was married?" Rex seemed surprised.

I'd admit, it was a little satisfying knowing something Rex didn't know. "That's what Ted Fowler said. He was a witness at their wedding. This was before he started the company, but maybe there are records."

"I'll add that to the list. I have an appointment with HR in the morning. My only concern is that they won't be that forthcoming about staff records."

Museum of Murder | 181

We chatted for a few more minutes before I heard the front door open and said my goodbyes. I walked into the living room to find my brothers-in-law there.

"How were babies?" Ivan went over and scooped his son out of the car seat.

Wally still kept his eyes on me.

"Fine. Have you ever noticed that they fixate on things?" I asked.

Ron and Ivan looked to Hilly for an explanation.

"They haven't stopped staring at Merry since they arrived," the assassin said.

As if to test their theory, Ron and Ivan started walking their sons around the room. But no matter where they went, the babies kept their eyes on me. I wondered what they did when I was in the kitchen earlier.

"We are so lucky!" Ron shouted.

"Yes!" Ivan set Wally back in the car seat. "Our babies are prophets, and you are the Great Pook Snork!"

Both Chechens stared at me, grinning like idiots.

"What's a Pook Snork?" Betty looked at the babies curiously.

Ron clapped his hands together as if he were praying. "Is a holy person! Is prophesied that two baby boys will find the Great Pook Snork, and he...or she..."

Ivan finished, "Is the second coming of the Mother of all Goats!"

I folded my arms over my chest. "You've got to be kidding."

Ron held up his hands with his fingers twisted around the other fingers like a mangled Vulcan salute. "We do not kid about this! Is very important legend back home!"

"She's the Great Pook Snork—Mother of all Goats?" Hilly's eyebrows went up.

"Congratulations," Betty deadpanned.

Hilly ran over and threw her arms around me. "I'm so happy for you!"

"I've never heard of such a thing," I said.

Ron nodded. "Is because only legend in Blasto Blasto."

"That explains why our sons found her!" Ivan paused and looked me up and down. "Although, I never thought the Great Pook Snork would be a *woman*."

"Is surprising," Ron agreed. "But very good that our sister is Pook Snork!"

I held up my hands. "So what does this Pook Snork, Mother of all Goats, do?"

"You are the bringer of justice to all!" Ron explained.

"That doesn't sound bad," I reasoned. In fact, I kind of liked that idea!

"All *goats*!" Ivan said. "There are many injustices against goats."

Ron nodded. "Is important job!" He looked at his phone. "Okay. We go now. Wives want babies back."

As they walked out the door, Ivan said, "Wait until we tell them about baby prophets!"

Hilly offered to take Betty home, and against my better judgement, I agreed. Hopefully I'd be able to undo any harmful suggestions, like kidnapping Conrad's dad to scare him into staying here.

After cleaning up, this Pook Snork went to bed.

The next morning, after a weird dream where I launched a goat legal defense fund that was funded by Sheldon McBride's ghost, I headed over to Riley's. Hopefully, he'd found something by now.

"All hail the Great Pook Snork!" Riley said as I walked in. "Congratulations, by the way."

Kelly looked up from her monitor. "Ron texted us both this morning to say how lucky we were to know you."

She said it in a way that sounded like she didn't think that was a good enough reason.

"Hey!" Riley said. "That's a big honor!"

That brought me up short. "You've heard of it?"

He went back to his monitor. "No, but Ron and Ivan were impressed."

Kelly added, "Babies can't see at that age. There was probably some light behind you or something."

I dropped into a chair. "Well, in order to find justice for all goats, I need to know if you've found anything."

"I spoke to Grigori," Riley said,. "And he says there are two Chinese spies in the area who've been operating here for the last few months. He wouldn't tell me who they were."

"He probably doesn't know," I sighed. "But that adds credence to the idea of a spy killing Sheldon for the drone and Britta for the drone-finding tech."

Kelly handed me a sheet of paper. "I found a marriage license for Sheldon McBride."

My spirits rose and then sank. "Wait, the bride's name isn't on here."

"Yeah," Kelly sighed. "It's very unusual. The county clerk I talked to about it was shocked. She says it's extremely rare, but she has seen it before once or twice."

I frowned. "They didn't have any other documentation on the marriage?"

Kelly shrugged. "She's looking but doubts it. Apparently the county clerk from that era died a few years back."

My eyebrows went up. "Suspicious death?"

"No, old age. She was one hundred and ten years old."

I thought for a moment. "Did the clerk think the license had been forged or altered?"

Kelly shook her head. "No. She believed the bride's name not being filled in was an oversight."

So we had Chinese spies and a mystery bride. The trouble was, how important was this new intel? I believed that spies could be behind this. But Sandy...whoever she was? She could just be a red herring and the blank spot on the marriage license a coincidence.

I looked at my friends. "What do you guys think?"

Riley spread his hands out. "If it's Chinese spies, I'd say leave it. It isn't our hunt anymore. I mean, I don't like it any more than you do. But this is above our pay grade now."

Kelly seemed to agree. "We do enough dangerous activities. And they still don't know who the latest victim is."

I gaped at them. "You guys love this stuff! Kelly, you ask to come with me all the time when I'm about to run headfirst into danger!"

"Things are a little different," Kelly said. "If you die, someone has to keep leading the troop, and we have Thinking

Day and cookie sales coming up. I'd prefer it if you didn't go after the killer, but if you do and get killed, then I'm on my own."

I put my hands on my hips. "I've faced off with lots of dangerous people! There's a whole museum to prove it! And those are just nine times I did that!"

"Cookie sales are a huge undertaking," Kelly said as she nonchalantly turned back to her computer. "The girls need one of us to be alive."

I threw my arms up. "The girls have shell companies, are running a shady city government, have 'guys' who provide things at the drop of a hat, and have connections to the Des Moines Russian mafia!"

"Yes," Kelly said evenly. "But who's going to keep them in check?"

"Clearly not us! Why are you so worried about this?"

My best friend gave me a look. "I overheard the girls saying that if anything happened to us, they would get Hilly to lead the troop. And since I didn't get into the Girl Scouts to train a bunch of children to be assassins, I need to stay alive."

She had a point. "Nothing is going to happen to me!"

"I don't know, Wrath..." Riley winked. "You're not getting any younger. And you're pretty rusty at spycraft."

I glared daggers at my former handler. "You and I are nearly the same age."

He grinned. "Yes, but in men that only makes us look more distinguished."

CHAPTER TWENTY-EIGHT

To prove how responsible I was, and to make sure I left things organized before what Kelly thought was my impending death, I spent the rest of the day with Hilly, cleaning out the old house, collating all the cookie sale packets, organizing the permission forms, and making notes on everything we had done, were doing, and had yet to be done for Thinking Day.

I'd fielded some emails from Conrad's mom, who was a lovely woman named Gunndis and had already shipped all the chocolate and yogurt we would need. Of course, then I had to find enough refrigerator space for all that yogurt, and it took a while before I called in a favor to the kitchen at city hall.

Hilly was absolutely no help at all, but she was entertaining and it made the day move quickly. She even picked up carryout for lunch and dinner after I gave her my credit card. By the end of the day, I sent photos to Kelly of all the things I'd done, accompanied by one word: *"See?"*

Then I collapsed into bed. Then Hilly woke me up and said I didn't live there anymore and would I mind going back to my house so she could knit all those sweaters in peace. And I went to bed again.

Rex called me late the next morning with what he'd learned.

"Apparently," he began "Someone sued the company years ago, saying Sheldon stole their ideas. Sheldon privately settled out of court as long as the records would be sealed. The plaintiff had to sign a gag order. No one knows who it is."

That was interesting! By settling, it seemed that Sheldon had admitted he'd stolen the ideas. Somebody would definitely kill for that. "Any other enemies?"

"He had a stalker. Again, no one knew who it was and Sheldon refused to call the police."

I reviewed the notes I'd been taking. "We have two unknown enemies with perfect motives. Make that three if you include the ex-wife." I filled Rex in on what Kelly had found out.

"Not necessarily," Rex disagreed. "The person who sued must have agreed to the settlement. And their claim may not have been that strong. They could've been perfectly happy with the agreement."

I wasn't sure about that. "Could that person be the stalker?"

"It's possible. Or it could be the ex-wife."

"Or…" I held up one finger. "It could be Brian Atkins. According to Audra, he was always jealous of Sheldon. Maybe he became more bitter as the years passed because Sheldon didn't hang out with him or acknowledge their friendship?"

"I'll look into Brian," Rex said after a moment.

"Good luck," I said. "I've left a couple of messages, but he hasn't responded."

"He could just be a private person," Rex reasoned.

Nope. That was not cutting it for me. "Too bad. That doesn't work with a murder investigation."

"That seems like something I should be saying." I could feel Rex smiling. "I should be home tomorrow. Soo Jin is shaving the victim soon. Once I have that photo, I'm heading back to HR. Oh, and I hear congratulations are in order!"

Oh no. Not him too.

"The Great Pook Snork! Sounds like a real honor."

"I don't know about that," I grumbled. "I mean really, finding justice for *every* goat? Seems like a lot of work."

We ended the call, and I thought about what he'd said about Brian Atkins. I was determined to find him before Rex did. I made up my mind: I was going to go to his house to find him.

It was daylight, but the house was dark. A lone light shone over the front door, but there was no light in the windows.

That didn't necessarily mean no one was home. I knew people who didn't turn lights on until they absolutely needed them. Brian could be frugal.

Or he wasn't home at all. Could he have left town at some point for vacation, visiting family or something like that? There was only one way to find out.

I got out of the van and pulled the baseball cap low over my face. After checking to see if any of the neighbors were looking out windows, I walked down the street as if on a stroll. At the end of the block, I turned right and then turned again into the alley.

It was a dismal winter day, and dark clouds hung morosely overhead. There was some loud buzzing coming from a streetlight. I should have Betty look into that. I worked my way down the alley, watching for doorbell cameras. I didn't see any. This wasn't that kind of neighborhood, I guess. There was no fence surrounding Atkins' place. It was pretty easy to slip up to the back door.

It was unlocked.

That wasn't too unusual. This was a small Iowa town. Rex didn't get many burglaries or break-ins. People trusted you to not just walk into their houses. But was Brian the same way? He was reclusive and bitter. Someone like that would most likely lock themselves up.

But Brian grew up here. Leaving doors unlocked would be second nature to him growing up. It was possible that he just never locked it.

Or he could be home.

There were two ways to play this if that was the case. I could knock and call out before going in. That would alert the neighbors, and I really didn't want to do that.

The other option was to just go in. It would be a quiet way to find out if anyone was home. I was trained to infiltrate all kinds of lairs and leave unnoticed. The only problem would be if Brian had a gun and shot me as I rounded a dark corner.

I didn't have time for this, and I didn't want anyone to know I was here. I slipped inside the kitchen and left the door slightly ajar behind me for a quick exit. If I did run into Brian, I would explain that I had tried calling and was concerned. It wasn't much of a story, but it would be enough to size up the situation and escape. Unless he was willing to talk.

If I thought the outside looked dark, I was surprised by how dark it really was inside. I took a risk and switched on the kitchen light. The light didn't even cut into the darkness of the next room.

The kitchen was tidy and sparse. A bowl, spoon, and small glass were in the drying rack. Everything else was clean. I went into the next room, which appeared to be a dining room and living room combination. Once again, I flicked on the light and waited. If someone was home, they would probably show up any second.

Nothing happened. I started to relax, pretty sure Brian was out. A quick glance out the window showed no one else on the street. I always preferred winter break-ins. No one was ever about outside to see me going where I shouldn't be.

I sniffed the air. It was clean, which meant it hadn't been abandoned long and there were most likely no corpses lying about for days. The main room was spartan and tidy, like the kitchen. There was no trace of dust anywhere. Brian kept the place clean, and recently too by the looks of things.

You can tell the personality of a person by looking around their living room. And from this one, I'd say Brian didn't really have much of a personality. The art on the walls were generic prints. There was one photo on a bookshelf that looked like it might be his parents. The books were all general fiction. I didn't see any genre titles.

The couch was in good shape but a bland brown. The flat-screen TV was smaller than most. I looked in the cabinet underneath and found it empty. He didn't have any movie DVDs. No gaming consoles. It didn't seem like the setup of someone who'd settled a claim of millions of dollars with Sheldon.

I ventured carefully down the hallway to find a generic bathroom, a master bedroom with no personal effects, and a closet filled with the usual clothes one might find on someone who lived here. The shelf had an empty briefcase and a hat.

The room across the hall was a sort of office. There was a small desk, and on it was a later-model desktop computer. A stack of the usual bills—which included water, power, and internet—sat neatly in a tray. None of them looked overdue.

The desk drawers didn't yield much other than a phone book, a calculator, some tax files from the past seven years, and various pens and pencils. I turned to the closet, opened the door, and did a double-take.

The back of the door was plastered with images of Sheldon McBride. Pictures that varied in age from youth to newspaper clippings that went up to the present. The photos were all cut and pasted onto a large piece of posterboard and appeared to have been haphazardly placed.

The top shelf had books about Sheldon—scanty biographies written by various journalists. There were also some notebooks and yearbooks. Beneath that, hanging on hangers were clothes like the ones the McBrides would wear. On the floor was a pair of canvas tennis shoes.

Could Brian be Sheldon's stalker?

A noise coming from the kitchen caught my attention. Someone else was in the house. I silently cursed myself for leaving on all the lights. I retreated to the desk and crouched down behind it.

No one called out. I kept waiting for a "who's there" but was rewarded with none. There weren't even any footsteps. Had I imagined it? I thought about the sound I'd heard and identified it as a door closing.

Maybe I'd be lucky and they entered, saw the lights, and left the house to call the cops. That was the kind of thing you should do in these circumstances. Movies and TV shows often depicted people going into their homes that had been broken into, but that was a terrible idea. It was better to stay safe outside and call the police instead.

I thought about my options. The police could come, and I could tell Troy or Joanna that I'd been concerned about Brian (there would be no point in lying to say Rex sent me, because he would've sent them), and when I found the door unlocked, I decided to do a wellness check. Sure, it would all sound suspicious, but I'd come out okay unless Brian wanted to press charges for B & E.

Minutes passed. No sirens. I think I would've preferred getting caught. Because this meant that they didn't call the cops and were waiting for me to emerge. Would it be Brian, ready to accost me or, worse, shoot me? Or was someone else having the same idea that I had in coming here?

That was an interesting thought, because it could mean that Brian was being watched. I pulled out my phone and texted Riley as to where I was and the situation. Of all people, Riley would understand and come to help me out. I suggested he come in the back way but to be careful. Then I stuck my phone into my back pocket and waited.

Still nothing. My phone hadn't even vibrated with a reply. It had now been twenty minutes, and whoever it was hadn't made a move. I couldn't stay here all day. I'd have to do something soon.

Perhaps the other person had left. They'd come in, seen the lights on, and fled. It was possible. I hadn't heard the door open and close again, but it could just be standing open. I'd have to make my way out.

There was a window next to me, and I hazarded a peek, in the hopes I could bypass going back through the house and just go out this window. Not a chance. A group of neighbors, each walking dogs, had apparently met up on the sidewalk in front of this house and were gabbing away as their dogs defiled Brian's front lawn.

Popping through the window at this point would be a bad idea. I cracked open the window, just a bit, to see if their conversation was heading to an end and they'd all move on.

"Did we tell you about our new grandson?" A woman held up a phone. "I've got three hundred pictures of him right here!"

"Ooooh!" the other woman cooed. "Let's see!"

Their husbands were busy ignoring what the dogs had just done in the grass.

I closed the window gently. Going this way was not an option. I could cross the hall and slip out the master bedroom window. Or I could just suck it up and go back the way I came. I looked at my phone. Riley hadn't read the text yet.

It was time to move. I tiptoed to the door and eased past it into the hallway. Flattening myself against a wall, I waited to see if anyone had heard. When there was no other sound or movement, I gingerly worked my way down the hall into the main room. The front door was tantalizingly close, and I glanced through the window.

The women were still going through the photos and the men were starting to look around them for anything that might have interest. They'd see me instantly if I went out through the front.

Crap. Oh well. No time like the present. I slipped through the dining room and paused in the doorway to the kitchen. All of a sudden, the door swung wide behind me, hitting me in the back, and I fell to the floor. Another blow to the back of the head caused everything to fade. My last thought was that this guy was impressively fast. Then I passed out.

CHAPTER TWENTY-NINE

The first thing I noticed was distorted sound all around me. It was dark, but a quick intake of breath told me I was wearing a hood. Pain at my ankles and wrists let me know I was secured to a chair. Oh right. I'd been hit from behind in Brian Atkins' house.

"Who do you think she is?" a male voice wondered.

"I don't know, but we've got her now!" another man chuckled.

The hood was ripped off of my head, and I found myself in what appeared to be a normal, ranch-style basement, not unlike my own. A fake Christmas tree that looked like it was bought at a Beirut garage sale in the 80s sat in one corner, surrounded by red and green plastic bins that were, should there be any doubt, labeled with the words *Xmas Decorations*. Next to it were a bunch of orange and black bins (appropriately labelled *Halloween Decorations*) with two large skeletons sitting on them, posed them as if they were waving hello to me.

Assorted furniture, cleaning tools, and an old tanning bed were piled against the walls. On my right was a washer and a running dryer. There was the faint whiff of *eau de I peaked in high school* and fabric softener in the air.

Directly in front of me were two men I'd never seen before. One of them was tall and heavyset, wearing a shirt that said, "*A Very John Denver Arbor Day Celebration 1997!*" The other was average size but wiry, wearing all black from head to toe. Both appeared to be my age.

"Great," I said. "You've got me. Now what?"

I wasn't usually strident with people who kidnapped me and tied me to chairs to be held in middle-class basements. But I was genuinely curious.

The tall one turned to his partner. "You didn't blindfold or gag her?"

The other one shrugged. "I'm out of duct tape. I used it all tying her wrists and ankles to the chair."

The tall one pointed at me. "But now she's seen us! Even though we're gonna kill her, that still can't be good!"

"Reg?" a shrill, angry voice shrieked from the top of the stairs. "Are you down there?"

I was about to call out that I was down here, when the tall man raced over, pulled a sock from the dryer, and shoved it into my mouth. It tasted awful but smelled like springtime.

"Don't come down here, Pickle Buns," the tall one called out. "I'm busy working on something!"

His partner snorted at the nickname, and Reg shot him a look.

"It better be something for my birthday, you idiot!" Pickle Buns shouted.

Reg looked at his partner and mouthed, *I forgot her birthday*, before answering, "It is! Don't come down!"

"Well then, see if the clothes are dry in the dryer and bring them up!" Pickle Buns said before slamming the door.

"We don't have much time," Reg said.

"You said she wouldn't be home!" the other whined.

"Don't give me that, Rog!" Reg exploded. "I didn't know she'd be home! And now I have to get her something for her birthday!"

Rog shook his head. "You should've thought of that before we brought our prisoner here. We could've done this at my house!"

Reg snorted. "Yeah, right! Your mom is way too nosy for that!"

While the family dynamics of these two was fascinating, I had other plans and places to be.

"Mmmmmm!" I mumbled loudly.

The two men looked at me.

"First things first," Rog said. "Let's deal with her, and then we'll figure out a solution to the birthday problem. Okay?"

Reg nodded. "Okay. Where's your brother-in-law's toolbox?"

Rog disappeared behind me and reemerged with a camouflage duffel bag. "I still don't know why we couldn't use yours."

"Because I didn't want any DNA traced back to me." Reg rolled his eyes. "Don't you ever watch *Forensic Files*?"

"So…my brother-in-law will get the blame?" Rog's eyebrows went up.

"I hate that jackass," Reg snapped. "And my wife loaned out my toolbox to the neighbors, so…"

Who were these guys? Why had they kidnapped me? I was pretty sure they planned to torture and kill me, which was unfortunate. My hands twisted in their duct tape snares. I had to think of a way to get out of here. Or at least to make enough noise to bring Pickle Buns downstairs. It was apparent these two didn't want her to know what they were up to.

Rog opened the bag and dumped the tools on the floor. He picked up a pair of tin snips and frowned.

I mumbled as loud as I could then raised my voice a pitch to a kind of keening whine that the angry Pickle Buns, if she'd been listening, might hear.

Reg walked over and took out the sock. "What? You have to go to the bathroom? Do not have an accident here on my floor!"

"Why am I here? Who are you working for?" I managed to say before he stuffed the sock back into my mouth. Why didn't I just scream? Because I needed the intel. Besides, now they probably thought I wouldn't, so they'd probably give me another chance to talk.

"The boss says you don't need to know," Reg said. "And the boss said to make it painful before we kill you."

I mumbled again. Reg complied by removing the gag.

"Look, I don't mean to be judgy or anything, but have you guys ever killed anyone before? Because you really don't appear to be the murdery type."

The sock went back into my mouth.

Reg looked at Rog, and they decided not to say anything. Instead, Reg joined Rog and his brother-in-law's tools.

"We're supposed to torture information out of her. We can use these tin snips to cut off a finger." Reg held up the snips.

Rog looked around. "Do you have a tarp or something? Because your wife will kill you when she finds out you got blood on the floor, not to mention when she realizes you didn't get her anything for her birthday."

Reg walked over to one of the orange and black bins and pulled out a Very John Denver Rocky Mountain High Halloween shower curtain. He then came over to me and tipped the chair to the right so Rog could slip the curtain under me. Then he tipped me to the left to get it on that side. Once he righted me, he went over and picked up the tin snips.

Taking off my finger would be difficult without cutting one hand loose first. That meant I could fight back. Why wasn't I panicking? Because it wouldn't do any good. And these nitwits seemed to think I'd be reasonable.

"We can't use these!" Rog said. "They're left-handed."

Reg's face fell. "I'm a righty too. What else is in there?"

Rog pulled out a pair of industrial scissors. "They're all left-handed! What the hell, Reg? How are we going to torture her if we're right-handed and the tools are left-handed?"

I guess it didn't occur to these two that somewhere in that bag had to be a hammer, which would be obviously ambidextrous.

I mumbled loudly.

Reg came over and pulled out the sock.

"Listen, not to demean what you're trying to do here," I said. "But this is obviously the first time you've tortured or killed anyone. Are you sure you want to go that route? Because once you do, you can't undo it. Besides, your boss should've provided you with a hideout and the proper tools." I took a chance. "I mean seriously, you can't even use a hammer if it's for lefties."

Reg shrugged. "I forgot my brother-in-law's a lefty. And you're right, this is our first time."

Rog's face grew red. "Don't tell her that! She won't be afraid of us if you tell her that!"

"Too late," I said. "Look, just let me go. I won't say anything. I was in the CIA. You can trust me."

None of that would've made sense to a normal person, but these guys appeared to be dumber than a box of cookies. Mmmmm…cookies. Why didn't I eat before getting kidnapped?

"I don't know," Reg said slowly as if he were actually attempting to think on the fly. "The boss would get mad."

"To hell with the boss," Rog said. "She's right! Let's just let her go! Even if we were able to pull this off"—he waved the tin snips—"which seems doubtful, then we'd run the risk of going to jail or worse!"

Reg warmed to the idea. "We might get kicked out of the Jaycees. I wouldn't like that."

"So cut me loose before your wife decides you're taking too long to get the clothes out of the dryer," I said, hoping to add another reason to why they should let me go. "And sneak out and buy her some nice jewelry for her."

Just because her husband had kidnapped me and had originally planned to torture and kill me didn't mean she couldn't have a nice birthday.

Reg nodded and dropped to a knee, tearing the tape and untying both feet and my right hand before stopping. He squinted at me. "Hey! Wait a minute! I think she might be tricking…"

He didn't finish his sentence because I stood and clobbered him with the chair that was still tied to my left hand. He passed out on the floor.

Rog dropped the tin snips and looked like he was debating whether to run or attack, when I closed the distance and knocked him out with the chair. After tearing off the tape on my left wrist, I dragged the unconscious Rog over to the unconscious Reg and tied them together using Christmas lights from the helpfully labeled red and green bins. Then I took pictures of my two captors to give to Rex once I was out of here.

The dryer buzzed loudly. After checking and realizing the clothes were still damp, I turned them on for ten more minutes.

"Thanks Reg!" came the voice from upstairs.

I spotted an exit door that I hadn't seen because it had been behind my chair.

"You're welcome!" I called out in my girliest voice and hightailed it out the side door.

It was always good to be helpful. I am a Girl Scout, after all.

CHAPTER THIRTY

Out on the sidewalk, I took a picture of the front of the house, figured out where I was, and jogged back to my van. Once inside, after regaining my breath, I thought about my next move.

I wasn't done with Rog and Reg—not by a long shot. For some reason, I didn't want to go to the police. It seemed to me these guys had never done anything like this before and were unlikely to do it again. I could scare them more myself than sitting in a prison cell would do. Besides, it could wait. Those guys were going to have a worse time explaining to Pickle Buns who the woman in the basement was and why her husband didn't have a present for her.

Brian was gone. Had he fled the state after killing Sheldon and Britta? That was a distinct possibility. Only on British cozy TV shows did people flee when they were innocent. Had he hired Rog and Reg? Why else would they be watching his house?

Let's say, for argument, that Brian was the one who sued Sheldon and stalked him. I really liked that idea because it might explain why he'd kill Sheldon's lawyer. Brian got the settlement payout. Then he stalked Sheldon to scare him because he couldn't do anything else with the lawsuit settled. In an act of impotent rage, he kills Sheldon.

Britta, the attorney, knew who had sued Sheldon and, let's say, who stalked him. She offered to come here with the drone-locating information because Brian lived here. Maybe she was going to blackmail him…or just accuse him of murdering Sheldon. So she was killed. Then he hired Reg and Rog to watch the house as he went on the run.

All of those puzzle pieces fit nicely together. It even explained the stalker-like closet. The only piece that didn't fit was the latest victim. Hopefully Rex would have an answer soon on that one.

Still, I couldn't rule out the Chinese spies or the ex-wife.

Or even Audra and Matt. I didn't know them. Not really. Perhaps I needed to visit Ted Fowler again. I should ask him about Brian and try to get more about Sandy, the ex-wife.

I took a deep breath. What was up with Reg and Rog? I'd never seen two men I'd trust less with torturing or killing anyone. I was definitely going to have to pay them a visit to see who their boss was.

I texted Soo Jin to ask her to send me the photo of the dead guy. Then I'd visit Fowler. But first, I felt like I had to do one more thing.

"Mrs. Ferguson!" Drew Phillips said as I walked into his office.

Getting into the museum was no mean feat. The line was the length of two city blocks. Ron and Ivan, who were guarding the door, said the third murder blew up the computer. They seemed to take that literally and were appropriately concerned.

"Please, have a seat," the museum director said. "What can I do for you?"

"I just wanted to see how you're doing," I made what I hoped was a sympathetic face. "You've had a really rough week. I think the mayor is worried about you."

It was more likely she was worried about Conrad leaving and having to hire a new museum director. But I didn't say that.

He ran his fingers through his hair, leaving it looking like a mad scientist. Not that mad scientists weren't fun. Most of them were. It was the ones who lived in a volcano and had pet sharks you had to worry about. And yes, they did exist. There were, in fact, two of them. Frederick the Fearless, who lived in a volcano off the coast of India, wanted to rule the world, while Orva Jane McPhail, who lived in a volcano off the coast of Seattle, was trying to teach penguins how to dance the quadrille.

"It's been a challenge," he said slowly, measuring every word. "I'm not too sure how I feel about it right now."

"It's fine. Triple murders are really rare here."

He stared at me. "There are three exhibits out there on triple and more murders!"

Oh. Right. "They're still rare, if you count all the murders we've had in town."

That seemed like the wrong thing to say.

I continued, "If you're worried about Conrad, there's no need. Kids have never been murdered here."

"I'm more worried about myself," he said, "working in a museum where there have been three murders."

I waved him off. "I'm sure they're all related to each other. Chances are extremely slim that you would be killed."

He stared at me. "But there is still a chance. I've been thinking that moving here was a bad idea."

I leaned forward. "You're not thinking of moving over a little thing like this!"

Drew's jaw dropped open. "A little thing like three murders—all in the place where I work? I am thinking that!"

This was not good. Had I made things worse by coming here?

"And then there's the gift shop!" He shook his head. "I didn't realize I'd have no say in what is sold there!"

"Ah. The girls are a bit overly enthusiastic about capitalism..." I started.

Phillips looked first left, then right, which was weird because we were in a small office. He lowered his voice. "I think they are selling stolen merchandise!"

Act casual... "Why do you think that?"

"The police came in and confiscated half the things in the locked cabinet! They said the evidence room had been raided! What kind of town is this?"

Damn. I'd hoped the girls hadn't done that. "Maybe this is all a misunderstanding."

Drew slumped in his chair. "Well, the police actually said they needed to compare it with items in the evidence room. But still—who does that?"

My troop, apparently.

"Listen, I can vouch for my girls. Trust me on this. They're good kids."

"Says the woman who has a mannequin in all nine exhibits," he snorted. The man got up and stood at the window.

"But Conrad really likes it here. And I'd have to sell our house here to buy another one somewhere else." He turned back to me. "Is it wrong to base a decision like this on how difficult it is to relocate instead of the fact that this town is very, very dangerous?"

"Absolutely not!" I might have shouted too eagerly. "Let me ask you a question... Have you ever worked in a museum that has had this kind of opening success? The line outside extends two city blocks! On a Thursday! In winter!"

Phillips sat down and thought for a moment. "No, not really. This is pretty exceptional."

I jumped on that. "Yes! Exceptional! Exactly! Where did you work before this?"

He looked like he didn't want to tell me. "Um, before this I was the curator at the Turnstile Museum in Chicago. Before that I was the acquisitions curator for the Museum of Cheese That Looks Like Jesus in Wisconsin."

"And now you're the Executive Director of the most successful museum in the country—as far as opening ticket sales go."

He looked like he might be buying it. "I guess that's true..."

I ramped up my enthusiasm. "And it's exciting! How many bodies did you find in the turnstile and cheese museums?"

"None."

"So every day is interesting! You never know what will happen! Isn't that a good thing?" I might have been piling it on pretty thick.

"I guess so..."

I pushed it over the top. "And it's educational!" Maybe too far. What did I think people were learning? "You could bring in Dr. Soo Jin Body, bus classrooms in, and she can talk about forensics! My husband could teach kids about detective work!"

He lightened up a bit. "Huh. I hadn't really thought of it like that. We didn't have much luck with education outreach at the other museums."

I held my hands out. "This is a huge career booster for you! You can create fascinating educational opportunities for students!"

Drew frowned. "Do you think it's okay to teach kids about that stuff?"

My troop would love it.

"Sure! These kids all watch TV shows with that stuff all the time. This is an opportunity to bring in professionals to do it right! I'd be willing to bet you'd get kids from all over the Midwest. The hotels in town would probably give you an honorary award for drumming up business! Like Taylor Swift's Eras Tour!"

Had I pushed it too far? I was just trying to make it relatable.

Drew smiled. "Thank you for that. I was pretty down before you came in here. And selling a house here would not pay for an equal house in Chicago. But now I see that this is a tremendous opportunity! I could really make a name for myself here! We'll stay!"

I jumped out of my chair and punched my fist in the air. "Great!"

He held up a finger. "There's only one condition."

I sat back down. "Anything! What is it?"

"Can you talk to Mayor Ava about hiring Ron and Ivan full-time? I'd really prefer them to be here more often. And I'd like a state-of-the-art security system and a panic room attached to my office. Can you do that?"

"No problem," I said. And I left his office, knowing it was doable.

Back in the van, I watched the line move from across the street. My phone buzzed.

"Mrs. Wrath," Betty said. "Excellent work. I'm going to nominate you for leader of the year."

"You bugged Phillips's office?" That would probably be a deal breaker unless we could convince Drew it was for his safety.

"Of course" came the answer.

"Aren't you in school right now?"

"Study period," Betty said. "We're not supposed to be on our phones, but Mrs. Diptich is really old, and I have a remote that turns her hearing aids off."

I sighed. "You need to stop doing that."

"I think she's asleep…"

"Bye," I said, ending the call.

It was a huge relief that Drew and Conrad were staying. And I mostly meant what I'd said in there. The education thing was a bit of improvisation, but it was a pretty cool idea.

My only issue now was to wrap up this case with no idea how to do that.

CHAPTER THIRTY-ONE

The passenger side opened, and Hilly climbed in.

"I just had the most amazing day!" She bounced in her seat. "I'm being forced to take time off because of a problem with my last assignment! Yay!"

"Which means you did something wrong or are in trouble," I summarized.

She thought for a moment and then nodded. "Yup. That pretty much sums it up. Awesome, right? I got bawled out by HR for like two hours on the phone! What have you been doing?"

"Nothing much. Just broke into a house, got kidnapped and held in a basement by two men who wanted to torture and kill me, and then convinced Betty's boyfriend's dad not to move away."

Hilly stared at me. "And you didn't take me with you? No fair!"

I paused. "To which part?"

"The torture and kidnapping of course. Should we go kill those guys or what? That would be the icing on the cake!"

Okay, so I toyed with the idea. Reg and Rog had expressed an interest in torturing and killing me, but that was as far as it got. It wouldn't hurt to scare them a little bit. And I did need to know who their boss was...

My thoughts were interrupted by a phone call.

"Hey babe!" I said brightly. "Any news?"

"Can I talk to him?" Hilly asked.

Why? I mouthed.

She shrugged, so I said no.

"HR doesn't have any idea who this guy is. He doesn't work for the company. It's not much, but it is something. They're letting me review some of Sheldon's and Britta's files, but it will take all night. I hope to fly home tomorrow."

Hilly reached for the phone, but I pushed her away.

"I wonder who our victim is?"

"I'm having Troy put out an APB, and Joanna is searching missing person files. Is everything good there?"

"Tell him you were kidnapped and we're going to *take the fish out of water*!" Hilly said.

"I'm sorry, I didn't hear that. What was that?" Rex asked. "It's a bad connection."

I attempted to distract him. "Hey, did you send the troops over to the museum to take stuff out of the gift shop?"

"I did. But that's only to compare it with what we already have."

"So the evidential stuff wasn't missing from lockup?" There was an overly hopeful note in my voice that I hoped he wouldn't notice.

"No, and I'd like to think they didn't take the real thing and replace it with counterfeit materials. Mostly I just wanted to make the girls think about the consequences."

"Good luck with that!" I snorted. "I've got to go, but can you send me the photo of the shaved man?"

Hilly cocked her head to one side. "Is that code for something?"

I ignored her.

"Sure," Rex said before ending the call.

"What are we going to do now?" the assassin asked.

"Since I'm on my own tonight and I haven't had lunch, let's get an early dinner at Oleo's."

Hilly's eyebrows went up. "And then we kill those guys?"

"Sure."

Oleo's was doing a brisk business, but we were able to secure a table because it was just then five p.m. I texted Ted Fowler to see if I could come see him and waited.

"Why's it so busy?" I asked the waitress as she deposited a glass of wine in front of me.

"The museum," the girl said in a bored voice. "It's been like this since they opened. The manager's thinking of opening it up for breakfast."

Oooh! That was exciting. We ordered food, and I sat back in my chair and relaxed a little.

"So you're in town for a while?" I asked Hilly.

She looked surprised. "How did you know that? Are you bugging my phone?"

"You told me about it literally ten minutes ago."

"Oh. Right! Well, I ran into a little trouble in Uruguay a couple of weeks ago. Nothing big. But apparently you aren't supposed to leave the body in the rental car when you return it. I totally forgot! That happens!"

It does happen. And the CIA frowns on that.

The burgers and fries arrived, and we didn't speak as we devoured them. Looking around the restaurant, I saw others delighted with what they got. Oleo's was doing well! Talking Drew into staying was definitely the right idea.

When I finished, I told Hilly about the visit with the museum director and realized I needed to let Ava know the list of demands. Fortunately, I didn't have to call or text because the mayor and her interns came in.

The hostess led them to a table and got their drink orders. The interns seemed happy. I wondered how they were settling in and was going to go over and ask when Ava spotted me first and came over. The interns spotted me and gave me a halfhearted wave while narrowing their eyes. It appeared that they weren't too sure about me.

She did not sit down.

"Madam Mayor," I said. "I'm sure Betty told you about my conversation with Drew Phillips."

She nodded. "We are already working on his list of demands. It's no problem. Do you want a key to the city or something for doing that?"

Hilly's jaw dropped open. "*They have keys to cities?*"

Sometimes I wondered how she got into the CIA.

"I don't know how you'd justify that." I waved the girl off. "No need to thank me. It's very important that we keep Betty happy. I do think you shouldn't let her bug Phillips's office. That might cause problems."

"Or..." Ava held up a finger. "We spin it as a security measure. I don't think Betty would like us to take that out."

"What would Conrad think of Betty bugging his dad's office?" I wondered.

Ava shrugged. "He never has to know about it. By the way, I came over to ask how we can make Conrad a Girl Scout."

"I'm not sure that's possible unless he wants to disguise himself as Connie instead of Conrad."

"He wants to do it as a boy. Break up sexism or something like that," Ava said. "Anyway, I just thought you should be prepared."

"And if Betty someday decides that she doesn't like Conrad anymore?" I asked. "And then wants him out of the troop?"

Ava looked conflicted. "We hadn't thought of that."

"We shouldn't make it a precedent," I said. "You girls are going to be into boys at some point, and I don't want to add your crushes to the troop."

"What if you made him like a mascot?" Ava asked.

"Or an honorary scout, like me?" Hilly suggested.

"You're not an honorary scout," I corrected her. "You just join us for stuff…often uninvited."

"I'm not a scout?" Hilly's face fell.

"Don't upset Hilly!" Ava rebuked. She looked over to the interns, who were bouncing in their seats as their food was delivered. "You can be a lifetime scout," she said to the assassin. "I'll send you the link."

"Okay! I'll have to look at it later. Merry and I are going to go kill a couple of guys."

Ava's eyebrows went up. "Hopefully not voters?"

"Don't worry," I assured her. "We're not going to kill them."

Hilly seemed disappointed. "We're not?"

"But we are going to scare them."

"Yay!" Hilly clapped her hands.

Ava went back to her table after saying it was better if she didn't know about that.

We paid the bill, and I checked my phone. Nothing yet from Fowler.

"Well, come on, Hilly." I stood up. "Let's go see two guys about a boss."

We parked out front and waited for the woman I presumed was Pickle Buns to back out of the driveway and peel off down the street. In the window, I saw two men sitting on the couch, playing video games.

Why did people leave their curtains open at night? Anyone could just walk up and shoot them through the glass. If these guys wanted to be taken seriously as gangsters, they had a lot to learn.

"Ready?" I asked Hilly. "We're just going to scare them. I've already knocked them unconscious once today."

"Fine!" Hilly pouted. "But we can have fun, right?"

"Of course!" I turned off the car and opened the door. "What kind of spies would we be if we didn't have fun?"

We walked up to the front door, and to our surprise, it was unlocked. These two were idiots, even if that went without saying. I opened the door, and we walked into the living room.

Hilly walked over to the curtains and pulled them closed while the two guys stared at us. Clearly they were imbeciles because neither one tried to take me captive again.

Amateurs.

I walked over to the men and stood in front of them, taking the handset from Rog while Hilly liberated Reg's from him. The men just gaped at us as if they were having synchronous strokes.

"Hey guys! Remember me?" I asked amiably. "This is my friend Hilly, who is a CIA assassin."

"Hi!" Hilly waved. She spotted the tool bag from earlier and walked over to check it out.

The men didn't move. I guess we didn't need to tie them up. That was nice. I looked over to see that they were playing an online game.

"Hey, I know this game! My troop plays it! Isn't it one of those games people play for years, building up levels over time?"

Reg found his voice. "Uh, yeah. We've been playing Orc Mountain Battlefield of Blood for ten years now."

"Got to the highest level ever," Rog said proudly. "We're about to become legends!"

"Hey." Reg pointed at Hilly. "Are you really a killer?"

The assassin nodded and pulled a hammer out of the bag. "Yup. I'm an excellent torturer too."

The men laughed.

"You can't use that if you're not left-handed," Reg said as he elbowed Rog.

"Yeah! You must be an idiot if you..." Rog started to say before Hilly, using her right hand, hit them both on the head with the hammer.

CHAPTER THIRTY-TWO

"Hey! How'd you do that?" Rog rubbed his head.

"She must be ambidextrous!" Reg marveled.

Hilly looked at me curiously. "What are they talking about?"

I laughed. "I know, right? It's a hammer! It doesn't do left or right!"

The guys' faces fell as they realized they'd been tricked earlier.

Hilly pointed at the monitor. "Boy, this one is really hard to do! You have to work for years to get to this level."

"Is everything saved to the computer and backed up in the cloud?" I wondered aloud.

"It is!" Hilly said. She looked at me, and I turned to the men.

"Who is your boss?" I asked.

"Mitch Needleham." Reg seemed confused. "We work at the lumber store."

Rog nodded. "Why would you want to know that?"

I pinched the bridge of my nose. This could take a while. "I meant the boss you referred to—the one who wanted me tortured and murdered?"

Hilly frowned and hit the guys in the head again with the hammer. "You're ignoring Merry. That's not very nice."

Reg yelped. "Hey! That was harder than last time!"

"Yeah!" Rog added.

"And next time, it'll be worse," I warned. "Who hired you to kill me?"

Rog narrowed his eyes, and Reg folded his arms over his chest. They weren't going to say anything.

"You know," I said to Hilly. "You could probably hit them all day. There's not a lot of brains in there, and their skulls are pretty thick." I turned back to them. "Sometimes, you have to do something that really hurts. Like destroy ten years of gaming."

"Ha!" Rog laughed. "Go ahead. Smash up the computer! It's all saved in the cloud."

"Do your worst!" Reg laughed.

"I believe," I said, studying the console. "That you can get banned for life for saying something threatening or very offensive. Isn't that right?"

"That's right," Reg said, a little confused.

"Yeah, so what?" Rog added.

I used the handset to enter an extremely terrifying threat. Looking back at the men, I could see the truth was finally dawning on them.

"How about something like this?" Hilly smiled as she added one of the most offensive things you could ever write.

Our fingers hovered over the controls.

"Who is the boss?" I repeated. "And I don't mean Mitch or Bruce Springsteen."

"No!" Reg screamed. "I don't know who it is!" He turned to his friend. "Tell them!"

Rog grew pale. This was far more terrifying than getting hit with an ambidextrous hammer being wielded by trained a killer. It's always satisfying when you find just the right leverage, isn't it?

"I…I don't know, exactly," Rog stumbled through the words. "The contact is always over text on my phone."

Reg pointed at a phone on the table. "It's that one!"

I picked it up. "What's the code to get in?"

"One-two-three." Rog looked nervously at the monitor. "It's all in there! The text to set this up and everything."

Sure enough, there was a long text stream from someone listed as The Boss. Not very original. The guys weren't lying, I guess. Still, they had kidnapped me and threatened me. I wasn't going to let them off the hook. And maybe this would keep them from diving into any further crime.

"Last question." I held up my index finger. "Did you get a nice gift for Pickle Buns?"

The men were openly afraid but looked at me with surprise.

"Um, no?" Rog said...or asked.

I shook my head and tsk, tsked. "Wrong answer, I'm afraid."

Hilly and I looked at each other before sending the messages.

"Noooooo!" the boys shouted simultaneously.

A message popped up on the screen announcing that the men were now banned from the game for life and their ten years of data erased from the system.

"You took out years of play!" Reg cried out.

"I missed all of my anniversaries for this game!" Rog choked.

The men stood up with looks of resolute fury on their faces. They pushed up their sleeves. I looked at Hilly, who was grinning and bouncing on the balls of her feet.

I sighed. "Okay, fine. But don't kill them."

The screaming was probably heard down the block. Hilly was right. That *was* fun.

CHAPTER THIRTY-THREE

Hilly and I went back to my house, ordered some pizza, and watched a new assassin series while Hilly cranked out lopi sweaters. It was funny and I enjoyed it, but Hilly was upset that they didn't use any dumpsters.

"But dumpsters are *your* thing," I reminded her. "They might have to pay you royalties if they were to use them."

"Ah! So that's it! I should make my agent include that in future contracts." She paused and made a note on her phone.

"You have an agent?"

"Well, duh! Doesn't everyone?" She rolled her eyes. "I keep getting offers from Hollywood to do my story, so I got the best in the business."

Was she kidding? "The CIA will never allow it. I'd be willing to bet that all of your assignments are classified and always will be," I reminded her.

She laughed. "Of course they are! It goes without saying that things would go badly for the agency if the world knew about the time I *clipped the tiger's claws* in Malaysia, or *skipped the mayo on the tuna sandwich for the marmot* in Estonia, or that time I *bundled home and auto insurance* in Idaho!"

Sometimes I really worried about her. "Yes, but selling the rights via an agent to Hollywood would be telling the world just that." Wait a minute... "Hold on. Idaho?"

Hilly looked at me as if I'd turned into a spider monkey. "What do you mean? Oh, and Idaho? Pretend I never said anything. Talk about being in the wrong place at the right time!"

I clicked off the TV. "Forget it. I'm obviously too tired to reason properly."

Ted texted to see if I could meet him in the morning, the pizza ran out, and I was tired of arguing with Hilly about something that would probably never happen anyway. With that, we said goodnight.

"Good morning!" Ted waved as I walked into Martha's.

He wasn't alone. One of his former students was with him.

"Hey Audra!" I greeted her as I sat down.

This was great! Everyone I needed to talk to was in one place where they had cinnamon rolls. I ordered some hot tea, but again changed it to water when Martha refused the tea, and then I turned to face the others.

"What is it you wanted to know?" Ted asked. "You said you had a question."

I pulled out my phone and showed Ted the photo of Britta Almondine. He studied it for a moment.

"Is that Sandy—the woman who married Sheldon right after college?" I pointed at the photo of the dead woman.

Audra took the phone and frowned at it. "I've never seen her before."

She handed the phone to Ted, who pulled a pair of glasses out of his pocket. "Let me see. I do better with glasses these days." He slipped them on and held the phone out at arm's length.

"That could be her. She was much younger than this back then." He handed the phone back to me. "How did you find her?"

"She's the second body in the museum." So Britta was the mystery Sandy!

The two of them looked at each other.

"They haven't said who the two other victims were," Audra said at last. "I wondered."

"Britta," I started. "Or Sandy as Ted knew her, was Sheldon's attorney. When Sheldon was killed, his drone went missing. Britta brought technology with her that would track the drone. She was killed at the museum, and the device she brought was never found."

Ted sat back in his chair and sighed with a note of sadness. "That's terrible. Two young lives thrown away. This killer is a monster." He paused. "Do you think this was all about the technology in the first place?"

My phone buzzed, but I put it back into my pocket. I could look at it later.

"Maybe. There have been Chinese spies reported in the area."

Audra and Ted looked stunned.

"Spies? Here? In Who's There?" Audra squeaked.

"Makes sense." Ted rubbed his chin. "The Chinese are usually in Iowa after agricultural secrets. Why not technology?"

"I have another question," I said. "Have either of you heard from or seen Brian lately?"

Ted shook his head.

Audra had a strange look on her face. "Like I told you before, we haven't stayed in touch. Why?"

"Oh nothing. He just hasn't responded to any of my messages. I went to his house, and he wasn't there either."

"He might be taking Sheldon's death pretty hard." Ted shook his head. "Those two were close."

Audra bit her lip. It seemed she didn't want to tell her old teacher that Brian was obsessively jealous of Sheldon. For a moment, I wondered why. She didn't owe Brian anything.

Or did she?

"Excuse me for a moment." Ted got up and waved at someone across the room. "Mr. Hughes owes me money from last night's game." He winked and headed toward a table full of old men.

I watched as he walked away and took this as an opportunity to ask Audra something.

"Why did you react so badly to the photo of you and Sheldon together in his college yearbook?"

Audra drew in a sharp intake of breath. She looked at the door, and I wondered if she was considering escape.

"It's no big deal," I assured her. "And I won't tell anyone. I just want to know for curiosity's sake." That wasn't entirely true, but I left it.

Her eyes searched mine. "You won't tell anyone?"

"I just said that." Didn't I just lie about that to her? Some people were so untrusting.

The woman looked down at her wedding ring and twisted it on her finger. "Matt and I were going through a rough patch—you know…different colleges and all. I visited Sheldon for a weekend. We flirted, and…well, you know. But it was a terrible mistake, and I told him that when I got back to my campus. I never saw him again." Her eyes were fixed on Fowler's back and her words came out like machine gun fire. "You won't tell Matt? He doesn't need to know."

I hedged but gave a nod to make her think that. "Is Matt jealous of Sheldon?"

She gave a strange laugh. "Of course not! That was a long time ago! I just don't think it's necessary to upset my husband with this."

This tidbit of intel was probably nothing and most likely, unless she was the killer, I wouldn't tell her husband. I wasn't vindictive unless you were a double agent. "Why haven't I met Matt yet?"

"He just has no interest in being dragged into this," she said a bit abruptly. "In fact…" She pushed away from the table and stood up. "I'd better get going. I said I'd meet up with him for lunch."

I watched her walk away and wondered, *Who goes to lunch at ten in the morning?*

Ted returned and sat down. "Sorry," he apologized. It was then that he looked at Audra's chair. "Did Audra go?"

"She said she had to meet Matt for lunch," I explained.

He laughed. "Who eats lunch at ten in the morning?"

An idea hit me. "Ted, can you tell me about Matt? I've only ever met Audra. It's like she's hiding him or something."

He smiled. "Matt's a good guy. Very quiet, but he does have a bit of a temper. He probably just doesn't want to talk about it."

Could Matt have killed Sheldon over a fling two decades ago? People had killed for less.

"What about Brian? Audra told me Brian was extremely jealous of Sheldon because Sheldon stole his ideas."

The old teacher's face fell as if the news disappointed him somehow. "Really? I don't think that's right. Brian and Sheldon were friends." He thought for a moment. "They were always lab partners in my class, and sometimes they disagreed on things. Maybe she's confused because of that?"

"She was very specific." I thought for a moment, drumming my fingers on the table. "If they were always lab partners, couldn't Sheldon have used Brian's ideas?"

Ted considered this. "It was a while ago, but I don't remember any long-standing animosity between them. I'm sure that she's remembering that wrong. Is it important?"

"It could be." I sighed. "Or maybe it isn't. I don't know."

"Tell you what," Ted said. "I'll invite their old chemistry and physics teachers to dinner tonight. We've been meaning to get together for a while now. I can ask them if they remember anything."

This could work. "It wouldn't be a stretch to bring up Sheldon, since the world knows he died here."

"I get to help you like Linda did!" Ted grinned. "I'll do it. And report back to you tonight or first thing in the morning."

As I left, I felt good about recruiting Fowler. Audra was adamant about Brian's jealousy. Was she lying? Could it be she was trying to take the heat off of Matt? It was strange that he wasn't with her yet again. Was it Matt who was jealous of Sheldon?

Did Matt kill Sheldon out of jealousy of Audra, or was he the one who sued Sheldon? Matt was an engineer—it was possible that Sheldon stole an idea or two from him. That would explain why he was so scarce. And if he did kill Sheldon for that reason, he could've also killed Britta for representing Sheldon.

I got back in my car and checked my phone. The picture of the third victim popped up. You know how on TV shows they used a picture like that to find out who they were? It had always struck me as odd because it was hard to tell who someone was when they looked asleep.

This guy looked pretty generic. It might have been easier to figure out if his eyes were open and he had some sort of expression. I was just blowing the image up to examine more closely when I got a text from Stewie.

Bird Goddess! Come quick! Chapel of Despair! Help!

I was there in a less than a minute, turned off the van, and ran inside. The Chapel of Despair was also known as the Old

Lutheran Church. Stewie and the other teen druids bought it a few years ago and fixed it up for their purposes.

The door was locked. I heard shouting coming from the other side. I thought for a moment. The door opened inward. It was a gothic, wood door. Not great for security, but it had the look the kids liked.

I kicked the door hard, right under the knob, and it caved inward. The side door opened to the level with offices, and I ran through the hallway, listening for the sounds I'd heard earlier. When I didn't find anyone, I ran up to the chapel, where I saw Stewie and Mike waving their arms at me.

"What is it?" I joined them a little breathlessly. "Are you guys okay?"

Stewie smiled and spoke through his clenched teeth as if he was afraid someone would hear. "They're waiting for you. Said they wouldn't leave until they talked to you!"

Mike gulped loudly, his Adam's Apple bobbing furiously. "They didn't find me menacing!"

My eyes scanned the chapel. I should've brought my gun. "Who? Where?"

"Two guys in the confessional." Stewie wiggled his red eyebrows.

That caught me off guard. "We have a confessional? In an old Lutheran church?"

Stewie looked offended. "Dred demi demons need confession too! How else are you going to get all the demony things you do off your chest?"

Mike nodded. "We got it from the Catholic church in Bladdersly. St. Uncumber's." He looked at Stewie. "What demony confessions do we have?"

"You know..." Stewie's fists were balled at his sides, and he stomped his foot like a petulant child trying to prove a point. "Stuff that demons do that they feel bad about!"

"Like what?" Mike's eyes went wide.

"I don't know!" Stewie shouted. "Stuff!"

Before they descended into useless slap fighting, I intervened. "Do you want me to kick their butts and throw them out?" I was a little confused about my role here.

"They said you have to go into the middle…thingy." Stewart pointed at a huge, three-box confessional at the other end of the chapel.

"Weapons?" I whispered. "What am I walking into, exactly?"

The boys looked at each other.

"No weapons. They actually seemed okay," Stewie said. "We'll send you with a protection curse."

Mike and Stewie held hands around me like I was in some "London Bridges" game.

"Guys, I'll be fine," I started to say, but they *shhhhed* me.

From the confessional, someone started to tap their foot in irritation.

"Curse this bird goddess with a shield of safety," Stewie made up on the spot. "And protecteth her from harmeth."

"*Not* amen," Mike said, and they dropped their arms.

"Not bad, but we have to make it more druidy," Stewie agreed.

I tried very hard not to roll my eyes as I strolled toward the confessional booth. They meant well. The group of awkward adolescents had never really decided if they were druids, part of a cult, or cosplaying demons. They were sweet kids though.

The booth was very gothic, with elaborate spires over the three doors. The one in the middle was the largest. Apparently I was playing the priest. I almost laughed, remembering how I'd actually pretended to be a priest in a very small church outside of Minsk, to hear the confession of a rather Catholic Russian spy who felt bad about the things he'd done, so he came clean with some nuclear plans to his priest…or, me. I think he went away feeling better (I know I did), probably because the only thing I knew of for his penance was to do Hail Marys. Hopefully he was done with the five billion, three hundred and sixty million, and five I'd told him to do.

As instructed, I opened the middle door and stepped inside. It was dark, but I took a seat on a black velvet chair and waited. It wasn't long before the two small shades opened on either side of me.

"You are Merry Wrath?" one man said in a German accent.

"I am," I said sternly. "And I've got a gun trained on each of you, so don't try anything stupid."

Damn. Once more I wished I'd brought a gun or two. Hopefully they'd fall for that.

"Makes sense," a man on the other side with a Spanish accent said.

No one spoke for a minute.

"Now that we've established that," I said. "What do you want?"

"We just want you to back off this Chinese spy thing," the German said. "We didn't kill Sheldon McBride."

"You are the Chinese spies?" It wasn't that I didn't believe them. It wasn't even the accents. Anyone could be a spy for anyone these days, and a couple of Chinese men roaming around asking strange questions about ag secrets would be noticed.

"Let's say that we are," the Spaniard said.

"I just said that," I repeated.

"Theoretically, let's go with that. In *theory*," the German insisted.

Great. Stupid spies. My favorite!

"Why should I *not* believe that you killed Sheldon McBride? You could be after the technology of his ethanol drone."

The German said, "No. We are here for something else. We just don't want you following us."

"And why should I believe you?" I wondered.

"I told you she wouldn't believe us," the Spaniard sighed. "But it's true. We aren't here for that."

"That's right," the German said. "We're here on vacation."

"Vacation? You came to Who's There for vacation?" I wasn't convinced. "What did you come here to do?"

"We just needed a break. You know, from being…" The Spaniard struggled to end the sentence.

"Chinese spies?" I filled in.

"No, not for that!" the German insisted.

"So you are Chinese spies, then," I said.

"You walked right into that one," the Spaniard hissed.

"I did not! Anyway, it's mostly true," the German said a little defensively.

"Guys." I cut them off. "Why am I here?"

"Because we heard that you are looking for us in the murder of Sheldon McBride. We just wanted to tell you that we aren't here for that," the German insisted.

"Because of vacation," the Spaniard added.

I pinched the bridge of my nose. "Okay, if I'm going to believe that, then why are you really here?"

There was a moment of silence before the German said, "You promise not to tell?"

"Why would I do that?" I challenged. "If you're spying on my country, I can't promise I won't tell."

"It isn't like we're here to steal secrets," the Spaniard scoffed.

"Or that we're Chinese spies!" The German said. "We're actually North Korean."

Ah. That explained a lot. "And you are here for? Look, if it isn't that important, I won't tell. I've been retired for years now and am kind of busy at the moment with a triple murder and a pair of terrified, if not confused, teen druids."

"Let's trust her," said the Spaniard.

"Okay," said the German. "We're here for a recipe."

This time I was silent. "For ethanol? For hybrid seed corn?"

"For something more important," the Spaniard said. "The Is That A Banana In Your Pants Sundae from Feeling Lucky's House of Delights."

They were so solemn, I tried to take it seriously.

"For Dear Leader," the German continued. "He loves ice cream."

That made sense. Kim Jong Un was notoriously strange and a serious foodie. Back in my CIA days, I'd heard he'd sent spies to KFC to get the Colonel's secret recipe and to McDonald's for the secret to their amazing French fries. Feeling Lucky's had the best ice cream, so it made sense to me.

"Okay," I said in a hushed whisper. "I'll help you out. Go to Feeling Lucky's and tell Kayla that the Bird Goddess sent you for the recipe."

There was a moment of silence again.

"That's it?" the German asked.

"That's it," I said.

"Well, that was easy," the Spaniard said. "You must wield a lot of influence here!"

"That's right, so after you get the recipe, you should leave town and never come back," I warned. Then I got up and stepped out of the confessional.

Two men emerged from either side. The German was wearing a sort of Tyrolean costume and looked a little like Baron Von Trapp in *The Sound of Music* when they went over the Alps. The Spaniard was dressed like a cowboy. They startled a bit as they saw me but thanked me and headed up the aisle.

"They're gone!" Stewie came running down the aisle with Mike walking slowly to keep up.

"That's right. They were just lost. Now guys, please remember to lock the door so this doesn't happen again."

"Were they spies?" Stewie's eyes went wide.

"Yup," I said. "North Korean." I brought my finger to my lips.

CHAPTER THIRTY-FOUR

"We can give up on the Chinese spies," I said as I flopped down in the chair opposite Riley. "They're just North Koreans here to steal an ice cream recipe."

Kelly laughed but stopped when Riley and I didn't join in. "Wait," she said. "Seriously?"

Riley nodded. "They're always doing that. Kim Jong Un is reputed to have the largest collection of junk food recipes in the world. So that theory is out."

"Where were you yesterday?" I asked as I held up my phone. "I texted you to get me out of a sticky situation."

He frowned. "I changed phone numbers last week. Too many women were calling all hours of the day and night. It got old."

I filled him and Kelly in on my adventures for the past twenty-four hours.

"I thought I heard screaming last night," Kelly said. "And hey, thanks for convincing Conrad's dad to not leave. I'm not sure about having school kids look at murder scenes, but our troop, if they hadn't seen it already, would love something like that."

"What are you going to do now?" Riley asked.

"I don't know. This whole Matt thing doesn't sit well with me. What do you think?"

He held his hands up. "Oh no. We've got too much work to do as it is. I told you, we're out of this one."

I looked at Kelly, and she nodded.

"He's right. We just got six new cases in the last two days. And they're rush jobs. You'll have to do it without me."

My jaw dropped open. "I can't believe this! You've never bailed on me before!"

Kelly leaned forward. "Look, normally, yes, I'd be on board. But in addition to work, I've got two church events this week, Finn's got a huge slumber party this weekend at the house, and we have Iceland for Thinking Day and cookie sales coming up."

"You'll do fine without us," Riley said. "You found the"—he held up finger quotes—"Chinese spies."

As much as I didn't want it to be true, Kelly was overbooked. And if she burned out, I'd be screwed.

"And you need to focus on the Girl Scout stuff too," Kelly warned. "I can't do it all myself."

"I did! I spent the other day getting things ready for all that! But I'll tell you what," I said. "Give me a couple of days. If I don't solve this, then I'll turn it all over to Rex."

Kelly and Riley burst into laughter.

My phone buzzed. Rex texted that he was landing in half an hour.

"Gotta go. I promise, I'll either pull this off or drop it all in Rex's hands."

They were still laughing as I walked out the door.

The entire half hour drive to the airport in Des Moines had my head spinning. This case was complicated. With the Chinese/North Koreans out of the running, there were still a lot of questions, like was Sandy actually Britta like Ted thought? If not, where was Sandy, and was she a suspect in her ex's murder? Where was Brian? Had he killed Sheldon and Britta out of jealousy? What about Matt? Audra was keeping him under wraps, or was he hiding because he was the killer? Or was it someone else?

Who had the opportunity? A thought came to mind…one I didn't want. What about Drew Phillips? These people were all killed in his museum. He definitely had opportunity, but where was the motive? He seemed genuinely shocked. But then, I'd dealt with people who were good actors before.

And who was the third victim? If we could just find out who he was and how he tied into this, we might crack the case. And then there was always the possibility that it just a crime of opportunity or was someone else completely who we hadn't even suspected yet.

I parked the car and went into baggage check.

"Hey babe!" Rex scooped me into his arms and kissed me.

"Hello yourself!" I said once I came up for air. "Are you happy because you cracked the case?"

He smiled and shook his head. "I just missed you. I'm used to you getting underfoot while I do my job. In a way, that irritation is rather comforting. Oh hey, that's my bag. Hold on."

He went over and grabbed his suitcase, and we walked out to the van. On the way home, I told him what I'd learned, leaving out the break-in and the kidnapping. Instead, I told him that Audra had told me what was in Brian's closet. It wasn't a great lie, but it would provide context.

"I just wish we knew who the third victim was!" I complained.

Rex looked at me. "North Korean spies after an ice cream recipe?"

"Oh yeah," I said. "They do stuff like this all the time. They're kind of food obsessed, which is weird for a country without enough food."

"I do like the idea of the museum being used for educational purposes," he mused. "It sounds like you saved Betty from a broken heart."

I told him about my idea regarding Drew as a suspect. This got his attention.

"You and I were thinking similarly. I had Joanna get his file from the city. Ava didn't even check his references. The application consisted of a kid's handwriting writing the name Conrad over and over. She must have met him online or something and worked her magic to score an interview."

My heart sank. "They didn't check his references? What if he really did it? Conrad will have to move to Iceland!"

Rex chuckled. "Well, let's not get ahead of ourselves. Not yet, anyway."

"We could adopt him," I said suddenly.

Rex stared at me. "It's admirable that you'll go to such lengths to keep your troop happy."

"Isn't it just?" I should tell Kelly he said that.

We got home, and while Rex went to the station, I felt guilty and decided I might as well take a couple of hours and read through the latest cookie sales info online—just to prove my cookie expertise to Kelly. Things didn't change dramatically from year to year, but there was usually a new price increase and a new cookie. Sometimes they would change the rules for cookie booths.

"Merry!" Rex shouted in my ear, and I jumped to my feet.

"You were napping?" he asked as he unstuck one of the cardboard cookie forms from my cheek.

"No, of course not," I lied. "I was thinking."

"Well, I hate to cut into your reverie, but it's late and I brought home takeout for dinner." He held up an aromatic bag from the Italian place in town.

I opened a bottle of wine, and we relaxed through dinner. Philby even joined us, sitting in one of the other dining room chairs, staring at us.

"When did we start letting the cat sit at the table?" Rex poured me another glass of wine.

"Shhh." I took the glass from him. "Just go with it. It could be far more dangerous not to let her sit there."

As if she knew what we were thinking, Philby jumped up on the table, walked over to my bread plate, and sat on the garlic bread while staring at me meaningfully. It felt like a threat from the Sicilian mafia—if the mafia employed cats who looked like Hitler.

"You said she shouldn't be up here," I complained. "I disagreed with you in her defense, and she still punishes me!"

We were cleaning up, which included peeling garlic bread from an angry feline's bottom (she seemed to think that was my fault too), when both of our phones rang. Rex went into the kitchen, and I headed for the living room. It was Ted.

"Waiting for my call?" He laughed.

Actually, I'd forgotten all about it. "Of course! What did you find out at dinner?"

"Well, you might be onto something. Mr. Dean, the chemistry teacher, and Mr. Glen, the physics teacher, both said they thought Sheldon and Brian had a somewhat adversarial relationship." There was a pause. "I don't know how I missed it. I thought I knew those kids."

"Maybe because you were closer to them and advisor of the Science Club?" I rationalized.

"I don't know, but you could be right. Dean accused me of seeing all of my past students through rose-colored glasses. And maybe that's true. But I'd rather remember the good things about them than the stupid stuff all kids do. Or I'm just a softy. Oh well, it hardly matters now I guess."

"Don't feel bad about it," I consoled him.

"It was fun, playing detective. It made retirement more interesting. Now I know how Linda Willard felt when she helped you. I don't know how often you'll need a science teacher, but if you do, I'm your man!"

A thought occurred to me. "Can I send you something on the phone? Let me know what you think."

"Will do!" he said eagerly.

I sent him the photo of the third victim. It was a long shot but worth a try since he was willing.

Two minutes later, he replied, "Why did you send me a photo of Sheldon?"

CHAPTER THIRTY-FIVE

It took me a moment to recover from the shock. I sent him the photo of the first victim.

"That's Brian Atkins!" Ted responded. "Are you testing me? Is this part of a sort of detective test?"

I thanked him in a fog and sat very still for several minutes. Various scenarios on how this could be possible bounced around my brain, searching for purchase. Was this even possible? Ted Fowler thought so.

If this was true, then Brian Atkins and Sheldon McBride must've changed places years ago! The photo of Brian was the face on Sheldon McBride's driver's license, and it was the face his company knew since the beginning.

Why would Sheldon agree to do something like that? Was it even his idea? Did he plan to switch back at some point, or had he decided to remain Brian Atkins forever?

And did Audra know about it? Did Matt? If they'd stayed in touch, then they had to in order to make the fraud work. Honestly, my head was spinning. I needed to sound this out on someone, but it was too early to talk about it with Rex, and anyway, he was still on the phone. I had to make sure I knew what was going on.

Mr. Fancy Pants, the king vulture, eyed me then my bag. He knew what I had in there. I pulled out my very last package of Girl Scout shortbread cookies from last year and crushed them, dumping them into a pile on his log. His mate woke up and, upon seeing me, went back to sleep. His chick, Hilly Pants, now a full-grown vulture, came over and checked out the pile of cookie crumbs as her dad guzzled them down.

"So you see," I continued with my rant. "Here we all were thinking Sheldon was Sheldon and dead guy number three was someone else. I guess I could've considered that it was Brian at some point, but now we know that Sheldon was Brian and mystery dude was Sheldon."

Mr. Fancy Pants looked up from his feast and cocked his head to one side. If you've never seen a king vulture, you'd think it was a cartoon drawn by a toddler with a full crayon box on a sugar overdose. Mr. Fancy Pants and I went way back, to a trip to Washington DC and the national zoo. He'd even saved my life once or twice.

Now he and his family lived at the Obladi Zoo in town, and every now and then I broke in, late at night, to chat. He was a great listener.

"The crazy lady's talking to birds again! Security!"

Dickie, the scarlet macaw, on the other hand, was a pain in the butt. The giant bird usually chewed me out, when he wasn't repeating the pathetic ramblings or phone conversations of his teenage caretaker.

"Orc Mountain Battlefield of Blood is real, Mom! I'm leading real battles for the fate of orc kind with my guild! I'm gaining valuable skills for real life!"

I ignored him and kept talking to my vulture friend. "If this is true, and I can't imagine Ted Fowler lying about it—he seemed very surprised—then how far does it go back? It must be after college, because of Aura. Unless she's lying and they'd switched before college."

"Orcs are real, Mom! You don't even know! If we're ever overrun, I'm your last line of defense!" Dickie shrieked.

I was starting to worry about Dickie's minder's mom.

I continued. "Which also means that Audra has known since the beginning. She may have been having an affair with Brian in college! Seriously! This is some mind-warping stuff!"

Mr. Fancy Pants finished his snack and allowed me to stroke his stubbly bald head a few times before going back to his nest and curling up next to his woman. Hilly Pants found a couple of crumbs her father had missed and chewed them. After a moment, she barfed. Then she fled to the other side of the enclosure.

"Why would I go to community college when I'm getting the best education here, in my room? And you hafta use more fabric softener on my socks! I need soft socks!"

It was time to go.

"Breaking into the zoo again?" Rex looked up from the TV as I walked in.

I plopped down on the couch next to him. "There's something you need to know."

Rex turned off the TV and adjusted to turn toward me. Martini's seemingly boneless body shifted in his lap, but she didn't stir. "Alright. What is it?"

I showed him the message I'd sent Ted and his response. I didn't say any more, in case Rex might have a different, better take on the whole thing. My husband was quiet for a few moments.

"Let me get this straight," he said slowly. "Sheldon McBride has always been Brian Atkins. And Brian Atkins has always been Sheldon McBride. And no one has ever figured this out since Sheldon was a recluse."

I nodded. "And I think it started before college and Audra knew."

"Because she was in that photo with him in the college yearbook," Rex finished my thought. "Why would they decide to switch places after high school?"

I reached over and pulled the unconscious cat onto my lap. She didn't even notice. "I don't know. Maybe Brian wanted to be Sheldon, he talked him into trading places just for fun, and it took? Audra said Brian was insanely jealous of Sheldon."

"What if she meant that Sheldon as Brian was really jealous of Brian as Sheldon?" Rex wondered.

The stalking closet! "Um, I should tell you something..."

Rex took the whole thing pretty well. I still left out the part about being kidnapped. We'd done more damage to Rog and Reg than Rex could with jail time.

"What if Sheldon always regretted changing places?" I suggested. "But things were too far gone for him to switch back?"

Rex's right eyebrow went up. "What if Brian was the idea man the whole time?"

"Oh wow! If that's true, then Sheldon couldn't switch back and take over. Because the ideas were his."

We sat there for a moment, each lost in our own thoughts. This was an unexpected twist on an already twisted case.

"Sheldon/Brian could've killed Brian/Sheldon," I started to say. "And Britta. But who killed Sheldon/Brian?"

"Audra or Matt?" Rex wondered. "You said Audra has been acting strangely and you haven't had any access to Matt."

"But why would she kill Sheldon?" I dropped the backslash. "She could've just left it all alone."

"Maybe as revenge for Sheldon killing Brian?" Rex asked. "I think I need to bring her and Matt in. He can avoid you but not me."

I really wanted to meet Matt, but Rex was right and I didn't want to push it. Besides, I thought I might visit Ted first thing in the morning to pick his brain on this. He was pretty smart and knew the people involved. Not well, but still, he might have come up with the same scenarios I did, or he might see things another way and I could use his perspective.

CHAPTER THIRTY-SIX

"He's not here," a tired young woman wearing rubber gloves and holding a dusting cloth said when she opened the door the next morning. "But he told me you'd come over."

"He did?" I was just feeling bad for not calling first, but Ted must have anticipated my confusion when he told me who was in the photos last night.

"Yup. I'm his cleaner, Vera. Ted said he had something for you in the den on his desk. You can go get it."

I was about to ask if she was sure, but it was possible that the photos I'd sent him might have made him think of something and he took off to check it out. It made sense that he thought I'd come over to confirm things. It was nice of him to leave me whatever it was. The man was efficient.

The desk in the den was empty except for a file folder and an envelope. Which one was for me? I didn't want to snoop. I liked the guy. I picked up both, when my phone buzzed. Sticking the envelope and folder into my left hand, I checked my texts to find one from Rex, saying Audra and Matt didn't go to work today and weren't at home.

Oh no! What if Ted thought what I thought and went over to confront the couple? Was Ted in danger? I shoved the file folder and envelope into my bag and took off for the van. Two seconds later, I saw Rex go by in a cruiser driven by Joanna. I decided to follow, thinking they were going to Audra's house.

A few minutes later, I pulled up behind them. Rex and Joanna got out of the car. He spotted me and sent his officer to the front door.

"What are you doing here?" he asked through the window.

"I think Ted's in trouble," I said quickly. "He's not at home. When you told me Audra and Matt were missing, I thought he might have come here to confront him."

Joanna joined us. "Hey Merry!" She looked at her boss. "No one's home."

"Come on," Rex said. "Let's check around back."

I started to get out of the car, but my husband stopped me.

"You stay here."

I was a little miffed to be left out. I'd been helping! And I was good in a fight. Rex knew that. Hey! Maybe he said that so I could watch for them coming back! Okay, that was probably a stretch, but it made me feel better.

Then I remembered the file and the envelope and pulled them from my bag. I hated hesitating if Ted was in trouble, but one of these had a message for me. If there was something sensitive in the other, I'd just have to pretend I hadn't seen it. Older people were sensitive about things that had personal information. I could probably even slip inside his house and return it without him knowing.

I opened the envelope and read it. Then I opened the file. And that's when everything came together.

"The back is locked, and both cars are missing from the garage." Rex appeared at the window. "What's that there?"

"Get in." I motioned to the passenger door. "We've got to go to the station and do a little research. I think I have an idea what happened."

It was a full house at the Museum of Murder that afternoon. Rex had called everyone involved to meet up for the big reveal, and I thought the museum was the perfect place to do it since all three murders took place here. The big surprise was that Drew also thought it was a good idea. My chat with him the other day had opened his eyes to the possibilities of this place, and he was only too happy to close the museum early and set up chairs in the lobby.

Mayor Ava, flanked by her interns, Pantu and Bal, who still eyed me a bit warily, were in attendance. Betty, Lauren, Inez, and the Kaitlyns were handing out fliers about the upcoming cookie sale. Kelly and Riley sat in the back. She was on a laptop, and they were whispering together. They really were busy. I'd be willing to bet they were just here to find out who did it.

Medea Jones sat in the front row wearing a lanyard with a press pass that she didn't need. Lucinda and her cameraman (the drone was absent) stood at the back of the room, waiting. The McBride Followers filed in and sat in the front row next to Medea, who, upon noticing how weird they looked, moved a couple of seats over. Audra entered with Ted Fowler, who gave me a cheery wave. If Matt was there, I didn't see him.

Rex stood next to me, while Joanna and Troy stood against opposing walls, waiting to hear who they should arrest. Kevin and the Hamlets stood at attention with their hands on their holsters.

Conrad came in, and he and Betty moved closer to the front. The other girls stayed near the door, ready to hand out fliers to any latecomers.

Ava came over and stood in front of me. The interns, unsure of what to do, came over and flanked her. "Before Mrs. Wrath tells you who killed who, as a representative of the government I want you all to know we are now the number-one most murdery small town in Iowa! Remember that at election time and that Mayor Ava did that for you!"

The crowd began to applaud as Ava and her contingent took their seats. Ted stifled a smile. Drew was enthusiastic. Kelly and Riley kept working on their laptops. I thought about how weird it was that this was something to be proud of.

Betty walked up and addressed the small crowd. "And there will be a discount today in the gift shop for everyone here of ten percent off all merchandise. If you are the killer, you get twenty percent. That is all." She went back to Conrad, who nodded as if this was the most normal thing in the world.

Drew looked uncertain. Maybe they hadn't told him about the sale.

"Who killed Sheldon McBride?" Medea barked out. "I have deadlines!"

I guess it was showtime. "That's the question. Everyone knows that Sheldon McBride and Britta Almondine were murdered here in the museum. But let me tell you something you don't know. Brian Atkins was also murdered here."

Most people didn't know who I was talking about and stared at me blankly. Ted and Audra looked sad but gave no other indication of what they thought.

"Here's a little history," I began. "Brian Atkins and Sheldon McBride were friends, growing up here in Who's There. One of them still lived here. And Britta, in case you don't know, was Sheldon's one-time wife and current attorney."

A few people raised their eyebrows at this information.

"Now that you know something about the victims, I can tell you something new. Sheldon McBride was actually Brian Atkins. Sheldon McBride hadn't been Sheldon McBride since graduating high school. The two men switched places and names before they started college. Ever since then, Brian has been Sheldon and Sheldon has been Brian."

A gasp went up among the crowd, and the McBride Followers looked like they were devastated.

"We're going to have to change our last names to Atkins?" Simon squeaked.

I shrugged. "Technically, you are the Brian Atkins Followers. All the ideas, inventions, everything, were his." I paused dramatically. "Or were they?"

"They were Sheldon's!" Sam shouted.

I sighed. "Sadly, they weren't. The ideas for the grand inventions were someone else's. That's why the two men were killed, along with Brian's lawyer, Britta."

People looked around the room curiously. Only one person smiled.

I looked at him. "Right, Ted Fowler?"

The teacher stood up and began to clap. "Bravo! I'd heard you were smart! I wish I'd been teaching when you were at Who's There High."

That was nice. Rarely was the killer so nice about being accused. Usually they lied or got angry. This one came with a compliment.

"Mr. Fowler?" Audra gasped. "No, that's not possible."

"Says the only other person who knew about the switch." I motioned to her. "I have to ask, why did they do it? I hadn't figured that out."

Audra looked suddenly like she hadn't slept in decades. "They thought it would be funny, at first. Brian was more social than Sheldon. For some reason, they thought that Sheldon McBride sounded like the name of a famous inventor. I always assumed the ideas were Brian's and Sheldon just went with it."

Fowler's face darkened. "They were *my* ideas. I'd shared them with the two-person science club. The Corn Hole car, the ethanol drone... Both were my ideas! I even drew up the plans for them!" He paused. "But I would like to say I had nothing to do with the rumored robot turkeys. That doesn't even make sense! What would you even use them for?"

I had to agree with him. The best thing about turkeys was that they were delicious. What would a robot turkey be worth?

"I know. You left a file on your desk with a rejected notice from the patent office, dated fifteen years ago, for the car. I read it by accident. You meant for me to have the envelope with the copy of an article from the newspaper twenty years ago, showing you, Brian, and Sheldon working on a project for the science club. You can see everyone's faces, and it's labelled correctly. Then again, maybe you wanted me to see the plans too. Is that right?"

Ted nodded. "I was going to fool everyone, but then the truth wouldn't come out. I needed everyone to know what had happened. Teaching is a mostly thankless job. Students rarely recognize the influence you had on them. These two took my plans and made them their own! Before I realized what was happening, Sheldon McBride...or rather, Brian, had patented my plans! He made millions!"

I jumped in. "You told me the truth about the third victim being the real Sheldon because you wanted me to think he'd killed Brian and Britta then himself."

Ted gave a small smile. "I really did. I knew they'd changed places years ago. I'd never said anything, suspecting the information could be valuable later. Tell me, did you think that Sheldon had killed Brian and Britta?"

I nodded. "Detective Ferguson and I did...for a bit. It was a brilliant plan. Why did you kill Britta?"

Ted shrugged casually. "She was the lawyer who made sure I'd never get what I was owed. Britta met Brian in school. They got married right after, but it didn't work out. I was invited to the wedding as a witness, and I thought maybe it was an honor. I'll never know, really."

"Even though the marriage didn't work out, they stayed good friends, right?" I asked. "At some point, Brian told her he'd gotten the idea from you. Then the two of them made sure everything was locked down so you'd never get a penny. That must have been an awful betrayal."

"I was stupid for sharing my ideas with a couple of kids," Ted admitted. "If they'd just shared some of the profit with me, I would've been fine. A shout out at some point saying I was an inspiration would've gone a long way. But he never did."

I felt bad for him. Teachers gave so much of themselves to their students, and in this case, all of his inventions.

"In the end," Ted said sadly, "I couldn't override my ego. Sure, Sheldon, Britta, and Brian were dead. But that still wouldn't give me the credit for the inventions."

"You first found out when you tried to patent one of them fifteen years ago," I replied. "That's what you'd left in the folder. Detective Ferguson called a contact at the patent office, who said you were rejected because the idea had already been patented. By Sheldon McBride."

Fowler nodded. "That was the worst day of my life. All these years, it just made me angrier and angrier. I'm glad I left that out for you to find. I'll go to prison, but at least the world will know that I invented those things." He turned to Medea. "But seriously, in the article, please don't say I had anything to do with the robot turkeys. I really don't want that on my record."

Ted walked over to my husband and held his hands out. Joanna came over and put the handcuffs on before leading him away. The room exploded in conversation as everyone talked about this incredibly confusing turn of events. I spotted Medea scribbling furiously and Lucinda talking to her cameraman.

Audra came over to us. She looked like she'd rather be anywhere else.

"I have a question," Rex said. "How did Sheldon deal with Brian's fame? Was he really jealous, or did you just say that?"

The woman looked down at her hands. "Sheldon was okay with it all at first. He loved the idea that he could be famous and someone else would do all the heavy lifting. And Brian was generous with the money. But Sheldon lived like a pauper. He bankrolled all that money and never touched it. And then he became bitter. I really thought he'd killed Brian. I had no idea it was really Mr. Fowler."

"What happens to Sheldon's money now?" I asked.

Audra shrugged. "No idea. He didn't have any family. Matt and I were the only friends he had, but in the last few years, he stopped talking to us. I thought the bitterness was getting worse. Hopefully, he left a will and it's going to a good cause."

The door opened at that moment, and a man in a wheelchair rolled in. He sketched a wave to Audra and waited.

"That's Matt. He doesn't like being in public in his wheelchair." She noticed the expressions of confusion on our faces. "He was injured on the job a year ago. We were in Des Moines seeing a specialist this morning. Matt's very self-conscious about it. That's why he never came with me."

"I'm sorry," I said. "But he shouldn't feel that way."

Audra smiled at her husband. "We're working through it." She walked over to her husband and kissed him on the cheek before rolling him out the door.

Medea ran over to me. "This is the scoop of a lifetime! I knew you'd somehow be my big story!" She looked at my husband. "Can I get an exclusive interview with you right now?"

Rex looked at me, and I nodded. They stepped away and began talking.

Drew and Conrad approached me. I noticed Betty staring at the boy from the wall where she'd stood.

"Quite a performance, Mrs. Ferguson," Drew said. "And to do the big reveal here at the Museum of Murder is quite a coup for us. Donations have gone through the roof in the last few days, and I suspect they will grow even more now."

"Does that mean you're staying?" I asked.

Conrad looked at his dad curiously. Apparently, he hadn't known this was a possibility.

Drew smiled and put his hand on his son's shoulder. "Yes. We are staying."

EPILOGUE

By the end of the day, Rex had the drone in his possession. Sadly, there was no video of Sheldon... or rather Brian's last moments. But the retired teacher turned killer agreed to plead guilty in court, so it wasn't needed in the end. He'd taken the drone to examine it, and it turned out it had followed Ted's ideas closely.

I took Ted some Girl Scout cookies in jail. I asked him privately about Reg and Rog. It turned out that they were former students of his who he figured were stupid enough to scare people away without injuring anyone. He was horrified when I said they'd planned to torture and kill me, but he didn't think they'd have actually gone through with it, and we had a laugh about how I'd handled the whole thing. He also had heard what sounded like screaming that night.

It was too bad he was a killer because I had liked the man. I couldn't imagine how I'd feel if someone had stolen my invention ideas and never gave me credit for them. He was surprised about Sheldon suing Brian over the ideas. Ted said he didn't feel as bad about killing them both after that.

As for Sheldon—he'd left his money to Who's There High School's science department. The current teacher, Mr. Reyes, was startled to get the check for two million dollars and was surprised that he now had to start a science club in order to use the money. Apparently, the man really didn't like kids, so he was in a bit of a quandary—but I was sure he would work something out.

The McBride Followers were devastated that their hero was, in fact, Brian Atkins and worried that they'd have to change their names to become the Atkins Followers. In the end, they decided not to because it was hard to do, but they did find a woman named Briana Atkins who was happy to make them her reverse harem.

Drew wasn't wrong about the impact the three murders had on the museum. Within twenty-four hours of the news going global, they'd raised ten million dollars, which should fund the museum for years. Or at least until Conrad and Betty went away to college.

Conrad's mother flew over a few days after the reveal and helped with everything, including a giant, papier–mâché Yule Cat. The beast was terrifying, and we had to stop Betty from making a small papier–mâché child hanging out of the cat's mouth, screaming in horror.

Gunndis was absolutely delightful and taught the girls all about her homeland. She made a huge backdrop for the display, featuring the strikingly beautiful landscapes of Iceland, and planned to give every girl who visited our booth a new, Icelandic name. Hilly finished the sweaters early. I had a feeling this was going to be our best Thinking Day ever.

The girls were also working on ways to make the museum more interactive. They'd made a video that started with: "In a world where murder lurks behind the door, but it's rare and the victim always knows the killer so it probably won't be you…" There were some questionable reenactments and issues with accuracy, like Tinkles having a past where the llama was a Basque Separatist, but I thought it had real potential.

Pantu and Bal did end up moving into my house. Ava had served me with an eminent domain order. I doubted that it was legal in any way, but I felt like I'd finally been able to make it up to the interns for the unfortunate thumbs-up thing at the press conference, back when Who's There wasn't the small town murder capital of Iowa.

"Merry!" Ron and Ivan burst through the front door a week later, lugging sleeping babies in their carriers. "We have best news!"

Rex walked in right when Wally and Azlan woke up. Their eyes immediately found and fixated on me.

"What's going on?" Rex scooped up one of the babies like a pro, but Wally's head swiveled until it found me and stayed staring, unblinkingly, at me.

Ivan was bouncing on his feet. "Blasto Blasto is sending holy man to confirm that babies are prophets!"

I moved around the room, making the babies' eyes follow me.

"What are you talking about?" I finally gave up and picked up Azlan.

His tiny mouth dropped open as he realized I was holding him. Yeah, Hilly and Betty were wrong. The boys didn't want to kill me. They liked Aunt Merry.

Ron handed Rex a letter.

"I can't read Chechen, guys," Rex said, adjusting to make it easier for Wally to look at me.

"It says that Father Yusov is coming here!" Ron took the letter back. "He is to find out if our babies are really prophets!"

Ivan nodded vigorously. "Is big deal! Huge honor! He is like pope of Blasto Blasto!"

"How is he going to do that?" I reached up and pushed the baby's toothless chin up, closing his mouth. It immediately dropped open again.

"Is big ritual," Ron said. "They use most revered goat in Chechnya."

"Is his name Father Goat?" I asked with more sarcasm than needed.

Ivan looked confused. "No. His name is Billy Goat." He looked at Ron, who spun his finger at the side of his head.

"I'm not crazy, you know," I said in an even voice so as not to startle the baby.

Ron and Ivan took the boys from us and strapped them into their carriers. "We have to go now."

Ivan nodded. "We need to buy special clothes for boys."

They walked out the door, but Ron was back in a flash. "Almost forgot! I have mail for you!"

He handed me a gigantic cloth sack and fled.

"Mail?" I lugged it to the couch and sat down to untie the ropes that closed the top of the bag.

Rex picked up a letter from the top. "Fan mail." He held the envelope out for me to see.

They were addressed to The Great Pook Snork. I tore one open and read.

Dear The Great Pook Snork, please help my goat Falafel. He has gotten into trouble with the law but is totally innocent. We need your help to get justice for Falafel!

I read more of the letters out loud to Rex. They all said almost the exactly same thing. Their innocent goat had gotten in trouble for everything from murder, to jaywalking, and in one case executing paratrooper invasions of Russia. Every letter asked for my help.

I finally tossed the letters onto the pile and leaned back on the couch.

"So," Rex said with a barely disguised grin. "Are you going to help these poor, innocent goats?"

"Not a chance," I said. "I've got Girl Scout cookie sales and Thinking Day coming up, and I'm going to avoid murder if at all possible."

Rex stood up. "I'm headed to the kitchen. Is there anything I can get you?"

"A glass of wine would go a long way to curry favor with The Great Pook Snork," I admitted.

My husband gave a little, courtly bow and said, "As you wish."

Hmmm…I could get used to this.

ABOUT THE AUTHOR

Leslie Langtry is the *USA Today* bestselling author of the *Greatest Hits Mysteries* series, the *Merry Wrath Mysteries,* the *Aloha Lagoon Mysteries,* and several books she hasn't finished yet, because she's very lazy.

Leslie loves puppies and cake (but she will not share her cake with puppies) and thinks praying mantids make everything better. She lives with her family and assorted animals in the Midwest, where she is currently working on her next book and trying to learn to play the ukulele.

To learn more about Leslie, visit her online at:
http://www.leslielangtry.com

Enjoyed this book? Check out these other reads available now from Leslie Langtry:

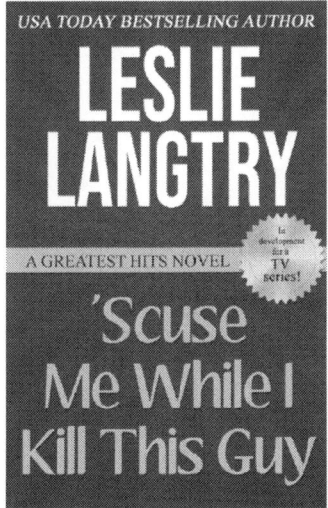

www.GemmaHallidayPublishing.com

Made in the USA
Columbia, SC
23 April 2024